COLD WAR

by

ERIC R. MCCLANE

The characters and events portrayed in this book are fictitious. Any similarity to real persons, living or dead, is coincidental and not intended by the author.

Cover design by: Eric McClane
Printed in the United States of America

TABLE OF CONTENTS

PROLOGUE — VICTORY IN EUROPE: THE END OF WAR IS NEAR

Tuesday, May 8th, 1945… V-E Day. America has seen the fall of fascism and the end of Adolf Hitler's Third Reich. And although World War II still rages on in the Pacific, the Nazi's unmitigated defeat has produced a much needed hope for a war-weary American homefront.

In Times Square, half a million of the *Greatest Generation* jubilantly gather in the crowded streets between New York City's finest high-rises, theaters and shoppes. Today's festivities celebrate the unconditional surrender of the German armed forces to the Allied Command. American flags proudly wave, banners with the word "Germany Surrenders!" flap victoriously in the breeze and commemorative newspapers clutched in celebratory hands bob up and down amidst the crowd. A fifteen ton replica of the Statue of Liberty stands pridefully at the intersection of Seventh Ave, 42nd Street and Broadway. Raised on platforms, tripoded NBC television cameras pan across the raucous mass, capturing this historic occasion. Although forever locked in the annals of time as a black-and-white film, there is a sea of vibrantly colored clothing matching the exuberant mood of the day. Whether they be dressed in wool suits, cotton dresses, gabardine pants, seersucker knee-length skirts, or any other socioeconomic 1940s fashion they can afford, they have one thing in common, they are all garbed in their finest attire. Men and women from all walks of life are here to rejoice and no matter their station emotions run high, as laughter and joyous tears fill the air. And although they're all keenly aware of Germany's surrender, the revelers still await the official word to unleash their true unbridled revelry.

Suddenly high above the packed streets, the mounted 10,000 watt Public Address loudspeakers crackle to life. A pensive silence falls upon the crowd. Movement stops and every ear listens intently. Then President Truman's radio address resounds through the streets like a clarion call to joy, "This is a solemn, but glorious hour. I wish that Franklin D Roosevelt had lived to see this day. General Eisenhower informs me that the forces of Germany have surrendered to the United Nations. The flags of freedom fly over all Europe." As he continues, the crowd goes wild. Cheers! Celebration! Streamers fall from the buildings' windows above. Loved ones and strangers embrace and a new day is born.

Three months later… August 30th, 1945. The Allied Control Council in Berlin coordinates the structuring of the four primary Allied-Occupation Zones: American, Soviet, British, and French. From these zones Germany will be rebuilt, and its population will be fed, clothed, and controlled. Nazi laws will be abolished, denazification will wipe out the Third Reich's deeply embedded culture, demilitarization will prevent Germany from launching a third world war in a century and the remaining Nazi resistance will be eradicated completely.

The occupation of Germany begins.

CHAPTER 1 — ALLIED OCCUPATION

February 17th, 1946... Hof, Bavaria, Occupied Germany.

Inside a US Special Services operated movie-theater, which somehow survived the war's nightly bombing raids, American soldiers relax and try to enjoy a double feature and some popcorn. For those who endured the horrors of war, their hyper state of readiness is now gone, and they find great solace in this small piece of comfort. The rest who rotated in as Occupation Troops have no idea of the blessing bestowed upon them by missing it all and are blissfully unaware of the importance of this simple luxury.

In the fully packed three-hundred seat cinema hall, a low murmur of frustrated anticipation gradually cascades across the crowd. It's been thirty-five minutes since the first film ended and some of the lower-ranking enlisted have to start duty within a few hours. Moments slowly pass without a single image, not even an entertaining cartoon plays for the troops. The only thing to look at besides each other is the plush velvet curtains inside the proscenium arch, covering the screen. A growing impatience grips the room. Some soldiers rise from their timeworn red-velour seats and holler up, castigating the projectionist with their rowdy disapprovals.

A finely dressed, well-spoken middle-aged usher wearing a tuxedo, gloves and a bowtie swiftly strides down the center aisle. Stopping abruptly, he pivots, straightens his tie, and addresses the hostile crowd, "Good afternoon, one and all… We thank you for being with us here today and we hope that you've enjoyed our first film 'Leave Her to Heaven'. I'm sorry that we've had some difficulties with the second feature, but we're trying to remedy the problem accordingly." Boos erupt, as he tries to explain, "The projectionist mistakenly loaded the wrong reel on projector two's platter, and he's been attempting to rectify that slight oversight as expeditiously as possible. The other minor problem that was in question has already been resolved, so I assure you that the main attraction will begin shortly. Please indulge us and be patient just a little while longer." More booing ensues. Expletives fly. Popcorn bombards him from every direction, "Thank you for you cooperation and we greatly appreciate your patronage." The barrage continues unabated. Wiping the butter-laden popcorn from his lapels, he tries to graciously bow out of the room.

As the displeased soldiers continue to yell, the curtain suddenly raises. Black and white 35mm celluloid rapidly clicks through the rotating sprockets of the Bell & Howell movie projector. The screen lights up and the crowd's curses turn to cheers. Flickering pictures of numbers counting down splash across the silver-screen. Then the image of *United News'* Screaming Eagle logo finally streams steadily overhead.

While the troops anxiously await the latest Rita Hayworth film to start, they're forced to endure the usual pre-movie Army generated newsreel. However, they're content just knowing that the film with America's "Favorite Pinup" is imminent. The newsreel continues and they watch as post-war Europe clumsily assaults the screen in a slightly sped-up comedic fashion, due to the documentary style 16mm non-sync camera's frame-rate float. There are images of US military vehicles shipping in pallets of much needed food and clothing, the Army Corps of Engineers rebuilding Germany's collapsed infrastructure, and Occupation Troops cheerfully assisting the local civilians. A nasally toned narrator barks positively slanted propaganda over the footage, "With the fall of Nazi Germany, the Allied Forces embark upon the ardent task of rebuilding a war-torn Europe... but no task is too large for these hard chargers." The footage then cuts to multiple perimeter locations surrounding Germany. The narrator ardently continues, "Our highly motivated Occupation Troops take strategic positions along the German countryside to squelch any remaining Nazi resistance and ensure a much-needed peace. These men are America's best." As the camera cuts between different locations, smiling and waving soldiers pepper the screen. Some wink, some give the thumbs-up, and others pretend to playfully shoot the camera with their hands posed like they're firing imaginary machine-guns. All are happy... seemingly. There is no anger, no pain, nor sorrow shown. The men of this generation refuse to display their mental scars to the world and even if they would the US Army would never allow it.

The overall tone of the reel changes to address the new enemy, *Communism*. Bellicose music ominously plays. A foreboding picture of the heavily armed Red Army dissolves into view. Football field long formations of massive *T-44 tanks* menacingly roll through Moscow's Red Square like unstoppable lumbering beasts. Infantry troops dressed in long woolen-coats march in perfect synchronicity, proudly saluting with their rifles displayed at left-shoulder-arms. Captured and converted Nazi *V-2 rockets* parade impressively behind banners adorn with the Soviet Unions' yellow *Hammer and Sickle* presented in a field of deep red. The show of force and cheering crowds are frighteningly reminiscent of the buildup of Nazi Germany. With zealous tenor, the narrator impresses, "Along the Eastern Front, tensions flare and former allies have now become adversaries. The Soviet Union, fearing that the United States will diminish its power as a totalitarian regime, continues to propagate a ring of fear throughout Eastern Europe. Communism must be stopped. Support the cause and join the effort. Reenlist and once again do your duty for America." The Soviet procession dissolves into a waving American flag. The Stars and Stripes snap pridefully against a rising sun. There is no subtlety in the message. The overt jingoism is the same strategy used to help defeat the Third Reich and it will be effectively employed throughout the Cold War.

Seated three rows from the back and on the end, a twenty-eight-year-old sinewy Corporal Joseph Anthony Lattanzi peers across the aisle at his sergeant. With a thick South Bronx dialect he facetiously complains, "Here we go again Sarge. Another bunch of assholes we're gonna have to deal with. Ya know, they should really give us a raise." Flashing a self-amused grin, his dark Italian eyes twinkle with sarcasm. "In fact, I think I made a mistake with reenlisting. I don't think I wanna do this no more. See what you can do about that, will ya?" He's always had a penchant for irreverent humor and at one time he thought for sure that standup comedy would be his ticket out of the neighborhood, but those dreams are long over. After the war, he's now just content with slogging through the day with another boring patrol, three square meals and a rack to fall into at night.

Sergeant Francis "Frank" McNeil is the typical thirty-eight-year-old everyman who was part of the huge wave that was drafted in 1942. And although he felt he was too old to enlist, he answered the call and left his family behind when the local draft board marked him Class 1C, 'Inducted Member of the Armed Forces'. Oddly, his age is not out of the norm; during the height of WWII the Army was continuously drafting men between the ages of eighteen to forty-one. During combat, McNeil's time in Europe spanned from the Battle of Kasserine Pass to the Battle of Nuremberg. Due to his prowess on the battlefield, he was reassigned to the 2nd Ranger Battalion for *Operation Overlord* and the invasion of Normandy. Like most of the men there, he feels like he did nothing special, just his job. Now that his tour is done, he's just another short-timer waiting to join the other eight million soldiers that have or will be shipped home during the fourteen months of *Operation Magic Carpet.*

Seated in the theater chair McNeil looks rough… not mean, just rough. He's acceptably unshaven for the time and has black wavy hair, with single curl that he fails to keep from falling down on his on forehead. His uniform is bit rumpled for an *NCO* and his boots look like they were shined with a Hershey-bar. He doesn't care. He did his job in combat. He does his job now. That's it. That's him, like it or not. Under the drooping eyelids of a former amateur middleweight boxer, his blue-gray eyes lazily drift over at Lattanzi.

Although he'll engage in conversation, his body language is naturally standoffish in general. And unbeknownst to him, he's always exuded an unintentional aura of irreverence; even Sister Bertilda-Ignacia didn't like his demeanor all the way back at Saint Xavier's grade school for boys. Flippantly he responds with a Lucky Strike cigarette bouncing in his lips, "What else are ya gonna do with your life Lattanzi?" His timbre has a deep resonance, and his words growl in jest with the slight gravel of a lifelong smoker.

Lattanzi thinks for a moment and then shrugs, "I don't know."

"Exactly..." Without even a smirk, McNeil glances at his watch and stands. As he does, a Merrie Melodies' cartoon-short featuring Bugs Bunny follows the newsreel and begins to play. Grabbing his *Thompson submachine gun* and helmet, the sergeant taps the cigarette ash on the floor and orders, "Come on. We're gonna be late." With the threat of Nazi resistance still lingering, most soldiers always have their weapons close at hand and McNeil's not one to leave possible enemy engagement to fate.

Astounded that they'd leave before the main feature begins, Lattanzi objects, "Late…? Our patrol doesn't start until seventeen hundred."

"Neuhaus wants us at fourteen-thirty."

"But they didn't even start the second movie yet!" Soldiers in front of them who are annoyed with the talking, turn back, and shush loudly. Responding, the corporal gives a flick of his hand, gesturing for the lower ranked individuals to turn around and shut up. As they turn back, the rest of the crowd roars with laughter at one of Bugs Bunny's antics.

Lattanzi looks back at McNeil and implores, "We're gonna miss Rita!"

"I don't think the lieutenant really gives two shits."

Shocked, Lattanzi points accusingly and states, "The lieutenant doesn't give two shits...? You knew before we came and didn't say a damned thing. You don't even care if you see her, do ya?"

"What am I dead? Of course I do. I just was hoping we'd be able to catch some of the movie before we had to leave. Unfortunately, it didn't work out that way. Just be happy we saw the first film." Although enforcing their departure, McNeil really doesn't want to leave. He's just an average guy like the rest of the men sitting here... and he was honestly hoping to get to watch Rita Hayworth dance across the screen too.

The corporal lightheartedly holds his chest, "That's just wrong Sarge. You're breakin' my heart."

Unamused, McNeil prods him along, "Let's go Lattanzi."

Indignant, the corporal dons his helmet, but wants to get in one more gripe before moving, "Ya know, this is some real bullshit. This never happened when we had morning patrol. Why'd the *LT* switch us?" *LT* is an abbreviation that servicemen use short for lieutenant.

Having played along enough, McNeil starts walking up the aisle and sardonically retorts, "Why don't you ask him?"

With a smirk, Lattanzi answers sarcastically, "Hey, that's real funny." Reluctantly, the corporal gets up and slings his *M3 submachine gun* over his shoulder. He starts murmuring to himself, "Ask him. I'll ask him... what'dya think I am, stupid?" Following, he jokingly quips, "Ya know, this job's really gettin' on my nerves."

As McNeil walks out, he glibly counters, "Well, there's always the Navy."

CHAPTER 2 — THE PATROL

Amidst bombed buildings, lightly falling snow dusts a squad of Occupation Troops on patrol. Thirteen men saunter through the cobblestone streets looking for any sign of possible resistance. Trapsing through the falling white, their standard issued uniforms create an odd looking silhouette of dark green. Each soldier wears an *Army M-1943* uniform, *M1* helmet and a long wool overcoat or parka. Some who were *Rangers* still wear their patches on their left shoulder, remnants from before the elite battalions were disbanded in December 1945.

Although they are on duty, they move in a two column casual route-step march; a style of marching that keeps the squad's correct spacing, but their steps are not in synch. Even though they look relaxed, they are mentally vigilant. Their machine-guns, submachine guns and rifles are lowered, but at the ready. Both McNeil and Lattanzi are former Rangers that are a part of this team, and for them this is old hat.

The thirteen move on, entering a more densely populated area. As they patrol further into town, they pass in front of decimated shoppes and homes in varying states of collapse. Blasted nightly by Allied bombing raids, this quaint village has been left in ruins. Beautiful architecture that once graced these streets is now marred or reduced to rubble. Some dwellings look like a young child tore into an ice-cream cake with their hands, whole chunks carved out by the bombshells' explosions. There is crumbling stone, cement, and wood buildings as far as the eye can see and nearly all the glass storefronts are shattered. Doors have been blown from their hinges and either hang damaged or lay in the street. Amazingly, very few buildings stand perfectly unmarred, but the ones that are undamaged appear as if the war just politely walked around them. They are a stark contrast to the devastation and a continual reminder of what was lost due to the unforgiveable folly of Adolf Hitler's psychotic ambitions. Unfortunately for the city's inhabitants, hardly any of these structures have been rebuilt since the start of the reconstruction; cleanup has been slow and laborious.

Off in the distance, a well-armed fireteam oversees the forced labor of German civilians. Exhausted local townswomen pull bricks from the wreckage and inspect them for cracks or chips. With each block scrutinized, they stack them in small piles, which the men promptly load into wheelbarrows and cart off to the Army masons. The majority of the population just picks up chunks of debris or shovels piles of dust from the streets. Demoralized and humbled, every able-bodied German must endure the grueling forced cleanup, to rebuild a defeated country that was brought to its knees by the world. Liberation from the brutal Nazi regime comes at a cost, but one that Germany must pay due to their role in the war. As the squad passes them, some villagers stare silently, some leer with disdain, but others smile their appreciation to the soldiers that helped free them from the yoke of Nazi tyranny.

On the edge of town, a stone bridge spans the Saale River heading East. The road on the other side leads miles out of Germany and subsequently into Czechoslovakia. At the bridge's closest boundary, four armed sentries carefully scrutinize vehicles and personnel traversing a guard gate checkpoint. Bookending that sentry post are mounds of stacked sandbags. And on one side, a Jeep mounted *M2 Browning .50 caliber machine-gun* covers the entranceway on the bridge.

Instead of crossing the river, the squad passes in front of the bridge heading further into the town square. A fledgling guard on post takes notice of the single silver bar insignia on the squad leader's helmet; it's an officer leading the approaching troops. "Good morning Sir," the young private squawks, as he snaps to attention and salutes. This gangly, pale-skinned, red curly-haired Private First Class (*PFC*) is the inexperienced leader of the three other naive privates manning the guard gate. It's a very typical situation for those new to the *Occupation.* When so many experienced soldiers are rotating out and homeward bound, many of the lower ranks have picked up the duties that would normally go to a Noncommissioned Officer (*NCO*).

Shouldering his *M2 Automatic Carbine,* First Lieutenant James Neuhaus cuts a return salute, "Morning... At ease."

At the peak of the lieutenant's salute, the young man noticed that the officer was missing the tips of his ring and pinky fingers. Not wanting to act like he saw, the sentry responds as nonchalantly, but respectful as he can, "Aye Sir." As Neuhaus draws closer, the *PFC* can see him more clearly. Along with the missing fingertips, a series of shrapnel scars run along the lieutenant's jawline, and a dime-sized hunk of cartilage is missing from his earlobe. However, his most severe trauma lies hidden below his uniform in a patchwork of grafted skin and burn scars. The *PFC* quickly tries to avert his gaze and cover once more, "Anything we can do for you Sir?"

Neuhaus' gait slows and his view intentionally looks past the *PFC* and falls upon something ahead. His forty-one-year-old stalwart eyes peer through the shadow cast from his helmet's brim. His eyes dart back at the young man and then at his nametag. From what he just viewed up ahead, the lieutenant's face is suddenly mired with alarm, but he musters up an affable smile to converse with his underling, "How are things Guthrie?"

The G.I. responds, "Fine Sir. Thank you. And you Sir?"

Ignoring the obligatory question, Neuhaus cordially orders, "Walk with me." His squad hangs back but follows at an acceptable distance behind.

The private responds and walks along with Neuhaus, "Aye Sir."

"Anything out of order?"

"No Sir."

"Signs of resistance?"

"No Sir."

"Are you sure?" The lieutenant asks like he already knows the answer.

Almost queasy regarding the officer's question, the private cautiously replies, "No sign of Nazis anywhere today Sir. Things have been pretty quiet."

Neuhaus stops and looks the private dead in the eyes. His stare nonverbally yells, "Really…?" Without needing a command, the squad follows Neuhaus lead and halts behind him.

"Um…" Dumbfounded, the sentry doesn't know what to say. He honestly thought he was telling his superior the truth.

The lieutenant points annoyingly to a freshly bombed café twenty yards up the road, and flatly states, "That was hit yesterday… midday. And do you know how I know that? Because that was one of the only pristine buildings left standing in this sector and I look forward to stopping for a coffee every day when we come through. And yesterday when we left morning patrol, it was still in one piece… but now, it's not. Do you want to explain to me how the hell that happened?"

Momentarily perplexed by the question, the young man stumbles to a standstill and provides the most obvious answer he can think to give, "Resistance, Sir."

"I know it was the resistance, Guthrie. I mean, how the hell did they blow up a building twenty yards from a guard post?"

"Well Sir… we uh… Motor-T from the 405th rolled through with provisions yesterday and… and they were in a hurry, so we helped them unload. That's when we --"

"--You left your post!?", Neuhaus pointedly questions, as he cuts him off midsentence.

Scrambling to blunt the truthful accusation, the young man blurts out, "Yes Sir. But it was just for a minute Sir. I'm sorry Sir… I'm sorry."

Annoyed, but trying to keep his anger in check, Neuhaus sternly replies, "They've been hitting us during the day across this whole sector… brazenly… out in the open… for over a month now. Do you know that?"

Timidly, the private mumbles through his answer hesitantly, "I… do… Sir."

The lieutenant barks loudly, "Then pull your head out of your ass and think before act! You think you can do that Private!?" Neuhaus unintentionally verbally demotes him, but it's enough for the *PFC* to take acute notice.

Hoping he's actually not going to lose a stripe, the young man instinctively snaps to the position of attention to answer, "Yes Sir! Absolutely Sir!"

Knowing the kid's shaken, Neuhaus looks him straight in the eyes and drives the point home, "This time there weren't any casualties. Next time, we may not be so lucky. Right…?" He puts his hand on the *PFC's* shoulder, "You gotta keep your head in the game, Guthrie. Understood?"

Ashamed, the soldier just nods in response.

"We all make mistakes. Let this one be your last." With a pat to the sentry's helmet, Neuhaus quips, "You better get back or they'll start thinking you ran off with some *fräulein* and mark you AWOL." He gives the kid a subtle smile.

Taking notice, the private feels a little relieved, "Aye Sir. Good day, Sir." Without hesitation, the sentry salutes and runs back to his post. As he hurries back, Guthrie thinks about how Neuhaus didn't sound or even seem like an officer. Little does he know; his feelings were technically correct. Even though Neuhaus now wears an officer bar, not so long ago he used to wear First Sergeant stripes. He was enlisted first. During the Battle of Salerno he was awarded the

Army's second highest commendation, the Distinguished Service Cross, for an extraordinary act of heroism while engaged with the enemy. Subsequently he was meritoriously battlefield promoted from an NCO to a 2nd Lieutenant. At the end of the war, he was promoted once more to 1st Lieutenant. The former is an honor and a moment in time that he still won't speak about today.

As Neuhaus starts the squad moving again, Sergeant McNeil gibes a simple statement past the cigarette hanging from his mouth, "Another stupid kid…".

Giving him a half-assed grin, Neuhaus responds, "Weren't we all."

McNeil concedes, with a nod.

Towards the back of the squad, awkwardly lanky, eighteen-year-old Private Michael Groves plods along with his six-foot-two frame moving like an uncoordinated newborn foal. He's thin, but strong and he shifts his *M1 Garand Rifle* around like it's a toy. His strength was forged through backbreaking labor he tolerated on his family's ranch back in Idaho. Groves is the typical rancher's son, who's accustomed to a day fully packed with hard work, from mucking horse stalls in the early morning to throwing hay bales far into the night. He was too young for the war but pined to see the world. And for many years he wished he could get away from that ranch and come to Germany… now he longs to have those days back. He can't stand the monotonous continual marching day after day, hour after hour. He wants excitement. Irritated with his plight, his once goofy boyish smile has been permanently replaced with a frown of frustration. Trudging through the snow, he watches with each step as his well-worn boots momentarily split open on the side, only to close and open once again. Snow and wet slowly seep inside the gap, drenching his sock. Perturbed, he looks up and taps his pale, dumpy cohort Private Ervalina on the shoulder.

Wanting to be more than he is, the Tennessee born and raised Bernard Theodore Ervalina scours the landscape looking for danger around every corner, wanting desperately to prove himself the hero he always wanted to be... just like his fellow Tennessean icon, Davy Crockett. However, he was never a hero back home. In his own eyes, he wasn't anything. In actuality, he was a just frecklefaced chubby delicate boy, who was incessantly picked on by his peers and reviled by his dominating father. Now he's an immature eighteen-year-old pretending to be a man. Looking over at his friend in the other column, he curiously questions with his Southern drawl, "What's goin' on Groves?"

Shouldering his *M1*, Groves grumbles, "I've had it with this shit."

"With what?"

As they continue to march, Groves points to his boots. He vents trying not to raise his voice too loudly, so his superiors don't hear up ahead, "Look at my boots. They're falling apart at the seams. My foot's freezin'. Can't get a good pair of boots if my life depended on it and I'm tired of it. I'm tired of the cold. I'm tired of marchin'. And I sure as shit can't take no more of this boredom crap. Marchin'... that's all we ever do here. I'm sick of it. I'm sick of all of it."

"What you need is some good Tennessee Whiskey to warm ya up... put ya in better mood.", Ervalina proudly advises of his state's famous liquor, as he rubs his belly in fond memory.

"What I need is some excitement and a new pair of boots."

"Well, something exciting might happen. The resistance has been blowing things up all over, so we'll probably see some action any day now."

"We couldn't get that lucky."

"You never know."

The wind begins to pick up, the snow falls heavier, and an exasperated Groves flips up his collar and rigidly scoffs, "*I do know...* and nothing's ever gonna happen. The Nazi holdouts only strike when no one's around. It's all about the numbers. They'll keep sneaking around blowing things up here and there, but they'll never engage us because they don't have the numbers. In a firefight, they lose... period It's that simple. We are never going to see any action. We're just gonna keep on marchin' around in the freezin' cold with our thumbs up our asses. Get used to it."

Ervalina looks at him shocked and dismayed. "That can't be right. I'm gonna ask."

"Who?"

"Lieutenant Neuhaus."

"You wanna ask the lieutenant?"

"Yeah... so?"

"Don't waste his time with a stupid question like that."

"He said we could go to him with anything?"

"That's not what he meant."

Indignant, Ervalina waves off his friend and shoulders his rifle. He also carries an *M1 Garand*, except his is the

M1E5 carbine with folding stock for lighter weight. Groves wouldn't give up his traditional *M1* because he didn't want the carbine's loss of accuracy and distance.

Jogging away from Groves' side, Ervalina shuffles through the snow up next to Neuhaus. No longer in one of the column formations, he walks along sideways and asks, "Sir, are we gonna see action anytime soon?" Astonishingly, his tone gives away that he actually wants to engage the enemy.

Taken aback, Neuhaus disregards the private's question and amiably states, "Take a look around Ervalina… this is pretty peaceful. Appreciate it."

"Sir, I didn't enlist just to tour Germany. I joined to fight."

From behind them, Corporal Lattanzi quips, "You're a little late asswipe…Where were you a year ago?"

Ervalina looks back, "Still in high school."

Snidely, the corporal condescends with oozing sarcasm, "And there lies your problem 'smartguy'. If nobody told you, the war's over in Europe. This is the Occupation. We try not to shoot people here. Didn't they teach you 'Boots' anything?" 'Boots' are what soldiers in the field call inexperienced newbies that recently left Boot Camp.

"Yes Corporal, they did!", Ervalina snaps with a look of rage. Lattanzi's tone burns at him. Throughout the private's whole life he's been dismissed and demeaned; he hates it even more now. Avoiding any further conversation with Lattanzi, Ervalina implores Neuhaus, "Sir, I was told that if we signed up for the Occupation we'd be clearing out the remaining Nazi *Wehrmacht*. Is that true or not?"

Not waiting for a response, Lattanzi cuts in, "Look around you Ervalina… do you see any Nazis?" Mockingly, the corporal motions his arm through the air like exhibiting the countryside like a gameshow host shows a prize. He continues sarcastically, "No… And do you know why there's no Nazis? Because we killed all their asses before you got here. So, don't be stupid… just shut the hell up and get back there with Groves."

Ervalina seethes. He wants to say something, but he can't think of an appropriate comeback. He knows he can't respond to an *NCO* with what he really wants to say, so he just silently mouths a two word expletive back.

Mildly entertained with the situation, Neuhaus interjects, "Settle down Lattanzi... he's just a kid."

The corporal retorts, "I was a kid when I got here *LT*, but I was never that stupid."

The lieutenant playfully asks, "Really…? So who was that stupid kid who charged a machine-gun nest without any backup?"

Lattanzi responds with an irksome tone, "Can't let that go, can ya *LT*? Three years later and you're still breakin' my stones. Ya know I survived that right?"

Neuhaus knows. He also knows that Lattanzi won the Bronze Star Medal for silencing that very machine-gun nest and subsequently saved both his and an advancing British platoon from being chewed apart by a *Waffen-SS' MG-42*. However, that doesn't stop the lieutenant from giving the corporal a friendly ribbing about being young and stupid, whenever he finds an opening. With a smile, Neuhaus shakes his head amused and turns back to the overzealous private,

"Ervalina, our job here is to help create a stabilized Germany and support the reconstruction effort. If we happen to see resistance, then we address it. But most importantly, we want peace… Right?"

Still angered, but needing to answer his superior's direct question, Ervalina begrudgingly responds, "Yes Sir."

"Good. Now fall in."

"Aye Sir." The despondent private hustles off and drops back next to Groves. As he does, his friend cuts him a look that says, "I told you not to ask." Unshouldering his rifle, Ervalina smirks back at him.

Up ahead, Sergeant McNeil nonchalantly takes off his helmet and taps it on his leg. The buildup of snow drops off. He dons it again, turns to Neuhaus and candidly repeats his point from earlier, "Another stupid kid."

Neuhaus laughs.

#

Further in the heart of the town, the squad moves more deliberately through the ruins. Rebuilding has begun here, but this area was so badly bombed, that the buildings look more like crumbling desert mesas than the esthetically built structures that formerly lined the street. Concealed within the fallen timbers, twisted metal and jagged concrete there are hidden tactical advantages to this type of cover from which to strike. Thus this area has seen an uptick in much more aggressive incursions by the resistance. Instead of employing their typical strategy of triggered demolitions, the enemy has changed their tactics. Contrary to Groves' frustrated overgeneralization of the *Occupation*, the Nazi resistance actually has been executing hit-and-run ambushes with small-arms fire, so that they can inflict damages and then swiftly disappear into the wreckage before incurring any casualties. The guerilla force has become exceedingly more brazen the more desperate they've become. The team is well aware of this fact, so they're more alert, but not overly concerned. Out in front, McNeil leads the two columns of soldiers undaunted. It's atypical for a sergeant to be on point, but if there's going to be action, he wants to be out in front.

The sound of clanking metal rings out from the side alley ahead, followed by young children's laughter. Even though the little ones shouldn't be here, the squad thinks nothing of it seeing how many kids try to find entertainment amidst the daily chaos. It's a dangerous situation, but one that has become a way of life for German children.

As the team passes the alley, they watch as five malnourished German tykes enjoy a game of 'Kick the Can', with a *155mm Howitzer* spent shell casing instead of an actual can. Their torn weathered winter-coats allow in the cold, but it doesn't bother any of them. Oblivious to the wreckage around them, they laugh and amuse themselves. Mid-play, a dirty-faced eight-year-old blonde girl notices the patrol, snaps to the position of attention and salutes them, holding it. Those that see her, salute her back with a smile. However, Neuhaus abruptly stops. With purposefully exaggerated steely eyes and scowl, he faces her. For a second, she thinks that she did something wrong and worries that her salute insulted him, even though she's seen American soldiers do it thousands of times. Then with a wink and a playful smile, he salutes her back with all the bearing and respect he can muster. Giggling, she runs off and joins the kids playing the game that's moved further down the alley. With a sense of warmth in his heart from the small interaction, Neuhaus grins and moves on. That little girl is just a small reminder to him that there's hope for American-German relations in the future.

#

The cobblestone road that the team's been following leads up to a bombed out train station. As they carefully approach, they scan the wasted vista and fully view the destruction. Alongside what remains of the station, the railroad tracks and ties have been obliterated by heavy ordnance. Huge ten-foot-diameter craters surround the area where Allied bombers attempted to level everything and cut off Nazi supply-lines during the war. An armored *Wehrmacht* engine, boxcars, transport flatcars and supplies are twisted into a derailed misshapen pile of steel and iron. Amongst the wreckage are the remnants of six *Panzer VI tanks* and three *leFH 18 mm Howitzers*.

McNeil looks back at Neuhaus, "The Engineer's haven't even started clearing this." He then points at the partially intact boxcars towards the tail-end of the train derailment, "Think we should inspect them?" Without a word, the lieutenant nods in agreement. Turning to the rest of the team, the sergeant commands, "Okay, spread out." The Engineers of which McNeil speaks is the Army Corps of Engineers. In the *Occupation*, they are a Regiment of combat engineers tasked with destruction removal and reconstruction of Germany. However, the countryside's devastation is so great that this is just one more untouched sector and who knows for how long.

As the men start to disperse, there's a sudden roar of a rapidly approaching vehicle behind them. Accelerating even faster, it heads straight for the group, instantly sparking their attention. Spinning around, they snap their weapons towards the sound, ready to ready to fire or dive for cover depending on the situation. All eyes instantly focus on the vehicle. Seeing all the hardware, a mud-spattered U.S Army *M38 Jeep's* engine quickly winds down to a slower pace, as it downshifts. It's an allied vehicle. They all relax.

It pulls up alongside the group, with the driver focusing intently at Neuhaus. With over a thousand escorts under his belt, the motorist passes them and expertly whips the vehicle around up next to the lieutenant. The soldier is a Tech-5 mechanic and who's also the general's personal chauffeur. He salutes and speaks up, "Lieutenant Neuhaus... General Buchwald wants to see you Sir."

Stunned by the unexpected words, Neuhaus briefly contemplates. *Why would the general be looking for me? Why did they track me down on patrol?* He can only mentally speculate. He responds, "When?"

"Now Sir."

Without hesitation, Neuhaus climbs into the headquarters bound Jeep. He yells back to McNeil, "Sergeant, finish the patrol!"

Without hesitation McNeil responds, "Aye Sir."

The Jeep tears off.

CHAPTER 3 — SOUTHERN COMMAND

An uneven stone-encrusted road slowly winds up the rocky hills of Weinheim to the wrought-iron gates of Vestenhaus Castle. This former Nazi stronghold fell to a small battalion of the 44th infantry division during a two-day long siege. It now houses the American Zone's Northern Strategic Command. High above the castle grounds on the citadel's spire, the *Stars and Stripes* emblematically wave on a flagstaff where a swastika once welcomed the Third Reich. Just below in the belfry, bells no longer ring in the castle's tower, instead armed lookouts scan the hillsides for encroaching insurgents. Surrounding the huge stone edifice, *M4 Sherman tanks*, razor wire, guards, and trucks mounted with *.50 caliber machine guns* prevent any incursions from piercing the Senior Officers' sanctuary.

Neuhaus' Jeep rushes up the hill and stops at the guard-gate for the security formalities. After his credentials are verified, he's waved through. His jeep passes through the gateway silhouetted by the setting sun.

#

Inside the citadel, arched hallways twist and turn throughout. Being led by an underling, Neuhaus proceeds to his destination. In front of him, broken remnants of an inlaid marble swastika encompasses the stone floor. His muddy boots stride over the crumbling remains, as he come upon ornately carved Gothic double doors. The escorting corporal opens them and steps aside, "In there Sir." He points to a single door at the end of the dimly lit hallway.

"Thank you Corporal."

#

Inside an elegant circular library, three men surround a large mahogany desk with a map unfurled on top. Temperate soft lighting cascades down from the chandelier above. While glaring down at the topographical depiction of the Soviet Zone, Brigadier General Buchwald confers with Colonel Tate and Major Kowalczyk.

Surrounding them, a triad of finely crafted amber wall-panels gleam a vigorous daily polishing. Hung on the panels, delicate Art Nouveau sconces accent the luxurious wood. In between them, floor to ceiling ornate bookshelves line the grand chamber, except where the previously seized French tapestries currently hang. Halfway up the wall, the bookshelves are intersected by a wraparound spindled mezzanine, which is accessed by a wrought-iron spiral staircase. This regal space was once designed for leisure and reflection, but now it's simply a war room.

The overweight, sixty-two-year-old George Mason Buchwald abruptly postulates, "Early morning, low level drop here…? I just don't know. I keep going over this in my head and there's too many possibilities for exposure. This southern ridge may offer a better avenue of approach." His barrel-chested large frame shakes in his dress greens, as his heavy finger jabs at a valley on the map. "Thoughts…?"

With indifference, wiry Major Clifford Kowalczyk shrugs his slightly hunched shoulders, and nods a half-hearted agreement. This is indicative of his character. Unfortunately for his career, he has intelligence and innate ability in the air, but lacks decisiveness in command. He was a brilliant pilot, and if he was as sure in leadership as he was in a cockpit, he'd be a Colonel by now. Even still, he's gotten by well. Kowalczyk's a handsome flyboy, who could have been a movie star if he had cashed in on his Cary Grant good looks before the war. However, his forty-three-year-old greying temples still don't detract from his beautifully rugged face, which can still stir a young lady's heart. Pilot wings and good looks go a long way in life.

Conversely, Colonel Orenthal Tate is an unattractive balding jackal with vaulting ambitions and knack for pithy repartee with those he perceives as lesser. The fifty-one-year-old Tate squints through his wire-rimmed spectacles and ponders the newly proposed location. For a moment he feigns actual consideration, although his mind was made up before he even looked. He presses, "I'll have to respectfully disagree General. *OSO* spent weeks on this strategy. It's solid. I think we trust the intel and proceed as planned Sir." The *OSO* is the clandestine intelligence agency Office of Special Operations, which was the precursor to the Central Intelligence Agency.

Buchwald contemplates and then grumbles, "Okay Colonel, we'll try it your way. I just hope your boys got *this one* right. We can't afford another fiasco." His allusion to Tate's team's last failures is a purposefully direct slight. The general doesn't appreciate the bureaucratic paramilitary agency that operates under its own rules and is swiftly becoming less influenced by the military chain of command. Most egregious to him is the fact that civilians are steadily replacing military officers and within a year the agency will be fully under civilian control.

Colonel Tate takes severe umbrage with the general's aspersion yet stands respectfully silent. However, his thoughts are not. *How dare you denigrate my team you bloated unintelligent windbag? You should be polishing my boots.*

Neuhaus enters through the doorway and stops just past the threshold. He snaps to the position of attention, salutes, and inquires respectfully, "You wanted to see me Sir?" As military etiquette dictates, he holds his salute.

Tate and Kowalczyk look over at the new arrival, acknowledge him and return salutes. Buchwald just waves Neuhaus in without looking up, "Come in…" Being more warrior than organizational brass, this general was never too big on protocol. Respecting decorum, Neuhaus finishes his salute, approaches the desk, and reassumes the position of attention. Finally peering up from the map, Buchwald sardonically questions, "Are you going to keep standing like that…?" As he turns towards Neuhaus, his full face in the light exposes a flattened nose and round fleshy jowls. He looks like an English Bulldog personified. "…At ease Lieutenant."

The Lieutenant responds, as he relaxes into the 'At Ease' position, with feet slightly apart and interlocking his hands in the small of his back, "Aye Sir."

Buchwald straightens up to his full six feet five and motions to the other officers, "Lieutenant Neuhaus, this is Colonel Tate and Major Kowalczyk from the Office of Special Operations." He motions back to Neuhaus,

"Gentlemen, this is the field promoted Lieutenant that I've been tellin' ya about."

Neuhaus extends his hand to the other officers. They shake. As a formality, he verbally addresses each of them, "Colonel... Major... It's a pleasure to meet you."

Annoyed, Tate angrily ponders in silence. *How could they bestow an officer's rank on a lowly enlisted grunt? Does he even have a degree? How insulting.* Then with less than subtle disdain Tate questions, "So Lieutenant, how does it feel to be awarded a battlefield commission and instantly bestowed an officer's rank? It's quite a remarkable honor wouldn't you say?"

Humbly Neuhaus answers, "It's greatly appreciated, but underserved Sir."

Tate smirks and wryly quips, "Well, you'd know best Lieutenant… wouldn't you?" Walking away, he lights a Chesterfield cigarette.

Irritated, Buchwald silently scowls at Tate.

Kowalczyk notices and attempts to divert attention from Tate's overt insult, "General Buchwald tells us that your team is the best of the best. He speaks very highly of you and your men."

"I appreciate the compliment Sir, but we didn't do anything more than anyone else over here."

Buchwald interjects flatly, "Don't be modest Lieutenant. Trust me, these two wouldn't. Generals don't give promotions for modesty." He chortles, as he grabs a cigar from the desk. Lighting up, he peers intently at Neuhaus and continues, "We have a problem, Jim. A big problem. We need the best… I've selected your team."

"Sir, a third of my squad went stateside when the *82nd* was rotated out. The replacements are inexperienced kids… not Rangers And the rest of us, we're just gettin' fat and lazy. I don't know what –"

The general summarily cuts him off, "I've seen who's left Lieutenant… Seven Purple Hearts, four Legion of Merits, two Bronze Stars and a Distinguished Service Cross. Are you really going to stand there and tell me that your squad isn't up to the task? I think you can handle this with a few new kids."

Neuhaus knows when to shut his mouth and what's already predetermined. He responds with a two word affirmation and becomes respectfully quiet, "Yes Sir."

Tate speaks up, "Lieutenant, have you heard of Operation *Wehrwolf*?" He intentionally pronounces the word *Wehrwolf* with a German dialect.

"Werewolf Sir?", Neuhaus asks dubiously.

"Not the howling beast from the Lon Chaney Junior movies Lieutenant." Tate over emphasizes the German pronunciation again, "*Wehrwolf… Wehrwolf* means Military Wolf in German. It means to hunt in packs, test the prey, find the weakness, become the apex predator … become the military wolf." He takes a deliberate drag from his cigarette while observant of Neuhaus' reaction. There is none. Exhaling, he resumes, "Operation *Wehrwolf* was Goebbels' last-ditch effort to stop the Allied Occupation of Germany. *SS* resistance and the Hitler youth were trained as assassins... hell bent on destroying us at any cost. For the past eight months they've been bombing low level targets and handing us minimal casualties from small arms attacks."

Neuhaus adds, "I know Sir. They've been hitting Hof for over a month now."

Dismissing his comment, Tate continues, "We don't consider them a real threat, but they've become quite an unignorable nuisance."

"And an overall pain in the ass embarrassment!", Buchwald coarsely inserts himself and speaks directly to Neuhaus. "Jim, we can't let this fester. Propaganda goes a long way, and the resistance isn't doing us any favors. We have a hundred and eighty-five billion in war bonds riding on America's image and it's imperative that we have a peaceful and positive reconstruction. With those fanatics running around, that just won't be possible. Truman's breathing down our necks and *Ike* wants this to go away... like *yesterday*. And now that you know the situation we're in, we'll tell you where you fall into all this. We've located what we believe to be one of their base of operations and a potential launching point for their attacks. Unfortunately, it just happens to sit along a nebulous area between the Czechoslovakian border and the Soviet controlled zone."

"Beggin' your pardon Sir, but if it's such a high priority target, why not just level it with a Mitchell or a *B-26*?"

"Soviet relations are strained. Tensions are high, demarcation lines are fuzzy, and the Reds are getting itchy. If we bomb what turns out to be a secret Soviet installation, our little Cold War gets a lot messier, and President Truman ends up holding his hand on his ass. We need an incursion team to get in there, assess the situation and do what needs be done. No mistakes. If it's the Commies… get intel. If it's the Krauts... leave nothing with a pulse." The General nods to

Kowalczyk, "Major…" Krauts and Commies were the common American serviceman's used derogatory slang for the Nazi and Soviet armies during the period.

Kowalczyk strides to the bookcase, grabs a manila folder, glances over at Tate, and then proceeds, "Our target is suspect at best. High Altitude intel has led us to believe that a small faction is holed up in a secluded farmhouse straddling the Allied and Soviet controlled Czech border." Reaching into the folder, he retrieves a black and white aerial photograph and holds it up for Neuhaus to see. "We were lucky enough to capture this during a *P-38's* early morning reconnaissance flight." The image is slightly blurred from the soft focus; recon flights take photographs with high-altitude cameras, while moving at extreme rates of speed. Captured in grayscale, a lone snow-covered farmhouse and oversized barn are barely visible atop of a mountainous cliff-face of white. Although equally obscured, an indiscernible immense metal object can be seen being dragged into the barn. Its frontend is already engulfed by the barndoors. Aside from the minor blur distortion, Neuhaus gazes at the photo silently astounded by the lens' magnification power, due to the picture appearing that it was taken from only a few hundred feet up. The major continues, "This homestead may look innocuous enough, but something very large went in that barn... and it's not farming equipment."

Across the room, sitting cross-legged on a supple Fritz Henningsen leather sofa, Tate taps the ash from his cigarette and speaks. With a self-aggrandizing tone, Tate's words ooze confidence, "The Nazis are there… Their command and control are there..."

Hiding his contempt, Neuhaus looks over at Tate to listen.

Tate, without ever breaking his gaze, continues deathly cold, "…I'm never wrong Lieutenant."

Buchwald's bellowing voice purposely commands the room; he's had enough of conversation, "Jim, General Eisenhower has authorized me to promote you to Major if you do this. How's that grab you?"

Neuhaus, "Thank you Sir, but I don't need the promotion. I'll do my job and let things fall where they may."

The General's laugh resounds through the room, "Believe that Tate...? You offer the man a double promotion and he pretty much turns you down." Incredulous with the idea this man may be promoted again, Tate's nostrils flare in disgust. He shifts uncomfortably in his seat. His thoughts race, as the 'continued insanity' makes him choke on bile. Still amused, Buchwald scratches his temple and points at Neuhaus with his cigar, "You're a dying breed son."

"I hope not Sir," Neuhaus jokes.

"Be ready to hit the silk at zero four hundred."

"Aye Sir. I'll assemble the squad."

Reserved, yet asserting in an authoritarian tone, Kowalczyk speaks, "I'll be leading your team, Lieutenant."

With a look of confusion and loss of decorum, Neuhaus blurts out, "You're what?" Stunned, he immediately turns to Buchwald. "No disrespect to the Major Sir, but you're putting an *OSO* officer in charge of a possible combat mission?"

The General calmly derides, "Well Jim… I really don't have to answer to you, now do I?"

"No Sir."
"Then get the hell outta my office... And Godspeed."

CHAPTER 4 — U.S.O. HALL

A converted German university's gymnasium acts as a *United Services Organizations* dance hall. *USO* halls were meant to be a soldier's home away from home, a reminder of the little pleasantries of life... laughing, eating, drinking, dancing and maybe even a show. Since the end of the war effort, these temporary facilities have been popping up at an ever more exceedingly expeditious rate. To keep tempers steady during the occupation and prevent the streets from running red with local civilians' blood, the need for entertainment is great. If men aren't happy or they're bored, they will distract themselves in the worst of ways.

Spread out across the polished wood floor, Occupation Troops in Dress Greens revel the night with booze and companions. The ladies of the Women's Army Corps "*WACs*" and American *USO* volunteers mingle happily amongst the servicemen. And since the fraternization orders were lifted, even some young German women have decided to attend too. They're all here for only one purpose… to have fun and enjoy life for a while.

On a dais at the back of the hall, a twenty-piece brass band, dressed in matching gray suits and black ties, blast out a bouncing salvo of swing notes. A piano, drum kit, an alto saxophone and an upright bass complete the ensemble. From behind cloth draped podiums, the ensemble wails their rendition of Benny Goodman's '*Sing, Sing, Sing',* reverberating the syncopated sounds through the rafters.

As the band delights the patrons with their lavish riffs, couples tear up the dancefloor with improvised versions of the swing dances... the Lindy Hop and the Eastern Swing. Legs, arms, and other body parts rhythmically bounce in a way that many of this provincial generation would consider immoral. However, those engaged in the dance don't care; they know what dancing is for… a prelude to romance, sex, or love.

Still dressed for patrol duty, Sergeant McNeil makes his way through the merriment and frivolity to the exuberantly animated bandleader. Stepping close, he taps him on the shoulder. The bandleader stops rocking with his trumpet and leans in. McNeil yells something unintelligible behind his hand cupped to the man's ear.

On the opposite side of the room, Lattanzi leans against the bar and watches for his potential mates, while boasting to Private Eddie Larson and Private Buford Falgoux.

Larson is a sandy-haired nineteen-year-old, with straightened pearly whites which are incredibly odd for the era. His parents had money back home and he was especially pampered, but he left all that financial comfort behind to serve his country, much to his mother's chagrin. Against her wishes, he now proudly displays his sniper tattoo with crossed rifles and the motto "One Shot, One Kill" on his right forearm. Just rotated in six months ago after his Military Occupational Specialty training, he's ready to hone his skills on something other than a target. His green eyes stray from Lattanzi to the passing women, as he listens.

The seventeen-year-old Louisianan Buford Jerome Xavier Falgoux has a slight overbite and ears that stick out like open car doors. He is incredibly green but has moxie. Wanting so much to join the war effort, he had his parents sign the age waver for him to come to Germany. The day after he landed, the armistice happened, and he was subsequently transitioned into an Occupation Troop. His penchant for tracking and his deadly accuracy at the rifle-range got him transferred to Neuhaus' team. Being one of the last to enlist before the ceasefire, he has yet to discover what it truly means to be a soldier in an elite light infantry squad. He's naive and gullible; a bad combination for someone half a world away from home.

Lattanzi continues, "I'm tellin' ya… It's all a conspiracy. First you got Pearl Harbor… A radar operator warned them that a huge blip was bearing down on them. They knew. They knew they were comin' and still they did nothin'. It's plain and simple… FDR needed an excuse to get us into the war. That's it."

In amazement, Falgoux ponders wide-eyed with his slight French-Cajun accent, "Is this true?"

"Come on… You don't really believe that do you Corporal? No way would our government do that.", Larson states emphatically.

"Larson stick to what you know… and that's nothing. Now shut the hell up and listen.", Lattanzi retorts.

Larson responds, "You're makin' this up."

Not answering, Lattanzi continues, "Get your head outta your ass. This is all true. Look, the powers that be let that happen. And then they follow that up by taking out

General Patton." The two youths stare in amazement at that last claim. The corporal continues, "Here's the facts. Patton opens his mouth about Ike and then suddenly he gets killed in a supposed *accident*... where his driver runs them into a huge *GMC Deuce*. How the hell do you miss seeing a two-and-a-half-ton truck!? That's some serious bullshit right there, my friends. Then *we* win the war and hand Berlin and half of Germany over the Commies? I'm tellin' ya, something stinks. Churchill nailed it man... it's the New World Order. And now --". Engrossed in the narration, Larson and Falgoux await his next hypothesis. Stopping mid-sentence, Lattanzi turns away from them, "Just a sec..." He downs the last of his beer, holds up a wad of cash, and motions to grab the bartender's attention.

As he does, Private First Class Jacob Chorin walks up and leans against the bar. He addresses the corporal in a familiar, but sarcastic tone, "Lattanzi..." Jacob Daniel Chorin is in his late 20s, of average height and build, with dark eyes and thick black wiry hair shaved up the sides. He purposely tries to blend in and conceal his lineage, due to the overt antisemitism that still lingers in the free world. For that reason, he wears a hidden *Jewish Star of David pendant* under his t-shirt, that reminds him of his Eastern European relatives that were slaughtered by the Nazis. And for those who know him, he's a bit of a hothead, but one hell of a fighter and deathly lethal with explosive munitions.

The corporal quips back in kind, "Chorin..." With a smirk, Lattanzi asks, "What are you doin' here? Don't you have some latrines to scrub?"

"I wouldn't want to take away the only job you're actually good at…", Chorin retorts amusingly. The two laugh out loud. Aside from always ribbing each other, Lattanzi and Chorin are good friends and have slogged through half the war together. Raising his hand in the air to signal the bartender, Lattanzi throws his other arm around Chorin's shoulder.

Leaning into Larson and Falgoux, Chorin nods towards Lattanzi, then gibes, "Just so you know, don't listen to the shit he's shoveling. He loves his conspiracies."

"Oh yeah, well here's a conspiracy about an ungrateful bastard who --", as Lattanzi goes to finish his comeback, the band stops playing and an ear-piercing sound of feedback rips through the dancehall.

Wincing, the whole room turns and looks to the stage.

On the podium, McNeil leans into the microphone, "Sorry about that." With a shrug of apology, he proceeds with a calm matter-of-fact tone. McNeil isn't the typical barking platoon sergeant, he commands with his demeanor, "First Squad... wrap it up. Debrief in fifteen minutes." Scanning his men across the crowd, his gaze hits each one and emphatically states that he means it. Walking away, he motions to the bandleader, "Well, go ahead Maestro."

The band begins to play again. Couples pair up and start to slow dance to the band's cover of Glenn Miller's "Moonlight Serenade". First Squad heads for the door.

#

Across town, Neuhaus exits the brownstone of a young fraulein with whom he frequently spends his time. He's dressed for the crisp night air. The frost burns off the streetlamps, as they illuminate a handsome boulevard teeming with activity, newly painted homes and busy shoppes. This avenue is one of the few fully rebuilt sections; looking at it you would never know the carnage that once took place here.

Locking the door behind, the lieutenant walks up to an idling military police Jeep that appears to be waiting for him. The driver is a military police Staff Sergeant. He's also one of Neuhaus' best friends from *The Battle of Bulge*. With a half-assed salute, he smiles, "Lovely night, eh Jim?"

Neuhaus returns salute, "Always… How ya doin' Hal?"

"I've been better, thanks to this one", with a nod to his prisoner seated next to him.

Slumped in the passenger seat, a disheveled Corporal Randall Scott DeVogler sits handcuffed, occupying more than half the front seat due to his size. Twenty-nine-year-old DeVogler is a walking oak, that most men step aside for instead of testing him. At six foot eight and three hundred thirty pounds, he could crush a man's skull with his bare hands. However, his kind soulful eyes reflect his true personality; he's a gentle giant with an unwavering sense of right and wrong.

The MP continues, "I brought him here instead of the brig, because he said he was one of yours."

"He is…", Neuhaus states. Dubious, he questions, "What did he do?"

"It took four of us just to get that behemoth shackled."

"What did he do?"

"Well, DeVogler here, thought it'd be cute to punch out a couple of officers."

Looking over at the embarrassed DeVogler, the lieutenant addresses him, "Did you do that Corporal?"

Flustered, DeVogler forces the words out with his thick Appalachian Missouri drawl, "Yes Sir... but they… they were tryin' to have their way with a young German girl. I couldn't let that stand."

Neuhaus stares for moment and firmly states, "You did the right thing."

"Thank you Sir."

"However, this is the fourth time that you've been busted in two months. You know you can't fight everybody's battles DeVogler?"

Undeterred, DeVogler straightens, "Someone has to Sir."

Neuhaus begrudgingly nods. He turns to the MP and orders, "Hal, take off the cuffs."

Uncomfortable, his friend responds cautioning, "Jim, if HQ gets wind of this, it won't be good for you."

Sternly, Neuhaus makes his point, "Remove the cuffs, Hal. DeVogler may be a lot of things, but he's not a liar. If he says that's what happened, I believe him."

"It's up to you Jim, but I tell ya… I saw the beating he handed those men, and it wasn't pretty. They're going to press charges and if it comes down to the word of two officers over a corporal, then…"

"I'll deal with them."

"Okay, it's your funeral…", the MP unlocks the handcuffs and removes them from DeVogler's wrists.

Rubbing where the bindings were, DeVogler smiles appreciatively to Neuhaus, “Thank you Sir.”

The lieutenant returns a warm grin, “You’re welcome.” Turning to his friend, he queries, “I hate to ask another favor Hal, but I’m running late… You think you could give us a lift across town?”

Without hesitation Hal genuflects in jest, “I’m at your service, your highness. Jump in.”

Amused, Neuhaus jokes back, “Keep it up and I’ll bust you down to private.”

“One could only hope, m’lord”, the MP continues with the joke.

As DeVogler ushers into the back, Neuhaus jumps into the passenger seat. Sitting, he looks back over his shoulder, “You know, one of these days those huge mitts of yours are going to get you in real trouble.”

Almost proud, “Sir, you sound like my momma.”

As the Jeep pulls away, Neuhaus yells over the chugging motor, “She must be a smart woman.”

CHAPTER 5 — THE BRIEFING

U*SAAF* Giebelstadt Air Base - Bavaria, Occupied Germany.

Sparsely located hangar-lights cast a flickering glimmer through whirling snow squalls that assault the night. A howling vortex rips through the expansive open vista, which provides no shelter from the turbulent winter winds. Intense gales rattle the multitude of impressive steel wings that line the airfield. A squadron of air defense *Lockheed P-80 Shooting Star* fighter jets sit ready to scramble and intercept any Soviet aircraft. Beside them, two *NAA T-6 Texan* basic combat trainers are covered with tarps, awaiting the next class of young pilots to rotate in from flight school. Further down, three *Douglas C-54 Skymaster* four engine transports are ready to move troops and civilian personnel if needed. A lone *OSO* modified, twin-prop *C-47 Gooneybird* is being prepped on the airstrip. On the other side of the runway, immense hangars house aircraft being reconditioned, fueled, or loaded with ordinance. Next to the fuel station, at the north end of the runway, is the command center.

#

Outside, the winds pound at the base, but inside this fortified briefing room the sound is hardly noticeable. Neuhaus stands in front of his seated twelve-man squad, who openly guess amongst each other what's the briefing's agenda. Their buzz fills the room. Behind the lieutenant is a chalkboard sized map of the Allied Occupation Zones and the Soviet cutouts. To his right, Major Kowalczyk awaits his moment. Observing everything, McNeil leans against a table in the back. Scratching his head impatiently, Neuhaus addresses the room, "Alright, let's have some quiet." The room quickly responds with silence. He continues, "Although I was hoping to take the Occupation easy, it seems General Buchwald has other plans. Major...". The Lieutenant motions to his commanding officer.

Kowalczyk pridefully takes center front. Convivially, he speaks, "Before proceeding with the mission overview, I'd just like to state a few words. You don't know me from anyone, but I need you to trust me and my leadership… and I need to be able to trust you. We are a team now. We are one. And although I haven't bled where you've bled, I have been in combat… many times. I've flown a hundred-and-two successful sorties with the 94th Army Air Corps Pursuit Squadron. I am a two-time Flying Ace. I've received the Distinguished Flying Cross for valor, and I've unfortunately seen my share of death. I'd like to avoid seeing any more. With that said, when I lead this mission, I expect everyone one of you to keep your shit wired tight and don't take any unnecessary risks with the group or yourselves. I want us all to make it home alive. When we embark upon this mission, my main concern is not the objective… it's you, my team." With a hint of winsome charm, he looks them all in the eyes, "I pledge to you my word… from now on, I will always have your *six*. I hope you'll have mine."

Lattanzi throws a look of 'can you believe this shit he's shoveling?' to Chorin, who responds by rolling his eyes.

Taken aback by hearing that the objective isn't paramount, McNeil stares questioningly at Neuhaus, who responds with a look of befuddlement.

Oozing sarcasm, Lattanzi's hand is suddenly in the air, "Excuse me Major…?"

"Put your hand down Lattanzi.", McNeil orders.

Looking back at the sergeant, but still playing to the room, Lattanzi sarcastically asks, "What Sarge? I was just gonna ask a question."

"No, you were going to be an asshole. Put your hand down."

Lattanzi puts his hand down, "Fine... But if my question turns out to be really important, it'll be on your head."

"I'll take that chance." McNeil motions to Kowalczyk, "Sorry 'bout that Major. Go ahead."

"He can feel free to ask his question Sergeant. We have no pretense here." With actual concern, Kowalczyk awaits Lattanzi's question.

Reading that the timing for his veiled joke has past, he defers, "That's alright sir, I already forgot what I was gonna ask."

"Oh… okay then, I guess we'll get back to it." A bit perturbed, the major moves on to the map. "Our mission is to wipe out a suspected Nazi resistance stronghold. Our objective is here... a small farm situated just along the Czech border." As he points to the map, the whole room looks around questioningly to each other. "We'll mask our approach behind this mountain chain." He then points to a doglegged-shaped range of mountains. "Three miles from the target, the *stick* will low level drop behind this ridge." Tapping the map, he continues, "We will then navigate the hostile terrain to the base of a ninety-foot precipice, where the team will ascend the cliff-face, infiltrate the contentious area and swiftly silence the target." He slams his fist on the map exaggerating his point about silencing the enemy.

Seated near the front is nineteen-year-old Private Walter Laskey; he has a naturally furrowed brow and a long-hooked nose, which he inherited from his father. His speech pattern is impaired with stammering, caused by the beating he took outside of Henry's Grill, when he was jumped as a teen. Along with his stammering, he poses a noticeable tic where his left eye and cheek squinch together rapidly when he's nervous. And although slight of build, he's strong for his size and also the team's ammunition bearer.

Next to him is Private Albert Turner, a twenty-two-year-old blonde, blue eyed brawny kid, who was drafted as a Marine during the last year of the war and later enlisted in the Army for the Occupation. And although he was unable to afford college on his father's butcher's salary, he's incredibly intelligent and speaks above his education. His words are chosen, and his speech is crisp. Math comes easily to him. Additionally, his bearing doesn't match his West Coast 'surfer-boy' good looks; he's seated rigidly, with his sinew stiffened and jaw locked. And although not conceited at all, he strives to escape the station where his lineage has placed him.

Disquieted with the premise of climbing a ninety-foot icy cliff face, Laskey leans over to Turner and whispers, "I don't… I don't… I don't like the sounds of that."

Momentarily breaking from his seated perpendicular form, Turner turns and glances over. As he does, a tuft of hair falls out of place. He instantly runs a comb through his platinum three-inch waves, correcting the minor aberration. In his moment of ease, Turner concurs a little too loudly, "Agreed… How are we going to ascend that massive obstruction?"

Hearing from behind, Lattanzi quips, "Hey Goldilocks, some of us are Rangers… and nothin' stops us. Besides two Ranger Battalions made it up *Pointe Du Hoc's* hundred-and-ten-foot cliff face, with Nazi lead rainin' down at them. I think we can do this." Glancing back at Lattanzi, Turner cuts him a look of contempt for the Goldilocks crack.

Enlivened by Lattanzi's comment, the major acknowledges the military fact enthusiastically, "Quite right Corporal. Those men at *Point Du Hoc* were fiercely determined soldiers who completed their impossible mission, in the face of insurmountable adversity. We will too. However, unlike those brave men, we are lucky enough to have the element of surprise. We will be quiet. We will be swift. We will be --"

Entering from the hall, a skittish radio operator runs in and interrupts, "Beggin' your pardon Sir, but Colonel Tate's on the line from *OSO*. He says it's urgent."

"Um… okay. Thank you Private. Tell him I'll be right there."

The operator responds, "Aye Sir". He salutes. Turning on a dime, he about-faces, and leaves as expeditiously as he entered.

Uneasy, Kowalczyk's mind races for a second then speaks, "It looks like you'll have to address any questions to Lieutenant Neuhaus. See you all on the tarmac." Not waiting for the lieutenant to give the command 'attention', he hastily exits for the awaiting call.

As the major leaves, Neuhaus steps forward, "If there's any questions, save them for the tomorrow. Go enjoy yourselves tonight." He knows this may be the last night for some of them, "Have some fun."

"Not too much fun…", McNeil grunts from the back, with his smoldering cigarette clenched in his teeth. Taking a last drag, he drops it to the floor and crushes it with his boot. "If I have to chase any of you down, I'm gonna put my foot in your ass. You got that Lattanzi?"

With a half-assed salute, Lattanzi replies, "Got it Sarge." *NCOs* are not saluted, and the corporal knows this, but he just wanted to make a smartass reply for McNeil calling him out.

"Right. Not too much fun", Neuhaus exclaims. "Gear up and lift off is at zero four thirty. Dismissed."

The jump team gets up and exits. Lattanzi strolls past McNeil, "It wasn't gonna be a stupid question, Sarge." Although the corporal was going to make a joke earlier at the major's expense, he tries to play it off.

Sardonically, McNeil nods to the door, "Get your ass outta here Lattanzi." The corporal shrugs and leaves. As the team files out, McNeil begins to follow.

Passing Neuhaus almost out the door, the Lieutenant discreetly calls out, "Frank...?"

McNeil stops dead with apprehension. Knowing this isn't going to be good, he pivots back and faces Neuhaus. His words are, "Yes Sir…?", but his subtext is "What's the bad news?".

"This operation may take three hours or three days… I have no clue. The major hasn't given us much to go on and we may all end up dead. It's a shitty position. I know you're homebound Friday, so technically you have the choice of not going, and I know I'm asking a lot but… I'd like you to go with us. I need your help… one last time."

The sergeant knew it was bad news and there it is laid out in spades. He knows he should just get up and walk out, but his friendship compels him to stay. Not really wanting to know the answer, he reticently questions, "Is that an order?"

"No… I'm asking a favor from a friend".

Visually disturbed, McNeil contemplates. He sit-leans against a table and shakes a new cigarette from a pack of Lucky Strikes. He pulls one out with his mouth, lights it up and slaps the lighter closed. The distinct toasted tobacco smell wafts through the air, as his exhalation of smoke encircles him. His mind vacillates. He's torn between the loyalty to his friend and his need to see his family. The decision finally rolls over him like a wave. He's made his choice and now he has to live with it the rest of his life, like it or not. "If it's not an order… then I'll have to say no."

Neuhaus doesn't yell, he just pleads his case, "Frank, we're shorthanded as it is… and almost half these kids have never seen real combat. This isn't going to be some normal 'Occupation' cakewalk. If I go down, we'll need someone else that the men will follow, especially with Kowalczyk 'thinking' he's in charge."

"After all you've been through, nothing's going to happen to you."

"That's bullshit… There's no guarantees and you know it. I need your help, Frank. Besides needing every able body I can get; I can't do this alone."

Standing, McNeil walks to the window and looks out into the dark of night. Holding his cigarette at his side, he taps the ash to the floor. Contemplating, his breath repeatedly fogs the glass with every exhale. With his back still to Neuhaus, he speaks softly, "I've spent four years over here. Four long years… I've done my time. I've had enough. In three days and a wake-up, I have Ginny and the boys to go home to… And a little girl I've never even seen before. Jim, do you really expect me to turn my back on that?"

Unnerved by knowing what the right answer is and what he must say, Neuhaus relents, "No, I don't."

"So, you're not ordering me?"

"No."

"I'm sorry Jim." Turning back, McNeil walks past his friend, out the door. "I'm through."

CHAPTER 6 — ZERO DARK THIRTY

Morning is here. Hours have passed and the weather has calmed, but a post-storm frigid air still assaults the thirteen men slowly amassing on the tarmac. One by one the squad assembles and drops their gear: Kowalczyk, Neuhaus, Lattanzi, Groves, Ervalina, Larson, Falgoux, Chorin, DeVogler, Herrera, Turner, Laskey and Schaefer… but no McNeil.

In front of them, the now prepped twin-prop *C-47 Gooneybird* sits on the runway, lit for boarding. Its distinctive markings have all been removed. The call letters have been effaced, the Air Corps insignia and stripes have been painted over and the aircraft has been coated in a nonreflective slate grey, to hide in the predawn sky. Unless it were shot down, no one could visually associate this aircraft with the United States. The ground staff grabs one of the starboard *Pratt & Whitney* propellers and hand cranks the blades with multiple revolutions. The pilot yells "Clear…" out of the cockpit window and the crew backs away. With a sudden metallic clang, the immense prop churns violently and then suddenly turns over. The engine chugs, as it spits exhaust into a steady rotating hum.

The time to embark has come. Distraught, Neuhaus repeatedly looks back towards the barracks and the hangar. He was sure that his friend McNeil would show, but to no avail, his plea went unheeded. Needing to proceed, he shouts to the men, "Alright… Fall in!" The men collect their weapons and gear, file in line, and begin to board. They're all dressed in similar light gray-green winter-gear. White camouflage uniforms weren't ubiquitous at that time and there wasn't any time to ship some to the team. Hastily climbing the two stepped drop-ladder, they enter through the jump door seated just behind the aircraft's portside wing.

Excited to start the mission, Kowalczyk watches loftily as "his team" boards. While watching, he notices something off with Neuhaus, "Something wrong Lieutenant?"

Responding hesitantly, Neuhaus' eyes dart towards to the hangar one last time and then back to Kowalczyk, "It's nothing Sir."

"We can't have you preoccupied when we hit ground." It dawns on Kowalczyk, "Is it McNeil? You could have ordered him to come with us." Seeing the distress in Neuhaus' face, without hesitation the major concedes, "Understood..." As the last of the squad enters the aircraft, he nods motioning towards the *C-47*, "Let's do this."

Affirming almost tentatively, the lieutenant responds, "Yes Sir." The major turns and approaches the jump door. Neuhaus falls in behind. The starboard engine races higher and its pitch levels to a smooth sounding whir. The second prop begins to turn. It's only minutes now until liftoff. As Kowalczyk climbs the ladder, Neuhaus comments, "This must be old-hat for you, huh Major?"

Kowalczyk looks back at him, "Not really. Being a fighter pilot… the goal was always to stay *IN* the aircraft, not jump out of it." He laughs, as he enters the fuselage. Neuhaus laughs along with him.

Over the turning engines a familiar voices yells out from across the tarmac, “I didn’t know this mission was going to be full of laughs… maybe I made the right choice after all! What do you think Lieutenant!?”

Delighted by knowing who it is, Neuhaus beams and spins around. McNeil runs up to the *C-47*, gear in hand. The lieutenant warmly jests, “Although you’re late, it’s nice to see you made it Sergeant.”

McNeil salutes, “Wouldn't be a party without me Sir.” He starts to walk to the ladder.

Neuhaus grabs his shoulder. Sincerity is wrapped his tone, “Thank you Frank.”

McNeil responds to his friend in kind. “Anytime Jim.” He takes a step up, looks over and smiles, “I couldn’t let a friend go alone.” Then with a nod, he climbs aboard.

#

As dawn breaks on the horizon, the *C-47* cruises at an altitude of approximately five thousand feet. Speeding at 140 knots, it banks west below the misty gray-white veil of Cirrostratus clouds and descends to twelve-hundred feet. When the jump is imminent, the aircraft will drop to its final six-hundred-foot low level altitude.

Inside the fuselage, the troop compartment rocks and jolts through the turbulence. Metal seats and floor offer the only comfort in this 20 x 6 steel tube. Dual glassed domes provide scant incandescent light, barely illuminating the space. The team sits silently relaxed. Some grab a power nap. Some eye the “ready” light. Some stare at the steel ribbed walls.

Neuhaus intently studies a map and reconnaissance photos, looking for the best avenue of approach for a ground assault. There's a plan in place, but if he missed something and there's a slight advantage somewhere, he wants to exploit it. Since receiving this mission, this is his twenty-second time going through multiple attack scenarios. He focuses harder… *Is there something there I'm missing?*

A few feet up the aisle, shoved between the bulkhead and ammo cans, Groves admires new combat-boots. He pokes his portly buddy who's sleeping with his head propped against his parka. Stirring Ervalina mutters, "What…?"

Self-satisfied, Groves replies quietly, "Finally got some new boots. What'dya think?"

Annoyed, Ervalina carps, as he closes his eyes again, "I can't believe you woke me up over some stupid boots. I need to be sharp when we jump."

"They're not stupid, they were a gift from Private Wenzyl in supply. She surprised me with them after the dance. I only mentioned them to her a few times… can you believe it?" Ervalina eyes snap open and he glares over at him dubiously, not believing his friend could've only mentioned the "stupid boots" a few times. Groves continues, "If someone gave you contraband boots from supply, how would you take that? I think she likes me. Do you think she'd do that if she didn't like me?" Groves lights up just thinking about the beautiful young *WAC* with whom he danced. Beaming, he asks, "So what'dya think?"

"I don't know. And I don't care Groves. Congratulations… whatever. I hope she makes you happy. Okay?" Ervalina rolls over towards the bulkhead.

"Fine..." Unhappy with how the conversation turned out, Groves leans back and rests his hands on his *M1*.

Further up front, next to the navigator hold, Private Turner combs his well-groomed hair. Chorin notices and shifts, leaning on his *M97 Trench Shotgun*. Not wanting to wake those sleeping, in a low volume Chorin speaks, "Psst... Errol Flynn?" Turner looks over. "That's not gonna do you any good on the ground pretty boy."

Lattanzi leans over and snatches the comb from the young private, "Gimme that."

"That's my good luck charm. I would like it back Corporal.", Turner asserts. That comb has been his good luck charm ever since he had a life changing moment in the seventh grade. Since that day, he's never been through any real milestone in his life without having that security blanket at his side. And to this day, he's never told anyone what the moment had been.

Exaggerating Turner's hair combing, Lattanzi sweeps his hair to the side, "Chorin… I have a stick in my ass, who am I?" Chorin chuckles. After finishing, he addresses Turner again, "Hey 'Gyrene', I thought you boys wore high and tights?" During the war, Gyrene was a moniker of respect that the Army used for valorously hard-charging Marines, even though Lattanzi now uses it mockingly.

"I'm a soldier now, just like you."

"Oh, so you're just like me now, huh?" Oozing sarcasm, the corporal shrugs while playing to Chorin, "Did you hear that Jake… he's just like me?" Without hesitation, he pulls down his parka collar, exposing multiple shrapnel wounds in his chest and lower neck. Turner slightly stunned attempts to keep from showing a reaction. Continuing, Lattanzi motions to Chorin, “Maybe he’s just like you too. Whatdya think… is Goldilocks here just like you?”

Amused, Chorin plays along. He pulls up his left sleeve revealing gnarly second and third degree burn scars. “Nope. Doesn’t look that way to me Corporal.”

Leaning in closely, Lattanzi asks Turner jeeringly, “What’s wrong with this picture? Look at him. Look at me. Are you sure you’re just like us?”

Annoyed and trying to control his temper, Turner ignores Lattanzi’s taunt, “Would you just give me back my comb Corporal?”

“Listen *Private*, I'll give it back when I'm damned good and ready.” Impressing the point that Turner’s a lower rank, his gaze burns with disdain. Again, he addresses Chorin, “Can you believe this guy?”

“I need that!”, Turner exclaims as he tries to snatch the comb away. Lattanzi recoils. As he does, the comb flicks from his grasp. It sails through the air, smacking a sleeping McNeil in the face. While still leaning against the bulkhead, the sergeant’s left eye pops open… then his other one. Without even a thought, he instantly glares over at Lattanzi.

The corporal doesn’t even try to fight it, “Sorry Sarge.”

McNeil doesn’t respond, except with minor look of irritation leveled at Lattanzi for his usual antics. He stands. Walking up to Turner, he hands him his comb, “I believe this is yours.”

“Thank you Sergeant.”, Turner gratefully acknowledges. He has his good luck charm back. Although he feels everything will be alright now, he still can’t figure out why both Lattanzi and Chorin have given him the heat since he joined this unit.

McNeil moves on. As he does, Lattanzi makes an "Oh shit" face to Chorin.

On the other side of the fuselage, on the floor, Medic Specialist *T3* J.W. Schaefer plays a game of solitaire to pass the time. Thirty-two-year-old John William Schaefer always wanted to become a doctor, but unfortunately life got in the way… the war got in the way. Drafted as a field medic for a mobile medical unit, he never saw action, but he tended to an incredible amount of carnage. Glaring out amongst the sea of light gray-green uniforms, Schafer's bleached white medic brassard with a bright red cross, screams a target.

On the way back to his spot, McNeil notices the armband. He approaches Schaefer, and quietly offers, "You might wanna take that off."

Confused, Schaefer looks up at him, "But Sergeant, that's supposed to keep me from being a target."

"Well Doc, the bad guys don't always play by the rules." McNeil sternly adds, "Take it off."

Although Schaefer is technically a higher rank, specialists don't have any command authority. Begrudgingly, he acquiesces and unties the armband, "Alright… Thank you Sergeant." As he walks away, McNeil stares out the starboard window and then glances at his watch. Something isn't right. He heads forward.

The team's second light machine-gunner, Corporal Armando Herrera gives his two cents to Schaefer with a deep rich Latino dialect, "Listen to the man mijo. The Sergeant knows of which he speaks. He'll get you through this. He's gotten us through worse." Twenty-five-year-old Hispanic American immigrant Armando Jose Herrera was an entrepreneurial young man before he was drafted in 1942. Like many immigrants he longed for the "American Dream" and worked sixteen hours a day as a mechanic's assistant, just to learn a trade. He saved every hard-earned dollar from that job to purchase his own auto-repair shop, so one day he could build a good life for the large family he always wanted. However, a short time after opening his shop, he received his draft letter and was forced to leave it in the capable hands of his youngest brother. Within a week he left on a transport-ship bound for Europe, while his proud parents waved a somber goodbye from the Brooklyn Naval Yard dock. Unfortunately they would never know that their son would eventually be awarded the Bronze Star for heroism, due to their fatal car crash a few weeks later. Just as tragic, his two older brothers fell to Nazi gunfire the same day that he saved countless lives and earned that meritorious medal. Although he is a man of few words, he speaks with integrity. He is a proud man… An honorable man.

Schaefer asks, "So, you trust him?"

"With my life." After making a such an emphatic definitive statement, he nonchalantly remarks about Schaefer's cards, "You have to put that Jack on the Queen." The medic is confused what a jack and a queen have to do with McNeil. Herrera points at the game of solitaire. Suddenly Schaefer gets that he's now talking about the cards, "Oh right. I didn't see that."

"You have to keep your eyes open mijo… always." His words have more subtext than just a simple card play.

Up front, McNeil passes Private Laskey eating a can of potted meat and proceeds to make his way to the lieutenant, who's still hunched over the map. Trying to grab his attention, the sergeant gives a hushed call, "*LT...?*" Still engrossed, Neuhaus doesn't notice. More firmly, McNeil tries again, "*LT…?*" Finally, lowering the map, Neuhaus glances up. Silently restrained, McNeil impresses, "This shoulda been a forty-five... forty-seven-minute hop. It's been almost fifty-five." Neuhaus snaps upright.

#

In the cabin, Major Kowalczyk stands behind the pilot and copilot, staring out the cockpit window. Anxious, the pilot watches as the mountainous horizon and the snowy landscape rush beneath them. With his hand poised over a red toggle, the co-pilot stares back at Kowalczyk. He awaits the order to activate the "ready" light. The pilot implores, "Sir, we have passed the drop point significantly. We've probably breached Soviet air space by now. What do you want to do?" Kowalczyk stands frozen, his mind racing. There is no certainty to aeronavigation in 1946. If you don't have a reconnaissance beacon dropped previously, navigation is a skill done solely by timing and math. A wrong decision could be disastrous.

Neuhaus bursts in, "What's going on Sir?" He doesn't respond. "Major...? Major!?" Kowalczyk snaps back a look. Indecisiveness washes over his eyes.

"I saw a glint."

"A glint? What the hell are ya talkin' about!? We've passed the drop! We're going into Soviet airspace Major!"

"A glint… a glint on the approach. It was binoculars."

"It could've been anything!"

"It was binoculars! And if I can see them, they can see us! Now be quiet Lieutenant, I'm trying to figure this out!"

"Figure it out!? If the 'Reds' spot us we're going to have much bigger problems on our hands than some glint!"

Almost speaking to himself under his breath, the Major contemplates, "Buchwald was right. This approach was compromised. What do we do…? What do we do…?"

Neuhaus beseeches him to act, "Major, give the damned order to turn around!" Silence from Kowalczyk. Not waiting any longer, Neuhaus barks at the pilot, "Turn this bucket around and get us back to the *DZ*! Now!" The copilot backs off the ready-light toggle.

Before the pilot has a chance to act, the Major yells, "Belay that order!"

Neuhaus interjects trying to talk some sense into him, "Sir, we are miles off course and in hostile territory! This is not going to end well!"

Ignoring him, Kowalczyk speaks directly to the pilot, "Hold your course!"

Enraged by the stupidity, Neuhaus beseeches him to listen, "We jump this far in enemy territory, and you might as well bury us before we get there! Give the order to turn around Major!"

"Stand down Lieutenant!"

"You are jeopardizing every man on this mission! This is not what the General ordered!"

"Stand down, damned you!"

Incensed, Neuhaus loses it, "You are disobeying the General's direct order and endangering this mission! Either turn us around Major or I'm relieving you of your command." Kowalczyk glares at Neuhaus, with burning antagonism.

The pilot and co-pilot look back and forth in total disbelief. Basically, pleading for an order, the pilot's hand is poised to jam the throttle, "Sir, we've definitely entered Soviet air space now. In a few minutes and we're not going to have a mountain range to hide behind."

Neuhaus grips the pilot's shoulder, "Turn back now!" Fiercely, Kowalczyk cuts Neuhaus a look, then leans over and slaps the green toggle... the "Go" light. Sudden clamoring echoes from the fuselage. In utter disbelief, Neuhaus curses under his breath, "Stupid son-of-a..."

With eyes searing, Kowalczyk seethes, "Your team's jumping Lieutenant. I suggest you do the same. And any more talk of relieving me and I'll have you shot for mutiny."

"You jeopardize my team one more time Major and you'll have to shoot me yourself... Sir." They glare at each other for a momentary eternity. Neuhaus breaks his stare and exits the cockpit.

#

Without the ready light, there is chaos. Men are jumping at sporadic intervals, just trying to get out the door. Those caught by surprise strap on their packs and sling their weapon scabbards. Frantically, they attach their static lines to the jump cable. Wind whips past McNeil, as he runs to the open jump door, to try to make order of the pandemonium. Quickly checking each trooper that approaches to jump, he yells the okay, "Go! Go!" Checked and ready, each one jumps into the open sky.

Ervalina steps up, with his helmet tilted and parka unzipped, trying his best to look like John Wayne. McNeil yells, “What the hell are you doin' Ervalina? You're gonna snap your friggin' neck.” He grabs the private’s chinstrap and yanks it tight. The sergeant yells about the parka, “Zip that!”

The private complies and smiles with obtuse zeal, “Finally some action, huh Sarge!”

McNeil shakes his head, yanks Ervalina’s parachute pack-straps tight, and sarcastically responds, “Yeah… must be your lucky day. Go!” He shoves him out the jump-door.

CHAPTER 7 — SOVIET TERRITORY

As an arising sun crests over the snowcapped sedimentary elevations, morning breaks. The valley below is still silent. Across the basin, mountainous fields are interspersed with colossal ice covered conifers and deadened ground foliage. Beyond the clearing, cutting into the forest, a half-frozen river meanders its way through jutted rocks, roiling into a crystal white cascade. Throughout the open snowscape, multiple boot prints lead to an ad hoc rallying point. Gathered underneath an outcropping of spruces, the men kneel behind cover and await in a heightened sense of alert. Their weapons are at the ready. Those who've seen battle know their situation and they know things are not good.

In the distance, Neuhaus and Kowalczyk trudge through the foot deep snow, with submachine-guns in hand. They follow the team's tracks. Crouching, they hug the tree line, attempting to obscure their movement from enemy eyes. Their labored breathing mists with each exhalation. As they approach the assembled team, McNeil steps up to Neuhaus and questions in a voice just above a whisper, "What the hell was that cluster? We had men spread out over miles." Neuhaus just shakes his head knowingly. The major interjects, "I want a rundown Sergeant, not questions. We need to move."

Irked McNeil answers deadpanned, “Silks are packed Major… Gear is stowed… We’re all locked and loaded, except… no sign of Falgoux.”

Exhaling in dismay, Neuhaus responds with fatalistic sarcasm, “Great...” He kneels. “We'll give him ten. Then we'll go find him.”

Kowalczyk shoots back, “We don’t have ten minutes. Ready the team.”

DeVogler squats with his *Browning M1919A6 Light Machine-gun (LMG)*, scrutinizing his field map. Being his size, he’s charged with lugging the 32 lbs. belt-fed .30 caliber brute. Even though it’s a modified lighter version of the original, it’d still be a task for a normal sized man to carry. Leaning the gun’s folding bipod against his shoulder, he surveils the surrounding topographical features, reads his wrist compass and checks the map again. Looking up, he offers the bad news, “Major, we overshot the landing by... I’d say probably nineteen or twenty miles.”

Irritated, Kowalczyk attempts to deflect, “I’m well aware Corporal. There were issues with the navigation calculations. Unfortunately, the pilot had to go on instinct.”

Lattanzi mouths off, “Instinct…? My eighty-two-year-old Sicilian grandmother coulda done a better job.”

“Zip it Lattanzi,” McNeil growls back quietly.

“We didn’t even get a ‘ready light’ Sarge. Something stinks.”

As Neuhaus goes to respond to the two, he notices movement in the clearing.

Not willing to wait, Kowalczyk is determined to move the mission forward, "Lieutenant, ready the men. We're moving out."

McNeil stresses his previous point, "Major, if we leave this point, Falgoux may not find us or –"

Not listening, the Major commands, "He can follow the tracks like we did. Mount up Sergeant."

"What happened to the team being your highest priority… Sir", McNeil's 'Sir' exudes contempt.

Visibly angered, Kowalczyk spews his order, "I said mount up."

No longer paying attention their conversation, Neuhaus speaks to himself as he looks out across the snow covered expanse, "What the hell's he doin'?"

Breaking from the other tree line, eighty yards through the clearing, Falgoux drags his chute still hooked to his back. Elated to see his squad, he frantically waves his arms and yells out, "Hey!" His voice echoes throughout the valley. Trees shake and a flock of black grouse take flight away from the intruder. The innocent young soldier doesn't realize the possible consequences of his actions. The whole team instinctively snaps into a defensive position, except Neuhaus who's been watching the entire thing transpire. Weapons forward, some drop prone in the snow, others move behind rocks and tree trunks for cover. Falgoux points to his parachute harness, "My release is stuck!"

Neuhaus rapidly moves his hand across his neck in a cutting motion, physically trying shut up Falgoux with his body language. Fighting to keep from yelling out and giving their position, he murmurs hoping for an unrealistic miracle of telepathy, "Stop yelling kid."

Trying to prove himself, Ervalina starts to move from cover. Groves grabs his arm, "What are you doing?"

"It's time for some action," Ervalina retorts, as he pulls away. Without hesitation, he scuttles up to Neuhaus' side, "You want me to help him Sir?" Neuhaus studies the inexperienced soldier questioningly. His look only reinforces Ervalina's resolve, "Lieutenant, I can do this." Neuhaus throws a glance to McNeil, who shrugs back a nonverbal "I don't know… maybe".

With some misgivings, Neuhaus gives Ervalina the order, "Stay low and don't run in a straight line. Go…"

Ervalina smiles. Here's his chance to be more than what everyone thinks of him. Determined, the young private tears off. Hunched with his *M1 Garand,* he zig-zags his way towards Falgoux. The team watches the horizon, ready to provide cover-fire if needed. Ervalina chugs as fast as his bulky frame will allow. Surprisingly, he moves rather swiftly for someone his weight. Falgoux sees Ervalina coming towards him, so he stops walking. He starts pulling on his harness, trying to free himself, "I can't get the damned har – ".

CRACK!! Rifle fire shatters the silence! A *Mosin M1938 Carbine rifle's* 7.62 caliber round tears through Falgoux's throat, spraying the air red. He's tossed to the ground. Clutching the wound, he gasps for breath.

At the outcropping, the team dives for cover and starts blasting wildly. Not knowing where the assault is coming from, they unload indiscriminately. Suppressing fire whizzes through the air. Bullets erupt from muzzles at varying pitch. Suddenly, a Soviet *Degtyaryov DP-27* light machine gun spits back at them. Rounds pummel their area. As the bullets hit all around them, tree bark is turned into wooden shrapnel, gear bags are ripped open, and the snow-covered ground sprays a crystalized mist. The team tries to shield themselves.

Seeing Falgoux wounded, Schaefer grabs his med-kit and leaps up to go assist. Midstride, searing lead grazes his leg. He drops screaming, "I'm hit!" DeVogler runs, blasting with his machine-gun, and drags the medic behind cover.

Feverishly, McNeil scrambles and pulls binoculars from his gear bag. He surveys the landscape. There… Above them on an ascending ridge, dug into an embankment, there's a Soviet small unit machine-gun pit. The pit is constructed of dirt dug before the winter, stacked timbers, and snowpack for concealment. It's like a foxhole, but larger to accommodate a fireteam. Three Soviet *Ryadovoy* soldiers lean against the embankment's edge; one has the *DP-28*, another the *Mosin* and the last has a *Federov Avtomat* light submachine-gun tracking across the field. McNeil drops the binoculars, levels his Thompson, and shouts, "Hundred twenty yards… three o'clock!" He blasts. Muzzles turn. Lock in. Lead pummels the target.

In the clearing, Ervalina is now beelining it to Falgoux. A burst of *Federov* lead whizzes by his head. He dives to the ground, not yet to Falgoux. Being only forty yards from the gun pit, he yanks a *Mk II 'Pineapple' Fragmentation Grenade* from his belt. Frantic, he pulls the pin. His face twists into a scowl of determination. Kneeling erect, he cranes back his arm to throw.

McNeil yells out, “Get down!!”

Searing lead tears into Ervalina’s sternum. Blown back from the force, the grenade bobbles. It explodes midair, shredding the young private’s face and torso.

Watching the remnants of Ervalina litter the white, McNeil blasts with his Thompson and charges towards Falgoux’s position. Shouting, “Cover me!” he crouch-runs, as projectiles pump from his barrel. Rounds spray the snow behind him, chewing at his heels. The team rocks the embankment.

As Kowalczyk focuses on firing a weapon he has no experience with, Neuhaus barks commands, “DeVogler! Herrera! Right flank… suppressing fire now! Move your asses!” Automatic weaponry like DeVogler’s *M1919A6* and Herrera’s *Browning Automatic Rifle* are used to overwhelm and suppress enemy fire, while opening an avenue of approach.

Lattanzi scrambles to his feet, “They’re too slow… I got this *LT*.” Darting into the trees, he slaps a fresh thirty round magazine into his *M3*.

Neuhaus yells for him to stop, “Stupid son-of-a… Lattanzi! Wait!” It’s too late, the corporal is already storming up the flank. Covering him, the lieutenant unleashes a stream of lead, as he curses to himself, “He’s gonna get himself killed.”

In the clearing, McNeil slides up to Falgoux and blasts off sporadic cover fire. Whipping out a Sulfa-Pack, McNeil fights to pull the kid's hands away from the wound, “I gotta do this kid! You’re gonna be alright!” As young private chokes on blood and gasps for air, he shakenly releases his hands. McNeil pours it on the entrance and exit wounds and shoves a pressure bandage on it. Deep red continues to spread beneath them. Looking him in the eyes, McNeil fights for the private's life, "Hang on kid!" Falgoux wheezes. The snow sprays up, as bullets hit inches away. McNeil drops over, covering him. Grabbing the *Thompson* again, he returns fire.

Deeper in the woods, Lattanzi rushes through the trees, jumping and dodging the foliage. The fastest on the team, he sprints through the forest, while trees blur by him looking like a picket fence. The sound of gunfire grows deafening, and he smells the powder residue in the air. He knows he's close. Ahead… the gun pit.

In the pit, the three Soviets fire, then duck, and repeat the process trying to dwindle the larger force. They've already taken two. Being in an elevated position, they have the military advantage. Their standard issued *Vatnik* wool long coats are covered in snow and dirt residue. As bullets slam the bunker's edge, more rains down upon them. The mid-level commander firing the *Avtomat* loses his *Ushanka* fur hat, as an American's bullet almost finds its mark. He drops behind cover. The machine-gunner pounds the team's position with the *DP-27*. As the light machine-gun spits death, spent casings clink off to the ground. The bolt locks back. Quickly, he drops the *DP-27's* disc ammo-magazine and locks in another. As he starts to pull back the charging handle, Lattanzi bolts out from the tree line blasting with his *M3*. Through the sound of gunfire, they hear him too late. The machine gunner bounces as he's chewed apart by the corporal's .45 caliber rounds. Continuing his onslaught, Lattanzi unloads from the flank, catching the mid-level commander in the jaw, ripping it from his skull. Blood erupts around his quivering tongue and sinew. As he falls away, Lattanzi tries to hit the third soldier. Unfortunately, he misses. Seeing an opening, the low-level rifleman spins the *Mosin* at his attacker and fires! In his haste, it goes astray. The large caliber round grazes Lattanzi's side, tearing through his parka, uniform, and flesh, while bruising his ribs and spinning him to the ground. An inch to the right and it might have been the end. The *M3* bounces away from Lattanzi's grasp. Wanting to finish the job, the Soviet bolts in another round and levels the weapon. Staring back, Lattanzi grabs his *1911 sidearm*, draws it, but doesn't have enough time to pull back the slide assembly. Knowing it's over, Lattanzi screams, "Screw you Trotsky!" The Soviet smiles as his finger starts to tighten around the trigger. *SHRAAAP!* Half the Russian's head explodes in skull fragments and blood. He slumps over. Lattanzi watches wide-eyed.

A hundred yards away, thirty feet up on a rock faced knoll, Larson backs off the scope of his *MKIII Enfield Sniper Rifle.* He waves the "Cease Fire" hand signal to the team, while yelling, "Cease fire! Cease fire!" The searing lead barrage abruptly stops. The team holds. Larson calls out, "All clear *LT*!"

As the team slowly get to their feet, Neuhaus yells back, "Nice shot Larson! Glad you joined the team!" As Larson slings his rifle to climb down, he gives the lieutenant the thumbs up. Passing Kowalczyk, who's still dug in behind a tree clutching his smoking weapon, Neuhaus acerbically jeers, “You can get up now Major. It’s over.” He walks out towards Falgoux.

In the clearing, a reddish black has pooled under Falgoux. McNeil, bathed in the young soldier's life, kneels next to him. He pulls back from the bandaged wound. Falgoux's eyes are fixed wide open, frozen in the terrified gaze from his last breaths. Neuhaus walks up and peers at McNeil questioningly. The sergeant subtly shakes his head "no". Knowing options are limited, Neuhaus gives an order he’d rather not, “Wrap them in their ponchos and police up everything that would point to us being Americans.”

“Aye Sir.” McNeil shuts Falgoux's eyes and yanks off his dog-tags, “His mother will want these.” He sees Schaefer limping towards him, with the help of DeVogler and inquires, “You alright Doc?”

Discouraged, Schaefer unintentionally groans, “Hurts… but I’ll live. It’s just a graze.” Taking a second, he follows up with an emphatic remorseful assertion, “I’m sorry I couldn’t help them Sergeant. I --”

“It’s not right, Doc, but shit like this unfortunately happens. You can’t blame yourself. Just take care of that leg, we need you.”

The medic nods an almost surrendering “okay” of acceptance, but it doesn’t change the way he feels. The team slowly gathers around, staring down at the dead. As McNeil stands, Kowalczyk approaches, “I’ll make sure they get all the appropriate medals for this.”

McNeil shakes his head in disgust, as he moves to Ervalina and retrieves his dog-tags. Fighting back rage, Neuhaus snaps up within an inch of Kowalczyk's face. He glares at him, wanting to strike, "This…" Slowly he backs away and utters angrily, "…is on you." Turning to Private Groves, he orders, "Groves... get something to make a sled."

Groves, still gazing upon the remnants of his buddy, stands silently still in the coagulating pool of blood. He's distraught and in disbelief. His eyes are locked on how strangely the red shines against his new boots. He thinks to himself, *this can't be real.* Although Neuhaus knows Groves is upset, he stares at the distressed private as if to gently nudge him along. Noticing, the Groves finally responds, "Aye Sir." He runs off.

Kowalczyk queries indignantly, "You're not going to bury them?"

Sill incensed, Neuhaus answers with derision, "Maybe it's something they didn't teach you in flight school Major, but you need to learn it… No man is left behind… Sir." As the Lieutenant turns to leave, Herrera calls to him.

Holding up the remnants of a *Backpack SCR-300 Transceiver Two-Way Radio* by a shredded wire, the radio operator proclaims, "*Lieutenant...* the *SCR-300* got wasted. We're cut off from HQ and unless the Nazi post has one, it looks like our trip home just became a lot more difficult."

Exasperated, Neuhaus laments, "What the hell else could go wrong?"

Pointing back to the gear bags that were ravaged with machine-gun fire, Herrera replies, "Supplies and gear were hit. And we chewed up a lot of ammo in that firefight Sir."

"That was a rhetorical question but thank you. Always with the good news, Herrera."

CHAPTER 8 — THE LONG MARCH

A blustery chill has gripped the snowcapped valley. Trees creakingly rock erratically, as each gust assaults their naked limbs. Amongst them, nearly hundred-foot-tall conifers sway, casting triangled shadows that dance across the landscape. Fourteen miles from the battle, the team humps over the harsh terrain, traversing natural obstacles that slowly drain the men's resolve. The long march has taken its toll. Unfortunately, the bright sun brings no relief to them amongst the bitter cold that has blown in. The team is exhausted, cold, and not ready for whatever lies ahead.

In wedge formation, the squad's silhouette trudges through the blinding snowscape. McNeil leads the group, his eyes locking on every tiny movement, aware that another Russian unit may be somewhere hidden nearby. Behind him, Neuhaus checks on his exhausted team, while handing out dried pork loaf and biscuits from *K-ration meal kits*. Bringing up the rear, Groves and Laskey drag the sled that holds what's left of Falgoux and Ervalina's corpses.

Walking up to Lattanzi, Neuhaus extends a slice of pork loaf, "How ya feelin' Corporal?"

"Thank you, Sir", Lattanzi takes the food and gnaws off a hunk of pork. Thinking for second about his condition, he continues, "Seven stitches… Some bruised ribs. I'll be sore for a while, but still invincible." The corporal slyly grins.

Amused, Neuhaus retorts, "You keep charging machine-gun pits like that, and you won't be for long."

"Ah… you know me Sir. I'm light on my feet. I just keep on dancin'."

The lieutenant's demeanor changes to a graver concern, "Honestly… Are you sure you'll be able to make it up that cliff-face when we get there?"

"Me…? Come on *LT*… Is the Pope Catholic?"

Neuhaus laughs, slaps Lattanzi on the shoulder and walks ahead, "Okay Corporal… give 'em hell."

"Will do Sir."

The lieutenant moves forward. Walking up next to Kowalczyk, he holds out some food, "Major…?"

Still angered with Neuhaus' lack of decorum and challenging his command, Kowalczyk contemplates. He knows that he could stop and dig into his own pack, but that would not be appreciated by the men he's trying to lead. In the few seconds since the offer, his mind has raced between indignant refusal and acrimonious acceptance. However, his body is in need of fuel, which pushes him past his vanity. Begrudgingly, the major takes it, but can only muster a nod of thank you, "Lieutenant…"

"Sir…", Neuhaus replies nodding back. Speeding up his pace, the lieutenant strides past the major and finishes providing rations to the rest of the famished team. Reaching point, Neuhaus walks with McNeil and states the obvious in jest, "You know, you really shouldn't be on point."

McNeil jokes back, "Should you?"

Neuhaus smiles and changes the subject to small talk, "How's the knee?"

The friends amicably banter back and forth, “Well, we marched all through Europe and the Army never sent me discharge papers, so I’m guessing they think it’s perfectly fine. How's your shoulder?”

“If I could feel it, I'd tell ya. Who said you get better with age?”

“Some old bastard with a sick sense of humor.”

They both laugh, as they begin to slog through higher drifts. They lean into the gale. McNeil would love to light up, but in this weather, it would be a blazing target. The few moments of silence are broken when Neuhaus interjects, speaking with a whispering serious tone only audible to those two, “We missed the drop zone because of Kowalczyk?”

Lifting his collar against the wind and precipitation, McNeil quietly responds, “I know.”

“How's that?”

“After the firefight, he pulled me aside and tried to pin it on Galeski and Rivers. They’re damned good pilots… They could have flown that drop in their sleep. There's no way they would've taken us twenty miles off course.”

“He wouldn't give the green light because he thought we were compromised.”

“Let’s hope he was wrong.”

Neuhaus responds deathly cold, “Let’s hope he doesn’t get us all killed.”

A frigid blast hits them in the face. McNeil closes his one eye and leans his head to the side, trying to deflect the cold. Neuhaus hunches his shoulders, pulls his wool scarf up and wipes the frozen vapor from his forehead. For a moment they collect themselves and then continue speaking confidentially. Neuhaus tries to speak through the snow hitting him in the mouth, “Frank… This is going to get ugly. What am I saying…? It already is… Look, when we get there – When things get worse --” The sergeant studies him, as Neuhaus attempts to convey how important this is, “If I go down, no matter what, you can't let him lead.”

McNeil contemplates the lieutenant’s words, wishing he had a different response, but he doesn’t. With a momentary pause out of respect, he reaffirms, “Like I said before Lieutenant, I'm just the sheepdog. I'm not the shepherd. That’s you and you aren’t going anywhere.”

Exasperated over not being able to change his mind once more, Neuhaus admits, “I guess it won't matter anyway when we show up there in broad daylight. The element of surprise will be gone, so in the end, there may be no one left to lead.”

“You got that right.”

They march further through the squalls in silence. Thinking about the losses and what they’re about to face, Neuhaus mind reflects on what could have been done to avoid this situation. *Could I have paid more attention to Kowalczyk? Talked the pilots into disobeying his orders? Taken over his command?* There was not one good answer for his military career, but he realizes now they may pay for his inaction with their lives. With nothing but cold, snow and whipping wind, he plays his failures over and over in his head. Not that it will matter in an hour, but he severely regrets the precarious situation that his lack of action has put them all in now. As he inconspicuously looks over at his friend, he also laments the position he put his friend in back at base. He wishes he hadn't made McNeil choose between his family and their friendship. With the weight of everything, his thoughts overwhelm him, and he becomes racked with guilt. Even though he couldn't take it back, he suddenly feels compelled to say something, "I'm sorry I got you into this Frank."

McNeil hears the words but doesn't understand. He looks at Neuhaus confused, "This is my job."

"No. You could have gone home to your family. I played on our friendship. That was wrong. I'm sorry."

The sergeant exhales and then answers, "There's a lot you should be sorry for Jim... the food, this weather, that bad haircut, bringing Major Asshole along, but not this. I chose to be here. That's on me. Besides, we're not dead yet."

Neuhaus reacts with a chuckle, "Yeah, not yet."

"However, even if we get the drop on the Krauts and make it through that, we still have a machine-gun pit with three dead Russkies back there. And if the Reds find them, they'll come lookin' for us."

"I know. I just hope we're gone by then."

#

A massive ninety-four-foot precipice stands at the base of a river. Even with the loss of life and time, they've finally reached the originally planned incursion point. Jagged protrusions thrust out from the cliff-face, bestrewed with cascading icicles each almost six inches in diameter. Running up ninety-feet-plus cliff-face, its crags split into intermittent smaller bluffs. In between the fractured rockface, fissures wind through the metamorphic stone subsequently ending on top with the snow encrusted ledge.

Across from the precipice's gravel base, a dense tree-line runs the length of the river. One by one the squad members exit from the trees' concealment. Silently, they rush the river's edge and gather behind rock cover. The horrendous last few miles have passed under their feet and now the group gathers exhausted before the mammoth precipice. Bringing up the rear, Kowalczyk follows Groves and Laskey, sans the sled and bodies. Speaking barely above a whisper, Neuhaus calls to Kowalczyk, "Where are the bodies Major?"

Heated, the superior officer responds scornfully, "Where I ordered the men to drop them. Back there… where they're going to stay until this is over. We can't drag a sled into battle." Knowing the major is right, the lieutenant reluctantly nods in agreement. Kowalczyk proceeds to point at the cliff-face, "And we're not going up that."

"Excuse me?"

"We've been compromised. It's too risky. We're going around."

"Major, if we go around, there goes our element of surprise... and that's if we even still have one. We do a full-frontal assault against a larger force, in broad daylight and it's over before it started."

"Then we'll wait for night fall Lieutenant."

"So, we can die a slower death? We can't start a fire without alerting everyone in a five mile radius and we can't huddle long enough to stay warm. So, all we're gonna be is one cold sorry-ass target just waiting to get shot or freeze."

Flustered, Kowalczyk's volume starts to rise as he asserts his authority, "We are going to follow the river's edge and proceed up the back face. That is an order." Confused, the team watches the dissension. They look at each other as if "What the hell's goin' on?". They all know that the mountain's back face is an open slow incline, that would take hours of meandering miles up to the top and subsequently end up with no cover and no element of surprise.

Neuhaus fights not to raise his voice, "Major, I know you were one of the best in the air, but let me inform you, things are little different on the ground. You call an audible and you're wrong... a whole lot of men end up dead. I'm telling you the only way to go, is up... as planned."

McNeil chimes in, "He's right Major. We go around and they will shred us to ribbons."

All eyes are on Kowalczyk. He's about to reaffirm his orders when he hesitates. He surveys their faces. Unfriendly faces stare back at him. He knows whose side they're on, but will they follow his orders? *It's not worth it to find out.* The major acquiesces, "Sergeant, get your climbing gear."

"Aye Sir." McNeil looks to the team, "Lattanzi's out with his ribs. Who's goin' with me?" They eye each other and one by one they volunteer. "I appreciate the enthusiasm, but I don't even want to do this." With a half-assed chuckle, he points to one private, "Larson…?"

"Sarge?"

"I need someone light and quick… and a sniper might come in handy too. You win." Dropping his pack, McNeil digs in and pulls out a three inch long, one inch diameter wooden dowel, with a leather strap. He hands it to Larson.

Baffled, Larson eyes it skeptically, "What's that for?"

Taking out his own, McNeil shoves the wooden dowel in his mouth like a horse's bit. He mimics tying the leather strap around his head for demonstration. Pulling it out of his mouth, “If we fall, we won't be able to scream and give away the team’s location.”

As Larson shoulders his sniper rifle, “That’s reassuring.”

CHAPTER 9 — INCURSION

Sixty feet up the cliff face, side by side, McNeil and Larson perilously free climb up the frigid stone. The only ropes they have are the ones on their backs, that they'll eventually drop to the team when they reach the top… if they reach the top. Their gloved hands fold around each crevice, hoping for a solid hold. Spiked iron foot crampons dig into fissures, raining ice and rock fragments with every step. Gently and quietly, they do their best to ascend the jagged rock.

As Larson reaches up blindly to a small ledge above, he inadvertently knocks a large Osprey who's perched scanning for prey. Its yellow eyes dart, its head rocks back and its five-foot wings snap erect. Showing its displeasure, the bird lets out its unmistakable screech and launches from its nest. The sheer size and power of the raptor startles Larson, making him lose his grip. His hand flails, his stepping foot slips and body yanks straight on his other arm. As he dangles above death, he unintentionally screams against the wood-muzzle, but fortunately the noise is muted. McNeil immediately grabs the private's arm and while straining against his own grip, he heaves. Larson regains his hold. Exhaling rapidly, he looks over at McNeil, with his eyes exuding the words "thank you". McNeil nods and they start to climb again. Foot by foot, they ascend higher.

#

At the top of the precipice a farmhouse, and enormous barn sit conspicuously silent, roughly a hundred and ten yards from the cliff's edge. Only rocky terrain and sparsely standing trees remain between the target and the team's impending assault. Concealment will be minimal upon approach. One guard could change the following hour from a surprise to massacre.

Fatigued, McNeil and Larson slide up over the cliff's edge on their bellies. They quietly remove their muzzles and catch their breath. Unslinging their weapons, they crawl for cover behind a downed tree, with the foot deep frosty snow chafing their faces. The howling wind hides the crunch from their movement. As they reach the deadened timber, they shuffle behind it and momentarily rest, exhausted.

Cautiously, McNeil peers up over the top of the log and scans the area. From where they sit, he has an obscured three-quarter view of the back and one side of both structures. Although the farmhouse looks commonplace, the massive barn looks oddly out of character for a local Slovak farm. Eerily, at neither the farmhouse nor the barn is there any activity… not a soul in sight. Even past the dwellings, where he's able to see, there's no one in front and with the team waiting below, they can't afford to move to get better recon. He watches carefully, as the minutes pass. Still there is no movement. His mind races over the possibilities. *Are they out front where I can't see them? Was Kowalczyk right, do they know we're coming? Are they hiding? Are they even here?* He needs to find an answer. He looks up at the two chimneys and notices there's no smoke. He breathes deeply over and over, smelling the air. Finally, faint but distinctive, the smell of wood burning for heat wafts subtly through the air. The sergeant whispers, "There's no guards making rounds, but someone's here. They're hiding their smoke for a reason. We may be walking into an ambush."

Moving steadily but silently, Larson cranks the sniper rifle's scope down to 100 yards and places the barrel through a crook between two branches of the downed tree. He views through the scope, the crosshairs gliding across the exterior of the barn. The side door for mucking out stalls is shut, and snow is piled up against it. Nothing has gone in or out. He trains his sight past both structures, towards the road leading to the front. There are no tracks in the snow anywhere, vehicle or foot. Speaking softly, Larson begins to narrate, "No movement. No sentries. No tracks." Still gazing through the scope, he trails left towards the farmhouse scrutinizing everything, but there's no sign of defenses. He tries to see past every tree possible, looking for a shadow or any motion. "Nothin' around the barn or that side of house. Yeah, something's definitely up."

McNeil breathes back, "Well, then they're hunkered down in one of them. I don't know if that's better or worse."

Larson continues his visual search left. Through the lens and reticle, he sees a three-foot tall, dilapidated picket fence… then the stacked stone framed edge of the farmhouse… then wooden shutters, with one hanging at a forty-five-degree angle from its lower hinge. Behind the broken shutter, a small glimpse is available through a shattered windowpane. He locks in on it. Suddenly, the flash of Nazi *SS* officer's winter coat's shoulder lapel passes by the window. Larson freezes and whispers to McNeil, "*SS*..." The

SS were Hitler's fiercest paramilitary unit specialized in neutralizing opposition.

"Are you sure?"

"Can't miss their double lightning bolts. I'm sure… but I lost him."

"Keep searchin'."

The private moves on with his scan. The crosshairs pass over a closed rotted backdoor, then over to another window. Nothing. Then further left to another window. There… Larson notices something. Missing shutters provide an unobstructed view into the inside. Not into the bedroom adjoining the window, but further back, beyond the bedroom's open door to the hallway. He looks deeper. Past the hall further into a storage room, two Nazis huddle around a small fire, with *Gewehr-41* rifles pointed at something obscured from his sight. Their uniforms are rumpled and cruddy from weeks of continuous wear. Their facial hair is overly lengthy from not shaving. They appear dirty, gaunt, and unwashed. Larson comments to McNeil, "We've got a low level brownshirt and a mid-level commanding *SS* officer, seated with rifles. I can't see what they're pointing at, but... they look really weak. I don't see them putting up much of a fight."

McNeil inquires quietly, "How many more?"

"None that I can – Wait…"

Previously blocked by the doorframe, an emaciated previously heavyset machine gunner with his *MG-42* leans over to hand one of the officers a cigarette. Nicknamed "Hitler's Buzzsaw" by the men who saw action in WWII, the *MG-42* is a formidable weapon. It's a devastating machine-gun that can fire five hundred rounds a minute and cut men nearly in two. His is a modified shoulder-strap carried offensive version.

Larson whispers again, “There’s a *MG-42* machine gunner.” Larson backs off the rifle. “That could be an issue.”

“Do what you can to take him out first.”

“Right…” Confused, Larson tries to resolve this in his head, but then questions, “Did *HQ* make a mistake? Doesn't make any sense Sarge. If this is an outpost, it’s a pretty easy target. They don’t even have a full complement… unless there’s more in the barn, but I didn’t see any tracks anywhere. There’re no guards patrolling for an assault. This can’t be right.”

“We came to do a job no matter what. If the odds are in our favor, I’ll take it. If not, hopefully there isn’t a platoon sitting in that barn waiting for us. And whatever supposedly important object is housed in that barn, let’s hope it’s still there… or we lost good men for nothing.”

“I just don’t get it. They’re all aiming at something inside. What the hell could be so threatening?”

Turning back towards the cliff's edge, McNeil responds, “Maybe whatever they’re worried about made our lives easier. Sometimes you just get lucky.” He drops his rope from his shoulder and taps Larson, “Come on.” McNeil crawls briskly to the cliff-edge and drops the rappel line over.

#

At the base of the precipice, the hundred-foot rappel line falls into the team’s view. Moving out from cover, Neuhaus runs to the rope, grabs it, steadies it for belay and motions for the squad to start the climb. DeVogler scans with his machine-gun ready to provide cover fire. Silently rushing the line, the team follows, with guns and gear in tow. Groves, Chorin, Herrera, Turner, Schaefer and Laskey each grab the line and start walking up the cliff-face hand over hand, with their feet against the rock. As Kowalczyk goes to climb, he looks at Lattanzi and whispers, "Go ahead Corporal."

Lattanzi responds just as quietly, "I'll just slow you down Major." He knows his wound and bruised ribs will make his climb incredibly slow. The corporal doesn't want anyone to be a target longer than they need to be, especially due to him. Kowalczyk nods an affirmative and begins the ascension. As he does, Lattanzi motions to DeVogler, who quickly waves him off. Lattanzi implores him to go first. Emphatic, DeVogler shakes his head "no" and points to the rope. Lattanzi knows that in situations like this his large friend is the firepower that protects the squad's rear. He also knows that Devogler won't ever back down or shirk his duty. With a look of concession, Lattanzi winces as he starts to climb.

#

Fifteen minutes have passed, but it seems like an eternity to the already spent soldiers. With the grueling climb behind them, they assemble at the top. As each man reaches the pinnacle, to save on weight and agility for the attack, they shuck off their eighty-pound packs. Only Chorin and Shaefer retain their rucksacks, demolitions and medical respectively. With the last trooper up, they silently crawl through the meager wintry cover, keeping their heads low in hopes that they'll reach their objective alive. Without a sound, Kowalczyk and Larson intentionally break off from the group and continue towards the east. As the squad reaches the property's edge, they hastily squat run and descend upon the house and barn, like ants surrounding a dropped piece of cake at a picnic.

Next to the farmhouse, Neuhaus, Herrera, Turner, Laskey and Groves creep into position. Leaning with their backs against the stone wall, they split into two groups and straddle the back door. Groves pulls a *MKII* fragmentation grenade from his belt and holds it up.

By the barn, McNeil, Lattanzi, Schaefer and DeVogler crouch at its side, as Chorin sidles up to the barn's oversized double doors. The forty-foot-wide doors are too big and cumbersome to successfully pull open and assault with any element of surprise. Chorin removes multiple *1lbs TNT Demolition Blocks* from his pack and affixes them to both doors. He wraps the positive and negative wires around the detonator's terminals and runs back to the group. Squatting, he gives the nod "ready". McNeil holds the thumbs-up to Neuhaus, by the farmhouse.

Relaying the ready, Neuhaus extends his open hand in the air, facing a crop of birch trees to his left.

Eighty yards away, nestled in the birch tree line, Larson aims his sniper rifle at the farmhouse's window. This time in a better position to see clearly through the window. Lying next to him prone, Kowalczyk watches Neuhaus by means of binoculars. Barely audible, he asks the private's status, "You ready…?"

Through the scope of the sniper rifle, Larson locks in on one of the Nazis, silently he responds, "Ready Major."

Kowalczyk acknowledges their status to Neuhaus, with a thumbs up. The Lieutenant nods back. The major speaks again to the private, "They're in position. On my mark…" Trying to keep the ocular lenses from fogging, he breathes very shallow, as he observes Neuhaus closing his fingers one at a time. The major counts down, "Five..."

Larson's finger rests on the trigger ready to strike. Through the scope, the low-level Nazi gets up from his seat and exits the room. The target is lost. "Damn it."

"What? Do I stop this?", Kowalczyk inquires.

As he asks, the machine gunner starts to trade position with the other Nazi and steps into Larson's view, "No. I'm good."

Kowalczyk shakenly continues, "Two... One."

CRACK!! Larson's *Enfield* kicks and a single searing projectile rips through the air. The window shatters and the *MG-42* machine gunner's chest distends. A spray of red mists the air, he jerks in short spasms and drops.

Herrera lets the spoon fly on the grenade. Cooks it. One... Two... He whips it through the window closest to the door. The senior *SS* officer screams for his men to move, "*Bewegen Sie jetzt*!" It explodes! The deafening sound and concussive blast rattles the walls, and a low-level Nazi is blown halfway through the other window. His shredded remains hang on the sill. The team charges the back door. Busting it open, they run in firing! More grenades detonate! In a flash, the blasts light up the inside through the windows!

Simultaneously the barn *TNT* detonates! The explosion pulverizes the outbuilding's oversized double doors, spewing forth smoke in a shower of wood and steel.

McNeil's team toss grenades inside. As they explode, they rush the outbuilding, unloading indiscriminately.

From the crop of birch trees, Larson waits for another enemy to come into view, while Kowalczyk quickly scans with the binoculars. Watching the whole thing unfold through the double lenses, he sees desultory muzzle flashes light up the barn. The sound of automatic gunfire engulfs the air. The distinctive pitch of the different caliber ammo resounds their location and concentration. Even at their distance, the extensive gun powder can be smelled in the air. Turning towards the house, the major catches the final muzzle flashes of the waning assault.

#

Inside the farmhouse's kitchen, the smoke gradually dissipates, exposing the destruction. Walls are riddled with bullet holes, cabinets torn apart, glassware shattered, and three *SS* riflemen lie in a twisted bullet-ridden or shrapnel mass on the floor. However, a fourth lives. A thirty-three-year-old Nazi corporal lays wounded next to the others, in a mixture of their and his blood. Not wanting to yell out in pain and alert the American's that he's not dead, he clenches his jaw and moves. Grimacing from his partially shredded thigh, he shoves his *MP40 submachine-gun's* stock against the floor, dragging the leg. He strains to sit up against the wall. Dropping the spent thirty-two round stick-magazine, he struggles to reload another. His bloody shaking hands unintentionally, but repeatedly tap the fresh magazine against the housing. Neuhaus walks through from a back room, draws his *Colt 1911 45*-caliber sidearm and fires! The Nazi lives no more.

Herrera and Laskey come down the stairs and intersect with the Lieutenant in the hall. Disconcerted, Herrera gives Neuhaus the lowdown on the second floor, “All clear Sir. Bad news though... No radio.”

Neuhaus laments sarcastically, “That’s just what I wanted to hear.”

Laskey interjects, “There was… there… there was no one up there, Sir.”

Herrera follows up, “No lookouts. No additional force. No one. You think the rest bugged out Lieutenant?” Looking about the room and then back at the dead, Neuhaus studies the aftermath. Something is off. He has a bad feeling about this. Lost in thoughts he hears Herrera, but it doesn’t click. Repeating himself, Herrera tries to get the lieutenant’s attention, “Lieutenant...?”

“Sorry… I don't know, but something’s off. We’ll hear what McNeil has to say about the barn.”

Groves yells from down the hall, “Lieutenant, you gotta see this!”

Neuhaus, followed by Herrera and Laskey, tear down the hall and speed into the far bedroom. This is the same bedroom where Larson was unable to see from outside what the Nazis were guarding against and where now two lay dead. As Neuhaus turns the corner into the room, he instinctively pulls back from the pungent stench of rotting death. He coughs, shoves his face in the crook of his arm and enters. Mildly choking on the smell of decay, Herrera and Laskey cover their faces too. This isn’t new death; this is a putrid days old decomposing death.

Across the room by an open closet door, Groves stands with his hand over his nose and mouth. A single bulb illuminates the closet; amber hues cascade down upon what's behind the open closet. Beyond the closet door is a rock wall riddled with bullet impacts, dried red striations and gaping eight-foot-wide blast hole. Half hanging from the hole, while partially leaning on the floor, there is an out of place three-inch-thick steel door torn from its hinges. Further past the blast hole, chunks of human flesh and denuded bone lay strewn upon a cement floor. And what used to be a Nazi soldier is slumped in the corner. His head and one shoulder are missing, ripped away in an eleven-inch half circle; it appears to be the mammoth bite radius from a huge animal. Trying to avoid the stench, Neuhaus steps through the hole, past the broken steel door. He looks inside, "Holy hell." As he speaks there's a slight echoing reverb. Deliberate, he turns to Groves, "Get the Major."

CHAPTER 10 — THAT'S AN ORDER

Groves leads Kowalczyk into the back bedroom, where Neuhaus awaits. The major fights to keep from retching. Indignant, Neuhaus stands next the hole, "You want to tell me what you make of that Major?" Not wanting to show weakness, Kowalczyk steps closer. Fighting his nauseous urge to flee, he steps into the closet and then cautiously proceeds past the blasted stone wall and steel door. He looks inside, as gore squishes under his boots. He peers at several human corpses' remains, then the ripped apart Nazi soldier and finally at the structure before him. A stone spiral staircase winds down three stories below. One story below, the light from the bedroom closet fades into darkness. At the bottom, a faint light emanates through a carved limestone archway. The closet was just a false front for a hidden passage to an underground facility. Shocked, he looks back at Neuhaus. The lieutenant questions again, "Well… Sir?"

As he considers his answer, the stench of rotting flesh overtakes him, "I have to get out of here.". The major belches bile in his mouth and hurriedly exits from the room.

#

Exposed brick and hand hewed beams surround a sparsely decorated kitchen. Worn butcherblock counters are littered with weeks' worth of empty Nazi rations cans. Dust and grime cling to almost every surface. Broken glassware lay strewn about the floor. Although completely anathema to their wartime polished image, cleanliness hadn't been a priority at this *SS* stronghold… their only focus was on surviving whatever's down below.

At the kitchen sink, the major leans over and shovels water into his mouth. He purposely glances at his watch and hangs his head. Neuhaus sets his helmet on the table, leans against it, and awaits an answer. Minutes rush by and not a word is spoken. The room is filled with an uncomfortable silence.

Suddenly, the tension is broken by Tech-Medic Schaefer entering, "Excuse me Sir." Observing the situation, he looks to Neuhaus to see if he should proceed, who promptly nods "go ahead". The med-tech goes to tell them the reason why he's here, but then decides instead to broach cautiously, "Do you need any medical assistance, Major?"

With his head still hung, Kowalczyk grouses back, "No…."

Trying to hurry this along, so he can get back to the major's answer, Neuhaus inquires, "What do you need R.J.?"

"Oh, right… Sergeant McNeil wanted me to tell you, the barn's empty."

"All of them are dead?"

"No Sir. There wasn't even a firefight. We stormed the barn, and no one was in it. And there was no sign of the Major's large metal object." Still nauseated, Kowalczyk cranes his neck back and leers at him. Trying to ignore the look, Schaefer continues speaking to Neuhaus, "Also, Sergeant McNeil said that he was taking the others to collect the gear bags and he'd be back shortly."

"Thank you, R.J., that'll be all…" Neuhaus thinks about what he saw in that room, "…but don't wander off. Things aren't copacetic."

"Aye Sir." Schaefer awkwardly salutes and turns to leave.

"Schaefer…"

The medic turns back to face him, "Yes Sir?"

"You don't salute in a combat zone."

Within seconds, Schaefer's eyes scan the room trying to comprehend that this kitchen could be a combat zone. Quickly mulling, he guesses technically the lieutenant's correct seeing that there was a firefight here. Most importantly, there may be more in this location. Respectfully he responds, "Yes Sir.", nods and exits.

As he does, Neuhaus places his *M2 auto-carbine* on the table next his helmet, "Major… I'm still waiting for some sort of explanation?"

Perturbed, Kowalczyk faces him, "Everything is as we expected. And I don't owe you any explanation… Lieutenant."

"Everything is as we expected!? There's a Kraut laying back there with his head bitten off! What the hell kind of animal has jaws big enough to do that kind of damage!? His head was bitten off Major! How the hell did you expect that!?"

The major angrily retorts, "Animals don't concern me."

"Okay, fine… but we have a bigger problem. If you haven't realized yet, this isn't just some impromptu hideout for a ragtag *Operation Wehrwolf* resistance force. This a fortified subterranean base... A Nazi stronghold that's been built over several years. And best of all, there could be a whole damned platoon down there waiting for us, for all we know. So, either I get some straight answers or I'm pulling my team out of here now."

Kowalczyk snaps erect and steps forward, trying to project an aura of power, "I think you're forgetting who's in charge, Lieutenant."

"And I think you're forgetting who the men will actually follow."

The major leers at Neuhaus. He's had enough of his insubordination and this situation. "That's the second time you've challenged my authority, Lieutenant… There won't be a third. Stand down and ready your team for recon. I want that whole subterranean facility scoured. Our objective is here. I want it found now!"

Neuhaus seethes. Inhaling to calm himself, he answers trying to retain decorum, "Major, I have two dead men, with the rest of the team cold and exhausted. I have no radio, limited rations, and a shortage of ammo due to a firefight we never should've been in, so right now my first concern is survival. When I have a better idea what we're up against, I'll be glad to lead them down there, but until then how 'bout you back off?"

The major's face twists in rage, "That was an order, Lieutenant!"

"Do you even care that we may be walking into an ambush!?"

"It was a small *SS* team ready to shoot whoever came out of that hole, so there's definitely not a large Nazi force down there! They're on the same damned team!", Kowalczyk gibes mockingly.

"Even still, you can't ignore that there's something bad down there! Maybe it's the Russians! Maybe it's some of their Kraut friends that went nuts from the cold! Or maybe it's whatever tore that Nazi's head off! I don't know... but, I'm not finding out the hard way! These men need rest! And so do I!" Pissed, Neuhaus grabs his helmet, slings his *M2* and storms out of the kitchen.

Following closely behind him, Kowalczyk barks, "I want that area reconned now, Lieutenant!"

Livid, Neuhaus spins around to face him. He abruptly stops and snaps back, "What happened to 'my men are my main concern' Major!? Or did you forget that already!?" Stunned, the major halts abruptly and pulls back at the sudden end to Neuhaus' gait. Kowalczyk stands locked, pondering his own words thrown back in his face. His demeanor changes and mind races. He has no answer, only shame. Taking notice that's he's shaken, the lieutenant softens, "Major, we'll go down there after the men are rested. We'll get it done, Sir. The mission will get done. Until then, have yourself a cup of coffee or grab some shuteye. Things will be okay." Kowalczyk embarrassed, sidesteps to pass by Neuhaus and walks down the hallway. As he does, he bumps into an approaching McNeil, who watches him stride away quickly.

Turning to Neuhaus, McNeil asks, "What's with Major Asshole?"

The lieutenant glibly offers, "His needs to live up to his Oak Leaves and it's conflicting with his words, so he's having a little crisis of conscience."

Half joking, half serious McNeil's words tease past his clenched cigarette, "And that's exactly why I wouldn't want Oak Leaves or any other officer insignia on my lapels."

Sarcastically Neuhaus quips, "Are you saying I made a mistake?"

"Not at all… the Silver Bar suits you. But don't let that go to your head."

The lieutenant shakes his head in amusement. Thinking this is a good place as any to rest, he slides down the wall with his back against it, taking a seat on the floor. Easing into a semi-comfortable position, he half-heartedly probes, "What's our situation?"

McNeil grabs a spot next to him, rests his *Thompson* between his knees and offers Neuhaus a smoke. With a polite smile, his friend waves him off. McNeil shoves the pack of cigarettes back in his shirt pocket and responds, "Laskey, Larson and Herrera are on first perimeter watch. Turner and Schaefer are boarding up windows. DeVogler and Groves are policing up brass and collecting the Kraut's hardware. And Lattanzi and Chorin are on the hole."

"I mean, what do you think Frank?"

McNeil scratches his head, takes a drag, and gives his honest opinion, "We are not in good shape. If there's opposition down there that's even larger than just a fireteam, then we have serious issues. We're not equipped to take on a subterranean base, where they have all the advantages.

Tunnels, barricades, boobytraps… who the hell knows what else. If we're up against that, it's gonna get ugly real fast."

Distraught, Neuhaus nods knowingly as he speaks the words, "I know…" Dropping his head in his hand, he rubs his forehead. Obligated, he feels he must ask, "And no sign of the major's object anywhere?"

"There was nothing in that barn. No Nazis. No trucks. No animals. Nothin'... And the surrounding area showed absolutely no sign of anyone bugging out."

"Could the snow have covered their tracks?"

"Possible, but unlikely. A quarter mile up from the entrance, there's a group of downed trees lying across the road. Nothing came in or out. If the Major's object was actually here, then it's somewhere still on this property…. But we haven't found it."

"Well, we need to find it and get the hell out of here fast. If the Russians discover their comrades at that machine-gun pit, they're going to start looking." Disconcerted, but knowing he has a job to do, Neuhaus reluctantly communicates his orders to McNeil, "After the men finish what they're doing, give them an hour's rest, and then get them ready to go below."

"You know we shouldn't be doing this?"

"Yeah, I know… Just get them ready."

"Aye Sir." As McNeil stands, he eyes his friend, and notices this is really affecting him, "You alright?"

"No. But are any of us?"

McNeil's face declaratively acknowledges his poignant question. He walks away down the hallway.

#

In what you could call a living room, Kowalczyk silently stands at the edge of the doorway observing the men. On the far wall, blocking out the windows, Turner and Schaefer hammer nails through makeshift boards rummaged from the barn and pulled from furniture. In the center of the room, he sees DeVogler and Groves sitting on the floor smoking and taking ammunition out of near empty Nazi magazines. Emptying each metal hull, they toss them in the corner and consolidate the ammo into others just in case the team must eventually rely on Nazi weaponry. With their backs to the door, they continue their conversation, unaware of Kowalczyk's presence. Groves sardonically states, "That guy doesn't know his ass from a hole in the ground." Kowalczyk knows they're talking about him. His guilt begins to twist into anger.

DeVogler retorts, "Yeah, well that doesn't excuse the chain of command. If Lieutenant Neuhaus follows him, we have to respect that."

Turner posits pragmatically, "DeVogler's correct. Kowalczyk is the commanding officer, and the chain of command is there for a reason. You have to respect it no matter what we may think of him personally or his critical mistakes."

Groves crossly objects, "Even if those mistakes cost us our lives?"

Schaefer adds his two cents from over by the window, "Hey, I'm all for following the chain of command, but this guy doesn't know how to lead. I mean… I know I'm green when it comes to combat, but I know what the dead looks like back there, and I don't have a clue what did that… I just know

I don't want to end up that way. This isn't good. It's not good at all. This guy just doesn't get it. And I agree with Groves."

The major's anger becomes rage.

Groves adds, "This isn't war. Nobody knows we're here. How many more of us have to get killed before the *LT* stops listening to that *OSO* flyboy and takes command?"

Holding back his ire, the major steps fully into the doorway and calls out very calmly, "Groves… DeVogler…"

Surprised, DeVogler and Groves pop up. The two others spin around. Turner snaps to the position of attention. They all quickly glance at each other. Their minds all echo the same sentiment. *Did he hear? How long has he been there? Does he know what we said?* Kowalczyk won't give away the answer to their thoughts. He surprisingly plays it cool. He just awaits their reply with a serene, matter of fact expression. DeVogler responds first, "What can we do for you Sir?"

Composed, their commanding officer gestures for them to follow, "DeVogler… Groves… You two come with me." Pointing to Turner and Schaefer, "You two, search the grounds for any sign of the object." He turns to leave.

They all reply in unison, "Aye Sir." DeVogler and Groves grab their weapons and follow, accompanying him out of the room.

As the three exit, Schaefer and Turner look at each other with relief. They must have gotten away with not being heard. Schaefer exhales and Turner runs his comb through his hair. Little do they know, he heard it all.

#

Corporal Lattanzi and PFC Chorin sit on the floor, *M3* and shotgun in hand respectively. They try to get a few minutes rest and recuperate from the morning's events. Their breathing is labored, as they utilize cloths tied over their faces to diminish the room's stench. Even though they've tried to remove all of the gore, the rancid reek of death is even more pungent now. The early encounter with Kowalczyk's boots breaking the coagulated crust of human remains on the closet floor released more stench into the air. Languid, they aim their weapons at the wall's blasted opening, which leads to the subterranean annex. They're a little less tense than they normally would be in hostile territory because they figure that any real threat coming up from below would be heard way before. Additionally, this is the start of a laborious guard duty in a vile situation and neither on them are happy for it. Lattanzi goes to complain to his friend.

Kowalczyk, followed by Groves and DeVogler, enter in the room. Their faces are covered too. His blood still boiling from overhearing the team's conversation, the major is now ready to let these two have the brunt of previously curtailed fury. He barks at Lattanzi and Chorin, "On your feet soldiers!" The two reluctantly stand. "When you're on watch, I want you attentive and standing at the ready! Do you understand me!?"

Annoyed, Lattanzi scoffs, "Does that go for when we're in foxholes too Sir? Because that may cause a real problem."

"I am in no mood, Corporal!"

Sarcasm exudes from Lattanzi's face as he starts to make a crack. Chorin, clears his throat as if to say, "Shut up".

His friend rethinks and quickly changes his tone. Trying to feign decorum, he answers mutedly, "Yes Sir."

Still incensed, Kowalczyk now turns to Groves and DeVogler. He's done away with the pretense and now's his opportunity to show them who's really in charge and who can lead. He points to 'The Hole' and growls, "Get in there now." Confused, they don't understand why he'd send only two men into the unknown. "Find where that leads. Find what we're up against. And find my ship." The men all take notice of the word "ship", and it didn't seem like a mistake. Maybe a mistake by letting the word slip, but his statement seemed genuine.

DeVogler probes, "Ship Sir?"

Playing it off, Kowalczyk sharply states, "The object DeVogler. The object. Our target. Find it and I want precise intel in less than an hour. Move out."

Reticent, both Corporal DeVogler and Private Groves acknowledge the command, "Aye Sir."

Chorin doesn't like the situation and speaks up, "Major, don't you think we oughta go with 'em Sir? They don't even make up a full fireteam." The major's eyes snap in his direction and sear his disapproval. The *PFC* nonverbally backs off the topic.

Not appreciating the circumstances either, Lattanzi follows up, "Maybe I should go let Lieutenant Neuhaus know."

Kowalczyk fumes and the words roll from his lips with a seething rumble, "This is my command. I make the decisions. Not the lieutenant."

"Ya but, the *LT* has experience with close-quarters warfare. He might --"

Cutting him off, the major spews from his lips, "One word to him, Lattanzi and I'll have you busting rocks in Leavenworth for the rest of the *Occupation*. Am I understood Corporal?" Silence... The major seethes and overenunciates each syllable, "Am I understood?"

The corporal understands him and has his number. He responds flippantly, "Yeah, perfectly…"

Focusing on his watch, Kowalczyk looks over at DeVogler and Groves, "Move out."

Apprehensive, they both move into the hole.

CHAPTER 11 — THE DESCENT

Cautious with weapons at the ready, DeVogler and Groves tread softly down the stone spiral stairwell. Except for the remnants of blood splatter at the entrance, bare bone-dry limestone walls surround the descending stairs. Leading, DeVogler chokes up on his locked and loaded *LMG*, waiting for what may be around each upcoming bend. For a moment, the 250 round ammo belt wrapped around his arm clinks. Groves grips his *M1 Garand* tightly, with a false sense of security almost as a talisman to ward of danger. Their shallow breathing reverberates a hollow trill. As silent as possible, they step carefully descending the three-story structure. Even still, they're unable to stop the muted sounds of gravel and grains of sand crunching under their feet. A third of the way down, the light from above is gone and they are plunged into darkness. Their only guide is the archway light below that can be viewed only by leaning slightly over the stone railing's edge. Hating the position that they're in, from the darkness Groves whispers to his cohort, "This is not cool."

Just as quietly, DeVogler chimes back with his smoky midwestern drawl, "Do you ever do anything but complain?"

"I think I have the right to complain. It's just the two of us down in this shithole and we have no idea what the hell we're walkin' in to."

“Well, bitchin' about it ain't gonna help us there, Hoss. It might get us shot if they hear ya, but it certainly ain't gonna help.”

As they take a few more steps downward, Groves can’t help himself but gripe, “So this doesn't bother you... that we don't know what's down there?”

“No.”

“Well, it should. We don’t know anything.”

“We'll know soon enough.”

The conversation stops and they continue to the bottom. Step by step they tread closer to the light. Stopping in the last of the shadows, they relax and try to suppress their quickened breaths. DeVogler nods forward and they advance. Breaching the light, the two ease up to the archway, momentarily stopping at the threshold. The large corporal strains to peer around the corner, his view hesitantly peeking past the wall's edge.

There’s no one.

Exhaling, he nods ‘good to go’ to Groves. *LMG* leveled, he angles through the archway, moving in a hunched position. Harsh overhead lighting illuminates a brick corridor lined with timber supports, that leads down to a ‘T’. Moving expeditiously, the two charge the end of the hallway. As they do, they pass two *SS* officers’ corpses with their throats torn out. Their *German Lugers* lie next to them, with the bolts locked back from exhausted magazines. Only quickly glancing and not taking time to stop, they make their way to the end where the ‘T’ branches off into two other corridors. They each take a corner, with their backs against the wall.

Ready for anything, they look cautiously peering around the corners. They look left and right.

Again, no one.

At the end of the long corridors are reinforced steel hatch-doors, with levers for door handles. Although the right passageway is clearly lit, the left ends in intermittent shadows as the maintenance bulb above the hatch flickers. Again whispering, Groves asks, “Which way do we go?”

DeVogler motions, “Left.”

“Why left? I have a bad feeling about left. I think we should go the other way.”

Annoyed, DeVogler whispers back, “Okay, then go right. What did ya ask me for?” Groves shrugs. Quietly, they head right. Silently, but swiftly they move to the end of the corridor. The hatch is slightly ajar. The two stand still. They listen. Nothing…

Private Groves swallows, losing his nerve. Not wanting to see what’s behind that door, he offers a ‘better’ alternative, “I say we say screw this shit, get the hell outta here and tell the major we didn't see anything.”

DeVogler shakes his head, “We can't do that.”

“We CAN do that. No one will know.”

“I’ll know. I'm not gonna lie, Hoss.”

Groves knows that DeVogler is as immovable in his character, as the nearly seven-foot frame he occupies. Annoyed and frustrated, he snaps, “Fine…” Begrudgingly, he raises his *M1* at the hatch, “You open it. I'll cover you.” DeVogler nods an affirmative. With his hand still on the grip, the corporal leans his weapon upright against his shoulder. Grabbing the edge of the door with the other hand, he yanks.

Metal screeches as it opens. Quickly, he steps back, reattains his hold on the weapon with both hands and gets in firing position. As the hatch swings opens on its hinges, DeVogler and Groves appear silhouetted by a dim light from inside. *CLANG!...* the hatch hits the wall.

Groves jumps, winces, and shushes, “Shhhhhhhhh!” DeVogler looks over at him amused.

Ahead of them is an open mess hall, with lit caged emergency fixtures on the ceramic tiled walls. There isn’t a lot of light, but it’s enough to see the layout. In the center of the mess hall are enough tables to allow thirty men to eat comfortably. Off to the right there’s a succession of four hatches, each fifteen feet apart, that provide access to other corridors. Each passageway leads to the labyrinth of tunnels and chambers, further in the belly of this installation. To the left is a metal staircase that leads up to a mezzanine above.

They move in. Four feet into the mess hall, DeVogler momentarily stumbles, as his boot hits something on the floor. He abruptly stops. Looking down to the left, partially obscured in the shadows, he sees a pile of fragmented skeletons and dried blood of Nazi soldiers… but there’s no flesh. Bite marks have marred the calcified remains. The bones have been gnawed clean. Something has been feeding on the cadavers. The corporal murmurs to himself, “What the hell did that?”

“Holy shit,” Groves exclaims under his breath.

A creak from the stairwell has DeVogler spinning his *LMG*’s barrel around at the staircase, checking to see that it’s clear. He looks… Nothing. Groves cautiously moves on to the hatches along the wall. Passing the first open portal...

then the second… and then… a low rumbling growl echoes from the third hatch. Whatever's in there isn't happy. They both snap their attention to it. Closing in, they lock their weapons on the doorway. The corridor is pitch dark. Their breaths quicken. Their hearts pound. Groves points to the door that's slightly ajar and reaches out. DeVogler nods. Shaking, the private's fingers close around the metal door. Quietly, he pulls it open.

Suddenly, a German Shepherd barks viciously and bolts from the room, knocking Groves on his ass. Hitting the floor, his weapon slides away. The dog takes off through the mess hall. DeVogler holds his fire, "You asshole. You scared the hell outta me."

Groves looks back, chuckling, "You were scared…? I almost shit myself."

Suddenly... A flash of an immense seven fingered hand with razor like claws jerks Groves into the corridor's darkness by his leg. As he's yanked in, he screams, and his hands grab the doorjamb. Fighting to hold on, he frantically kicks with his free leg, "DeVogler!!" Corporal DeVogler drops the *LMG* and dives, grabbing Groves' hand. Spinning in place on the floor, he shoves his feet against the wall for support and heaves. His hulking frame strains. Groves snaps taught, "It has my... It has my leg!" Like a rope in a tug-of-war, he wrenches back and forth as the two powerful forces tug to have him.

From beyond the doorway, the thing that has the young private grunts disproving growls and spits its frustration in the fight for its prey.

DeVogler, "Hold on!"

Groves screams at the thing, as he kicks desperately, “Get off me! Get off!” His eyes pegged with fear, he yells back at DeVogler, “Don't let me go DeVogler! Don't let –” The sound of gnawing flesh cuts him off midsentence. He screams in utter pain, “Ahhhhhhh!!!” With the crunching snap of bone, he comes yanking back to DeVogler, with his leg ripped off above the knee. As deep red spills beneath him, Groves screeches out in pain, “Agghhhhh!!”

DeVogler hand scrambles to grab his weapon. Clutching it, he spins. Face twisted in anger; he fires blindly into the doorway! As the belt of ammo chugs through the light machine-gun, an ungodly guttural roar echoes from the corridor. Pounding footfalls tear off away from them. Dropping his weapon, DeVogler yanks off Grove’s web-belt and lashes it around the eviscerated knee, trying to slow the arterial spray. More screams of pain wail from the wounded private. Hastily, DeVogler stands and heaves him over his shoulder in a fireman's carry. Snatching up the *LMG*, DeVogler bolts through the mess hall as fast as his large frame will allow.

#

In the bedroom, Lattanzi and Chorin stand near the blasted wall and listen intently at the hole. The major isn’t in the room. Thinking they definitely heard something, they lean in further to hear. Indiscernible faint muffled sounds resonate from the three stories below. By the time the sounds have gone from the corridors to the stairwell to this room it’s just a muffled remnant of its original source. “There it is again… Did you hear that?”, Lattanzi questions.

While still trying to listen, Chorin replies, “I heard something. I just can’t tell what it is.”

“Was it gunfire?”

“I not sure. It’s a long way away.”

Lattanzi looks around to make sure Kowalczyk isn’t within earshot, “I’m not sure either, but I’ll tell ya what I am sure of… somethin’ stinks. Something’s definitely up with Kowalczyk. He sends them down there without a full team. Then he keeps checking his watch over and over again. What the hell’s his rush? We’re cut off from HQ. We have a seventy-plus-mile hump through freezing weather to get home. We’re not going anywhere fast. And did you catch that ‘ship’ comment?”

“Yeah… that didn’t seem like a slipup.”

“He’s hiding somethin’.”

Chorin examines Lattanzi’s words, rolling them over in his mind. It adds up, “I know I give you shit about being a conspiracy theorist, but this time… We’re on the same page.”

“Well, we gotta find out what –"

Abruptly rising up the from stairwell, DeVogler’s deep voice reverberates through the air, as he calls out, “Medic! Medic!”

Providing possibly needed cover fire, Lattanzi aims his *M3* at the hole. Chorin also readies his weapon and cranes his neck back towards the bedroom door, “Schaefer! We need you in here! Schaefer!”

Charging up the stairs by pure adrenalin, DeVogler carries the wounded private, only aware that Grove’s screams have turned to fading moans. He repeats again, “Medic!” His pounding feet grow closer. The two emerge from the hole in the wall. Exhausted from the climb, DeVogler drops Groves on the deck and bends over to catch his breath. Hitting the floor, Groves awakens from his almost passed out state. He screams again.

Lattanzi and Chorin now kneeling at the private's side, try desperately to save him. Frantic, Lattanzi yanks off his belt and fights to wrap it around the existing blood-soaked belt, which has yet to fully stem the flow. Chorin pulls out a sulfa pack and pours in on the wound. Quickly cutting strips from Groves' shirt with his combat knife, Chorin fashions a makeshift bandage and tries to do his best field dressing, "Get his leg tied off!" He then yells to DeVogler, "Get over here and hold 'em down!" Still screaming, Groves flails and his bleeding stump slams the floor. Rushing over, DeVogler grabs the leg and shoves him down. Finally, Corporal Lattanzi's able to sinch the belt tight. Groves eyes bulge and his neck striates, as he grits his teeth against the pain. Looking at the life slipping away, Chorin exclaims, "Stay with me Groves." He yells to the hallway, "Medic! Schaefer!" Angered, he barks, "Where the hell is he!?" After hearing the commotion, Kowalczyk rushes into the doorway. Freezing in his tracks, he sees the carnage. He stares in horror.

Grove's life pools under them. He begins to shake violently. Lattanzi reacting, "He's going into shock!"

Chorin yells again, "Medic! Schaefer, we need help damn-it!"

Pushing past Kowalczyk, Neuhaus and McNeil charge inside. In an instant, the two survey the situation. The lieutenant fills in the room why the medic isn't here,

"Schaefer and Turner went outside with us… they should be right behind." He then questions, "What the hell happened?"

As they all try to hold down a convulsing Groves, DeVogler looks at him with guilt, "He was attacked."

McNeil yells out the door, "Schaefer hurry up and get your ass in here!" Turning back, the sergeant watches as the leg still pulses streams of red. It's slowed but still flowing. He rushes over, "Lattanzi, grab something for a tourniquet." Not waiting, the sergeant shoves his fingers in the stump and squeezes off the artery. Before Lattanzi can get up, Medic Schaefer and Turner come running in. Medical bag in hand, Schaefer drops to the floor, breaks open a morphine capsule and jabs it into Groves' leg. A moment... Groves stops shaking and his breathing becomes labored.

Lattanzi shouts, "What the hell took you so long!?"

Schaefer flustered, "I'm sorry... I had to grab my bag."

Incensed, Chorin spews his frustration, "Sorry doesn't cut it asshole."

Having enough of their bullshit, McNeil halts where they're going, "That's enough!" Then addressing Schaefer, "Can you help him, Doc?"

Schaefer is silent. A wave of self-doubt and trepidation rushes over him. His insecurity of only ever working on men in medical units and never in a combat situation, paralyzes his voice and actions.

Knowing Groves is losing time, McNeil pushes, "Doc…!?"

Still frozen Schaefer utters, "I don't know."

"Doc!"

"Okay, okay... yes. Maybe. I need to get him on the kitchen table to work."

Before McNeil can respond, Neuhaus orders, "Turner... Chorin… help them get Groves in the kitchen. DeVogler… Lattanzi... over here."

Turner and Chorin respond, "Aye Sir." The two move in and each grab an arm. McNeil continues to pinch off the artery and clutches the leg. Schaefer seizes the other leg. The four lift Groves simultaneously and carefully move him out of the room. DeVogler and Lattanzi back away and approach Neuhaus.

Neuhaus looks to the senior corporal, "What happened Lattanzi?"

"Don't know Sir. DeVogler was the only one down there with him."

The lieutenant turns to DeVogler and without verbally questioning, he awaits an answer. Although undeservingly, the huge corporal is riddled with guilt over what happened to the young private. He answers with shame in his voice, "He was attacked. I shouldn't have let him go first."

"What attacked him DeVogler?"

"I don't know. It was dark. It grabbed him out of nowhere. I didn't see it."

"It was only you two?"

"Yes…"

"What the hell were you doing down there?"

If someone's wrong or not, DeVogler doesn't believe in throwing people under the bus, but he also won't lie either. Apprehensive to speak, DeVogler exhales with uneasiness and offers up the truth, “The major sent us after his object. He said it was a ship.”

Neuhaus gaze snaps to the major, probing. As he does, Schaefer enters the doorway covered in Groves’ blood. Everyone looks to him. He just shakes his head “no” and walks out. Only moments have passed, but he bled out. Groves is dead. The lieutenant turns and leers at Kowalczyk. The major stares back indignantly. His eyes betray his former words… it was never about the men; it was always about the ends justifying the means. It was always about the ship, no matter what. Neuhaus’ mind churns and his blood boils. Lattanzi adds fuel to the fire, “We offered to give them support *LT*, and the major said ‘no’. He sent them down there alone.”

Neuhaus’ thoughts focus on the years of war, watching “Top Brass” sacrifice good men for their egos. This was all just another lie leading his men to spill their guts for some officer’s glory. It pushes him over the edge. Like a flame to gasoline, the lieutenant explodes and charges the major. Enraged, he slams Kowalczyk against the wall by the hole, “You lying bastard! You knew! You knew all along, and still you sent them alone!”

Squirming under the force, Kowalczyk wails, “You're assaulting a superior officer!”

Not caring, Neuhaus persists, “Whose ship is it Major!? The Nazis’? Russians’? Whose!? And what the hell attacked them down there!?”

Kowalczyk grabs his underling’s shoulders and struggles to push him off, “That’s classified!”

Neuhaus slaps him upside the head, grabs his hair and yanks his head to look at the blasted hole. “Classified! Your classified got a man killed! How many more of us were you willing to sacrifice down there!? How many!?” Although he yells the question, in his heart he knows the answer; they’re probably all dead already.

“I'll have you shot, you insubordinate bastard!”

Neuhaus ignores him, “How many more of us have to die!?”

Trying to play on the men’s duty to honor, the major implores, “Are you men gonna let this happen!? You are soldiers in the United States Army! I’m a major damn you! Arrest him! That’s an order!” Lattanzi and DeVogler just stand in silence and watch. From all the commotion, McNeil runs in unprepared for what he’s witnessing. Kowalczyk loses it, “This is mutiny! I’ll have you all shot!” His eyes sear with rage. Spewing venomously, he turns his fury back to Neuhaus, “Stand down Lieutenant!”

“Who else is expendable!? What the hell are you after!?”

“I said stand down!” Kowalczyk draws his *1911 .45 caliber* sidearm and shoves it in Neuhaus’ ribs. Lattanzi and DeVogler draw their sidearms, leveling them at Kowalczyk.

McNeil raises his hands warily and tries to calm the situation, “Okay… Everybody just relax. This doesn’t need to happen.”

The major pushes the lieutenant back a few steps with the pistol muzzle, “It already has.”

Neuhaus' eyes burn, "You're not killing from a cockpit now Major. You're staring a man in the eyes. Go ahead… do it."

Kowalczyk wants to pull the trigger. He wants to shut this insubordinate asshole's mouth permanently. His hand shakes. His finger tenses on the trigger. But he's not stupid, he scans the hardware pointed at him and eases up. Still pointing the weapon at Neuhaus, "This is bigger than the two of us… Bigger than all of us. This is National Security, something you don't have a damned clue about."

McNeil reaches out towards Kowalczyk, "Give me the pistol Major."

Neuhaus antagonizes, "No. Pull the trigger."

Tense, McNeil beseeches, "That's not helping *LT.*"

The major is even more resolved, "You are impeding with the strategic interests of our country, and I have a mission to complete with or without you." He taunts, "Preferably without."

Irate, Neuhaus taunts, "Then do it. Just tell me what's so important down there that you're willing to sacrifice my team?"

Bound by confidential restraint, the major only reveals his motive, "I can tell you this Lieutenant, that ship contains technology much too important to let fall into the hands of the Soviets. And 'yes', I am willing to sacrifice all of your lives to make sure that doesn't happen."

"You sorry bastard."

Mockingly, Kowalczyk retorts, "No… not sorry in the least. It's called duty."

From behind, Turner who snuck in the room lunges for Kowalczyk's sidearm. The major hears the attack, pivots, and fires! The large caliber tears across the fleshy part of Turner's bicep, spinning him stumbling to the ground. In the major's momentary lapse of focus, DeVogler swings and lands a crushing right hook to Kowalczyk's jaw. He drops like a sack of dirt. The corporal quickly follows up by kicking away the major's weapon. With the possibility of being shot now neutralized, Neuhaus takes command. He looks Kowalczyk in the eyes, "You caused the death of three of my men and now shot another, your time's up Major." Talking to the rest in the room, "Tie him up."

Dropping military etiquette, McNeil questions his friend, trying to promote some rationale through the insanity of the situation, "Jim… how are we going to explain this?"

"I'll worry about that later.", the lieutenant nods to the corporal. DeVogler grabs the major by the collar, yanking him from the floor and slams him up against the wall. Neuhaus looks to Turner holding his arm in pain, "You okay Turner?"

Wincing, Turner acknowledges, "Yes Sir."

"Thank you for that."

Suddenly with a massive shuddering growl, a huge silhouette erupts out of the closet's blast hole and buries its massive jaws into Neuhaus' neck. The shaggy hide upon its head, muscular shoulders, and striated barrel chest undulates violently, as its lips retract from its opening jaws. In a shower of red, it drags the lieutenant kicking and screaming back into the darkness. The team was only able to catch an isolated flash of the beast, as it emerged and retreated. Only a sliver of light provided a glimpse of the bright warning variations of its mottled leathery skin. Yet it's bioluminescent eyes still pierce the darkness as it draws him back into the wall.

Both Lattanzi and DeVogler turn and fire! "*LT*!" Even wounded, Turner draws his sidearm and unloads. Rounds riddle the wall and inside the hole.

McNeil yells over the fury of gunfire, "Cease fire! Cease fire! You're gonna hit the lieutenant! Cease fire!" As the last of lead pummels the wall, there's silence again. Running towards the sound of gunfire, Chorin and Schaefer scramble in, weapons at the ready. They contemplate all the smoking barrels, with no bodies.

Confused, Chorin inquires, "What happened? Where's the lieutenant?"

Distraught and despondent, DeVogler responds in disbelief, "He's dead. The *LT*'s dead. It ripped him into the wall."

The men in the room stand stunned. They can't believe what they've seen. Even though the pain of watching his friend dragged to certain death is crushing, McNeil knows what must be done. He orders stridently, "Alright... Reload, get your shit together and saddle up. We're goin' after *LT*. Chorin… grab the rest of the team outside."

"What about the perimeter?", Chorin puts forth with clear intent. "Someone needs to watch for a Soviet force."

The sergeant knows he's right. Attack may be imminent if the Russians have found their fallen comrades. Also Herrera, Laskey and Larson can't stay out in the elements much longer; they need to be relieved by other personnel. He thinks about the best solution and then yells to the senior corporal, “Lattanzi... Take perimeter. Swap your weapon with Herrera and send them all in. We’ll need everyone we can spare.”

Lattanzi isn’t happy to be leaving the hunt, but he won’t second guess this man he truly respects, “You got it Sarge.”

Turner stands and interjects, “Sergeant… I’ll take watch.” All the room looks to Turner questioningly. “With my arm, I’m effectually impaired and wouldn’t be any help to the team down there. However, I’d be able to execute the perimeter watch effectively and without reservation.” Unconvinced, McNeil studies the private and considers the problematic task ahead of them. Following up, Turner offers cogently, “If you consider all the disparate variables at hand, this is the best tactical solution, Sergeant.”

McNeil starts to visibly give in. He’s right, it is the best solution. “You sure you’ll be able to handle the *Browning* with that arm?”

“I won’t let anything get past me. Neither the Russians… nor that thing.” Although they say nothing, both Lattanzi and Chorin have started to see Turner in another light. They still aren’t fond of him, but his actions have spoken volumes.

“Alright, take watch. Lattanzi, you’re with us.” He turns to Schaefer, “Doc… patch him up before he goes out.”

Schaefer nods.

Before another word is spoken, Kowalczyk clears his throats and proceeds to insert himself. Actually fearing his fate, the major asks directly, “And what of me?”

McNeil purposely doesn’t answer him. He just glances at DeVogler and sarcastically asserts, “Make sure the major's comfortable. We wouldn't want him impositioned.”

“Absolutely...” DeVogler drags Kowalczyk across the room and forcefully shoves him into the wooden kitchen chair, that a Nazi was previously using for watch.

McNeil walks out.

CHAPTER 12 — ELEVEN HUNDRED HOURS

Seated at a desk, in an upstairs bedroom, McNeil furtively scribbles a goodbye letter to his wife and children. He knows his odds. The thought of never seeing them again eats at him, especially knowing this was self-inflicted and wasn't for a true cause like winning World War II. Setting down the pen, he stops writing. With his elbow on the desk, he drops his head in his hand and laments the choice of choosing his loyalty to his friend over going home to his family. Lighting up a smoke, he gazes out the dirt encrusted window situated next to the desk. The sun's warm glow is backdropped by an incredibly serene winter sky. The storm never hit and the beautiful tranquility surrounding them in no way reflects the chaos that resides within this dwelling. Amused, he ruminates about the irony. He takes another drag, picks up the pencil and continues to finish the note. As he does, Schaefer enters the room, "Sergeant…?"

McNeil turns around to face him and waits for him to speak.

"I sutured up Turner's arm and bandaged the wound. He's waiting downstairs for you."

"Okay. Thank you.", McNeil nods his appreciation, with the cigarette still hanging from his lips. Schaefer doesn't leave. The sergeant starts to turn back to his letter but notices the medic's lack of movement, "Something else I can help you with Doc?"

Hesitant to speak, Schaefer equivocates, “I’m not a combat medic and this is just my opinion, so please take it for what it is… and I wouldn’t say this if I didn’t think it actually needed saying.”

“Out with it already.”

Schaefer shifts uncomfortably and nervously expresses his concern, “I don’t know if going after the lieutenant is prudent. From what the rest of the men described of the attack and with my knowledge of zoological behavior and human physiology; I’m not very hopeful. If we find him, I doubt he’ll be alive. And if somehow he is, he's going to need real medical attention, not just a field dressing. We have nothing here that will address his type of wounds. I don’t know if it’s worth risking everyone’s lives, given the most likely outcome. And I say that with the utmost respect for Lieutenant Neuhaus. I just thought you should know that before you made a definitive decision.”

McNeil takes a deep calming drag. Smoke roils and the ember glows. He sets his smoke on the edge on the desk, with the ashes hanging off. Trying to keep his composure, he exhales and answers in the most nonjudgmental way that he’s able, “Doc, he’s part of this team and we have no idea if he’s dead or not… or what condition he may be in, so we’re going down there and we’re going to get him.” He follows up emphatically, “We never leave a man behind.”

“I understand.”

“Most importantly… He’s my friend.”

Embarrassed by the interchange, Schafer nods and turns to leave. McNeil stops him, “We’re gonna need you down there Doc. You do whatever's necessary to feel fully prepared, but we need your head in the game. It's important."

The medic turns to face him. He looks him in the eyes and gives an earnest response, "I know that… I know. I follow orders just like everyone else. I'll be ready."

"Good. Don't worry… Things will be alright, Doc."

Schaefer chuckles nervously.

"Something funny about that?"

"No… no, it only struck me funny because you always call me Doc. I'm just a simple medic Sarge, that's all. I'm not a real doctor. I wish I were."

"You heal right? You save soldiers' lives right?" Schaefer nods an affirmation. With sincerity in his eyes, McNeil drives home the point, "Well, that's good enough in my book." Modestly, Schaefer smiles appreciatively and exits the room. He yells to the leaving medic, "See you downstairs, Doc."

Without hesitation, the sergeant goes back to finishing his goodbyes. He ponders for a moment, hoping to pen just the right words that will provide his family solace and let them know how much he loves them if he doesn't make it back. Hurriedly, he jots down a few more lines, erases, and then finishes the letter. Pensive, he reads over what he wrote. *Wow, this is terrible.* This is not what he wants to leave his family. With a humph of disdain, he crumples the paper and tosses it on the floor. Quickly he jots down a one succinct line. The letter reads, '*You were everything in my life, I'll miss you and I love you all'*. Folding it up, he puts it in his chest pocket and buttons it closed for whomever finds him dead.

Getting up from the desk, he grabs his smoke and peers out the window again. Seventy yards away Herrera patrols the Southeast ridge, slowly pacing through the deep snowy perimeter with his *Browning Automatic Rifle*. McNeil cranes his neck forward left and right to better see around the obscured corners of the window. As he looks for Larson and Laskey, his breath momentarily fogs the glass in a rhythmic succession. Gently inhaling and exhaling, he doesn't notice… fogged then clear… fogged then clear… fogged then clear… Minutes pass, as he waits for them to come into view. They don't. His thoughts shake him. *Can't worry about them... everything's copacetic. They just must be on a zone watch instead of a walking three-sixty rotation. You think. You don't know. What if it's worse? It's not something worse. Hopefully it's not something worse. What if that thing made it outside? Son-of-a-bitch...* As his mind races through the possible worst-case scenarios for those men, his breathing quickens and pulse pounds. Abruptly, the quickened repetition of his misty respiration on the glass finally grabs his attention. *What the hell's wrong with you? You need to calm down. If something happened, Herrera would have heard or seen something. You gotta stop this shit, you have a team to lead. Get it together, McNeil. Get it together.* Pulling back from the pane, he exits.

#

Gathered in the living-room, a few of the men await their new team leader, Sergeant McNeil. Lattanzi looks out the window and sarcastically inquires, "What'dya think Major… your good buddies at *OSO* gonna come save our asses?"

Kowalczyk is bound to the wooden chair, with his hands tied behind his back. He responds sardonically in the corporal's vernacular, "They may save *my ass* Lattanzi, but they certainly won't save yours from a firing squad."

Grabbing another chair, Lattanzi pulls it across the room and places it in front of the major. He spins it around backwards, sits and leans on the backrest facing him. "You know, you're a pretty funny guy for someone who just shot my friend."

Turner, out of habit runs his comb through his hair with his good arm, while mentally questioning, *We're friends now*?

"Come on, you can tell me the truth… You wanna shoot me too Major, don't ya?", Lattanzi taps his finger on the butt of his .45 in its holster.

With an acerbic dose of rancor Kowalczyk fires back, "Nothing would give me greater pleasure then to see you shot for munity Lattanzi, but then I'm not the one holding the gun… am I?"

DeVogler stands to the side, watching this unfold, while contemplating whether he should step in. The rest watch unsure. Lattanzi cocks his head to one side and then quickly thrusts his hand downwards towards the handgrip of his sidearm. The room holds its breath… *Is he going to shoot him?* Their eyes are locked. Subtly, the corporal's fingers graze past the sidearm and reach into his cargo pocket. He pulls out a package of crackers, eats one and holds one up to Kowalczyk's face, "Cracker..? I found these in the kitchen. They're pretty good. You oughta try one." The major doesn't respond, he just leers at the corporal. "No…? Not hungry?

Okay.", Lattanzi jests, as he shoves another cracker in his mouth. While chewing, his intonation exudes sarcasm, "So what are we gonna do with you Major? I have to say, thus far your actions have been quite unbecoming of an officer of your prominent stature. Ya know, you've made some really big mistakes. First, you give some dumbass orders to the pilot that take us twenty miles off course, which endangers the mission. Then you drop us into Russian territory where two of our men get killed and we waste a whole shitload of ammo. You follow that up by getting Groves killed. Then you pull a gun on the Lieutenant, only to top that by shooting poor Turner over there… which that in and of itself is pretty messed up. And after all that… this mission will most probably fail, and we'll all end up dead. So Major, how come I get the sinking suspicion that you may not be playin' for our side?"

Hearing everything from across the room, McNeil makes his presence known, "Lattanzi, cut the shit. We don't need that now. We need answers."

The corporal stands and pulls his chair away, "Right… got it. We're all ready when you are, Sarge."

Now with his *Thompson* and a Nazi *MP40* he retrieved slung over his shoulders, McNeil approaches Kowalczyk, "Is there anything you can tell us to give us as an advantage down there?" There's no response. "This is your one chance at redemption Major. Give me something I can use." Still no answer. The major looks up at him indignantly. McNeil tries another tactic, "Look, we can argue about how we got to this point, but there's one unmistakable fact… if we don't make it back, you're just as dead as we are." Silence. Unslinging just his *Thompson*, McNeil heads for the door, "Okay, have it your way." Without turning back, McNeil commands, "Turner, it's time… switch with the team outside. Chorin, watch the major. If that prick moves, shoot him. Everyone else with me." Enraged, the sergeant strides off. His anger resounds through the room, as each footfall pounds the wooden floorboards.

As McNeil goes to breach the living-room's threshold, Kowalczyk unceremoniously speaks up, "The ship is an alien spacecraft." Stunned and disbelieving, the sergeant stops and turns back to face him. The whole room goes silent. "We didn't find this facility from one of our high-altitude flyovers. We were made aware through pure luck."

"What about your photo Major?"

Enjoying every minute of this game, Kowalczyk beams while teasing out the truth, "That was a taken from a Zeiss gun-camera that was mounted on a *Drachen* kite balloon. It was taken by the Nazis the day that they found the spacecraft. Lucky for us, this facility's commanding officer decided to memorialize that momentous discovery with much celebration, fanfare, and photo documentation. The one you saw was most plausible with our story." McNeil silently seethes at that comment, as the major continues, "You should see the other photos… astounding and marvelous. Even still, it's remarkable that a top-secret facility took the uncalculated gamble of drawing attention to themselves, simply for the Third Reich's glory and their astonishing hubris… but then the Nazis were never a humble people." The *Drachen* which Kowalczyk references was a tethered mini-blimp, which could function effectively from almost ground level up to six thousand feet. It was utilized by the Germans in WWI and II for military observation or as anti-aircraft barriers. And gun-cameras are exactly what they sound to be; they were cameras mounted on aircraft's guns to take periodic photos or aerial motion picture footage, during bombing raids or dogfights.

McNeil is still incensed, but willing to play the game, "Okay… So if nobody knew about this place, how'd you get your hands on the photos?"

"Two weeks ago while doing a routine sweep of the Czech border, just outside of Waldsassen, one of our patrols came across the frozen remains of a dead propulsion engineer. He was found partially inhumed beneath an errant snow drift and in his pocket was a handwritten note. The note chronicled his escape, provided a rough sketch identifying the location of this underground test facility and it closed with an impassioned plea … he implored the Allies to intercede with the Nazi's research and destroy this facility at all costs. And clutched in his arms was a tattered briefcase, with files detailing an ongoing clandestine program that was to reverse engineer the crashed spacecraft's technology. Even more incredible, he carried something truly remarkable... photos of captured extra-terrestrial beings and a smashed interstellar vessel." The major glances at all of them, impressing his point. "Although the war had ended, this unknown facility continued to pursue their Fuehrer's goal… total global domination, but with their newly acquired alien technology."

Arcing with his hand, Lattanzi points to all the men and then points repeatedly at Kowalczyk, "I knew it! I knew something stunk from the beginning! This was a total setup!"

"Lattanzi…", McNeil snaps his name. The corporal quiets.

Kowalczyk proceeds with his narrative, "That ship is the same as the unidentified objects we started observing buzzing the Trinity Test Site in New Mexico almost a year ago. Right after our first atomic test, they suddenly started appearing from White River to Roswell. They seemed to watch, maybe study... we didn't know. But they definitely didn't seem friendly. Each time the Air Corps scrambled to intercept, they escaped with ungodly speed and agility." They all listen intently. Every man is riveted, as he continues, "And then suddenly after months of running, they stopped and started engaging us. Without them losing even one craft, they took out squadron after squadron of *F-80B*s, with unmitigated ease. Our most advanced jets were no match for them in dogfights. They were unstoppable." He takes a deep breath and reveals his own anecdotal close encounter, "Top brass called on the best of the best to stop these things. Every Flying Ace that engaged them, ultimately ended in defeat. I myself was knocked out of the sky within the first thirty seconds of combat. In all of my years, I've never seen anything like it. They are superior in every way. And right now, below us is an absolutely frightening technology. If that technology is fully realized and ends up in the hands of our adversaries, we're done for… America ceases to exist. However, if we can possess it, we will become the world's only military superpower. I don't know what knocked that alien craft out of the sky to let the Nazi's get their hands on it, but I know it's here now and we have to find it. That engineer risked his life to stop them. He knew the danger of their project succeeding. And now we find ourselves here... at the mercy of our precarious situation. You… me… and your team."

Miffed, McNeil's rugged scowl burns into Kowalczyk, as he walks closer towards him, "So the whole damned thing was a ruse? You lied to get us here?"

Without any remorse, Kowalczyk gives him a pithy retort, "Oh no Sergeant, we didn't lie to get you here. If you've forgotten, you're owned by the United States Army… we could have just ordered you here. We lied to ensure this mission's success."

"Unbelievable…"

"Let me ask you McNeil, what do you think would be more motivating for a successful mission… The narrative of a threatening rogue Nazi faction that needs extinguishing or some fanciful story about spacemen and their crashed alien ship?"

Now animated, McNeil raises his arms in frustration and seethes, "So you dropped us in here without a clue of what the hell we were up against!?"

"You were on a need-to-know basis."

"And if the whole damned team was wiped out!?"

Pulling against his restraints Kowalczyk leans in, his voice pragmatic, "We're all expendable Sergeant… that includes me. This is too important. It has to be stopped."

"If we're all dead, then the Army hasn't stopped anything!"

The major leans back. "That's not quite accurate Sergeant." McNeil doesn't like the sound of his remark, there's something foreboding in Kowalczyk's tone. The major offers unemotionally, “Following six hours of radio silence, *HQ* will launch a heavy bomber with a significant payload onboard. And roughly forty-five minutes later… an atomic blast three times the size of Nagasaki will level this area. This will be stopped, one way or the other.”

Lattanzi erupts, “Holy shit, they're gonna friggin' nuke us!”

McNeil glances at his watch. *10:17.* They were supposed to touch down at zero five hundred hours. A little over five hours have passed. *Eleven Hundred is the Zero Hour.* Ignoring Lattanzi, McNeil questions Kowalczyk, “Are you tellin' me that in a little more than an hour, we're all fried?”

Kowalczyk responds matter-of-factly, “If we fail to radio with the stand down code, they will assume that the only way to ensure that technology doesn't fall into the wrong hands is to make sure nothing's left. If there’s no contact by eleven hundred hours, they’ll implement the alternate solution. Between prep, liftoff, and flight-time… in the next hour and a half, give or take, we will reach 7200 degrees Fahrenheit and the *Operation Wehrwolf* ‘sympathizers’ will be blamed for an atomic mishap. There'll be no record that this team ever existed.”

Chorin approaches and vents to McNeil, “This is bullshit! We don’t have to listen to that asshole and stay here to die. We can bugout now and run.”

With a deathly cold assurance, Turner speaks pragmatically from the corner across the room, “We won’t make it.” Everyone in the room turns towards him.

Both annoyed and questioning, Chorin snaps back, "And why the hell not?"

Turner steps away from the wall where he was leaning, and addresses them all, "Nagasaki had a blast radius and firestorm of roughly five kilometers. The average man runs that distance in thirty minutes. If the major's correct, triple that. Throw in deep snow, parkas, boots, exhaustion… and that doesn't even take into account the radiation cloud's drift, with the prevailing winds…" He emphasizes each word, "We won't make it."

Pissed, McNeil one-handedly grabs Kowalczyk by the collar, "Why the hell didn't you tell us sooner!? Why!?"

Sneering defiance, the major counters, "Like Chorin said, the team would have run, and that technology would be lost forever. I wasn't going to let that happen." Rage boils in McNeil. His breath deepens, his teeth clench and he wants to strike. Kowalczyk sees the anger in his eyes and tries to deflect, "Honestly Sergeant, would it have mattered? We had no radio. No way to contact them. Not to mention, I tried to hurry Neuhaus. He didn't listen. I tried to get you to talk to your friend… talk some sense into him, but you just stood idly by and did absolutely nothing. You watched as your friend ignored lawful orders, struck a superior officer, and ultimately wasted the precious time you wish you had now. Hate me all you want Sergeant, but your hands are just as dirty as mine. But this isn't about us anymore…" His demeanor changes to a solemn frankness, "It's about your team now. And if you want to save them… the clock is ticking. I suggest you find a radio."

The words hit home. McNeil knows he's right. Easing up, he lets go of the major, "DeVogler, cut him loose."

Muttered exclamations of disbelief resound through the room. One voice speaks up the loudest… Chorin, "Are you friggin' kidding me Sarge!? You're letting him go!? That asshole pointed a gun at the *LT* and shot Turner!"

Lattanzi whole heartedly agrees, "That's right Sarge." The other voices make their agreement known.

McNeil sardonically snaps back, "Well, lucky for me this isn't a damned committee." He points to the other room… the entrance to hell, "The fight is in there! We are running out of time and need to find a radio or a transponder before our asses get cooked. There's something huge down there. I don't know what it is, but I know that it took out most of this facility's armed complement and it doesn't have even have so much as a scratch on it. Now it wants us all dead. So, it's all hands-on deck. We can't even afford a perimeter or a lookout. Like it or not, the major is coming with us… period. We're gonna split into two fireteams and find that radio… or die tryin'. Now, I don't want to hear another friggin' word about it. DeVogler, cut 'em loose. And the rest of you, saddle up." The sergeant storms out of the room.

CHAPTER 13 — WHERE IS IT?

The whole team has amassed in the back bedroom, even those who were previously on perimeter watch. Although the room has been cleared out, the stench of death has yet to subside. Some slightly wince, others cover their face with their hands, but all try not to choke on the smell. As they await the descent, the pungent smell is a keen reminder of the unbridled ferocity they're about to be up against.

Broken into two fireteams, they get ready to descend into the stone stairwell that leads to the tunnels of the facility. Fireteam one consists of Sergeant McNeil, Corporal DeVogler, PFC Chorin, PVT Laskey, and T3 Medic Schaefer. Team two is made up of Corporal Lattanzi, PVT Larson, PVT Turner, and T5 Herrera. Those low on ammo now carry a Nazi weapon as a backup.

At the mercy of his underling, Kowalczyk stands in front of McNeil hoping to go with his team. The sergeant hands him one of the dead Nazi's *MP40 submachine guns.* Surprised but pleased, the major acknowledges McNeil trusting him with a weapon, "Nice of you to give me the benefit of the doubt."

Ignoring him, McNeil addresses the two teams, "If he aims that at any one of us, shoot him. No questions asked." Turning to Kowalczyk, McNeil quips, "Don't make me regret this." He then points to Lattanzi's team, "You're over there."

Poised with the dead Nazi's *MG-42 machine-gun*, Lattanzi jokes and grins, "Looks like you're with me, Major." He checks the ammo belts inside the mounted ammunition box, as he nods a sarcastic 'over here' to the major. Annoyed, but not willing to challenge due to his situation, the major acquiesces. He steps in line behind Lattanzi. He may no longer be in charge, but he won't let himself be relegated to stand behind privates.

Without a word, McNeil moves silently forward into the breach and disappears. The two teams follow him into the blood splattered closet, through the blasted wall, past the broken steel door and down the stone spiral staircase.

#

Now below the farmhouse's ground level, the temperature begins to drop. Condensed water drips and creates a soft echo, as each droplet pelts the rock floor. The team is a discontinuous moving silhouette against the fading light from the closet up above. They keep their flashlights stowed to prevent becoming an easy target. Weapons raised; they step quietly. As they move down through the spiral shaft, they use each sense on heightened alert. Their eyes strain to peer through the dim lighting. They listen for heavy footfalls or obscure sounds to tip them off to an invader's presence. Against the waning smell of corpses, they even subtly sniff for any faint signs of the wretched beast. McNeil, leading the pack, whispers back, "If we encounter that thing or more Krauts, watch your fire… we're in close quarters."

With the sergeant still turned around, DeVogler notices something in the darkness and points to a section of wall a few steps below. Quietly he solicits McNeil's attention,

"Check that out Sarge." McNeil looks, trying to discern what he sees. Lugging the *LMG*, DeVogler moves by him and rashly takes out his flashlight. He shines it in a four-foot diameter jagged hole in the limestone wall. Uneasy, DeVogler makes his concern known, "This wasn't here when Groves and I came through."

Stepping down, the sergeant peers in, "Shine it down there." The flashlight beam stretches back and fades into an immense steel superstructure. The light can't reach across the span that is at least three hundred feet wide. What is illuminated is lightly rusted heating and cooling pipes, electrical conduits, machinery, and catwalks that hang from the inside ceiling above. DeVogler's beam changes direction downward, following the supporting metal architecture. The light creeps over steel planks, grated landings, and perilous walkways, as it tries to light three stories below. The two men scan, looking for any sign of the lieutenant or the beast. Nothing. As McNeil pulls back, he sticks his hand in something he hadn't noticed before, something wet. Raising his hand, he passes it in front of the flashlight beam… blood. Speaking just above a whisper, he makes a fair assumption, "It must've taken the *LT* down through the superstructure. Alright… douse the light."

DeVogler complies and responds just as quietly, "Where is it?"

"I don't know."

"We gonna follow it in, Sarge?"

Annoyed, Chorin pipes up, "Yeah, that's real intelligent genius... we're gonna follow it in there. That's gotta be forty feet in the air."

The big man faces him and points, “You best shut yer mouth, Hoss.”

Chorin barks back at the much larger man, with an attitude that doesn’t fit his size, “I don’t sweat you.”

“Cut the bullshit.”, McNeil rumbles as he starts down the stairs. “We’ll look for the *LT* after. Right now we need to find that radio. Let’s go.” The two stare each other down before moving on. The two teams begin the descent again.

#

Below, where the long-arched tunnel comes to a ‘T’, the teams diverge. Before parting, Lattanzi and Chorin shoot each other a look of “stay alive”. The two friends then nod an acknowledgement and turn back towards their respective teams.

Lattanzi’s group follows the same route that eventually lead to Groves’ attack. McNeil’s heads into uncharted territory. Filing into each passageway, each team moves into an echelon formation across the eight-foot-wide corridors. The staggered formation’s angle provides an excellent range of vision and field of fire for each member. A tactical advantage severely needed in this close quarters scenario.

Securing his grip on the *MG*, Lattanzi winces from the weight pulling on his previously bruised ribs. He snorts and shakes it off. Rapidly and nimbly as he can carry the large machine-gun, Lattanzi rushes towards the open steel hatch. Driven by the need to succeed, he closes on it quickly. Kowalczyk, Herrera, Larson, and injured Turner attempt to keep pace quietly. In an almost negligent fashion, the corporal hastily glances in and charges in fearlessly. The rest of the group follows.

Nervous, Schaefer looks back. He watches as the last of Lattanzi's group silently passes through the other steel hatch, into the darkness. Exhaling, he focuses back on what lies ahead… deliverance or death. Fifteen feet ahead, a sickening strobe of light from the failing maintenance bulb above assaults the hatch, which is closed and secured. Approaching it, DeVogler levels his *LMG*. Chorin's fingers adjust on the pump action of his shotgun, securing his grip. Laskey steadies his *M1 Carbine* to ready for engagement, but mentally prays for none. McNeil on point, holds up his fist. The team stops, their weapons poised to strike.

McNeil points to the door and treads closer. The team holds. Although moving as quietly as possible, the sergeant's boots make a muffled scuff against the brick floor, with every movement. His breath quickens. He sidles up to the hatch. The flickering light from above cascades down upon him in an alternating wash of harsh white and then darkness. His face grimaces as he reaches out and realizes that the hatch's lever will take two hands to open. Slinging his *Thompson*, he grabs with both hands and yanks. It barely moves. Straining to open it, the steel screeches, and the release gears clang under the force. His face elucidates his displeasure with making so much noise, but it's unavoidable. If they were hoping to stay stealthy, that's no longer an option. Anything within earshot knows they're there. Suddenly, the noise stops. He looks back at the team and shakes his head in half apology-half disgust. Without a word, he continues. Pulling on the cold steel handle, the hatch opens. Retrieving the *Thompson* from his shoulder, he aims into the black and cautiously proceeds through.

CHAPTER 14 — FEEL THE HEAT

A white tiled four-foot-wide service corridor stretches sixty feet in front of McNeil's team, as they cautiously enter. McNeil, DeVogler, Chorin, Laskey and Schaefer file into the tightly confined passageway. It's lined on both sides with rough-cut pine wooden doors, that are mounted on wrought iron hinges. They listen. No sounds come from within. No longer able to move in echelon, the soldiers break into two-by-two cover formation, except for Schaefer who covers the rear.

They converge on each door in twos, rushing the rooms. Each doorframe shatters one by one, as one-man kicks it open and the other one covers. Team members leave each room empty handed and then assault another. Steadfast, they move forward praying that just one room will yield a radio or some other form of communication. Slam after slam there is nothing… Nothing to halt the coming ruination. Until only one door remains.

At the end of the passageway, the men gather in front of the last door. Silent, McNeil eases up to the jamb. He can feel heat radiating through the lumber's slats. He listens. A mechanical hum resonates a slow cadenced thump. He turns to the group and mouths, "Furnace room." The men all raise their weapons, sighting in on what may be waiting behind that door. Holding up three fingers, McNeil counts down silently dropping one finger at a time. Three… two… one! Violently, he smashes the door open with his foot and then recoils into a shooting position. The team charges the room ready to unload. As they race inside, they realize that this isn't just a furnace room; it's a foundry in an immense chamber, which houses a vast superstructure. It's the same framework that they previously looked down upon from the stone stairwell above. Unopposed by any adversary, the men stop just inside the door behind an oil pump for cover. Scanning for anyone or anything, they view the massive room.

In the northeast corner, an industrial smelting blast furnace periodically fires up its burners and exhausts off-gas through its flue. Large swaths of its bronzy glow illuminate isolated sections of the enormous machinery. Hanging above on a transfer rail is a bucketlike metallurgy ladle for pouring molten alloys. Alongside the furnace, a fifteen-foot-long fuel tank and its supplemental reserve sits covered in condensation. Behind are mammoth boilers and a retrieval system. Further behind are slag-waste railcars and ore-minecars situated along the far wall on a track system. The tracks lead to a sizable steel bulkhead and blast-door. On the opposite corner of the furnace, chlorofluorocarbon cooling units, ductwork and twelve-foot fans push cool air throughout the facility. Weaving through the middle of the forge is a maze of pipes that climb brace-work and scaffolding into the superstructure. Slightly rusted steel I-beams support the exterior walls up to the roof. Anchored into the roof on the far wall, woven in amongst the pipes is an oblate spheroid water tower, where the outside aquafer is pumped in to deliver pressure for the whole facility. It also supplies the coolant for the furnace and the personnel's potable drinking water. Along the walls and ceiling, service lights provide harsh luminescence to the areas around them.

Pointing up at the service lights, Chorin whispers to McNeil, "Sarge… those weren't on when we looked in here before."

"I know." The sergeant responds with concern in his voice. He thinks to himself, *Something ain't right.* His eyes dart through the light and dark, trying to catch a glimpse of anything moving or even a silhouette.

Chorin creeps over to a forged stack of freshly machined metal. He picks it up, feels the weight in his hand and tries to bend it. It's too light for steel, too strong for aluminum and the wrong color for titanium. He whispers back to McNeil, "Sarge, I don't know what metal this is, bit it ain't normal. What the hell do you think they were building with it?"

McNeil can't speculate at the moment, "Chorin, get back over here now."

For a moment Chorin doesn't understand the sergeant's urgency, "What…?"

Then… Amidst the low rumble of the giant burner, Lieutenant Neuhaus' coughs suddenly bursts through the air. Although hidden by the multitude of structures in front of them, the labored voice is unmistakable, "Don't…" He trails off coughing.

The whole team locks in on the sound, except Schaefer who takes off running towards it. McNeil whisper screams, "Doc!! Stop!!".

The medic doesn't listen. He speeds towards the coughing, as it gets louder. Not stopping, Schaefer rushes the scaffolding yelling back to the others, "It's the Lieutenant!"

In somewhat disbelief, McNeil mutters to himself under his breath, "Damnit…" Jumping up, he barks orders to the men, "Keep alert and cover him." He charges after Schaefer, as the men swiftly move into position.

Now past the large obstructions, the medic can see the lieutenant clearly. Thirty feet across from him, Neuhaus hangs limply from a cooling pipe. Stripped of his shirt, it's tied around his hands and then wrapped around the pipe. His bloodied body hangs from his ensnared wrists above him, with his feet suspended seven inches from the floor. A red, almost black stain pools down his parka and soaks the Army-green wool undershirt where his neck was bitten. His ammo belt is missing. Schaefer shouts, "Hang on Lieutenant. I'm gonna get you down." Neuhaus doesn't acknowledge, only chokes up blood. The medic reaches him and tries to untie his binds. "You're gonna be okay *LT*. Hang on."

CRACK!! CRACK!! CRACK!! Suddenly... hot lead streams from above. It chews into Neuhaus, and Schaefer is rocked by the rifle fire. A kill shot rips through the medic's forehead and shatters his skull. Fragments of bone ting off of a metal duct next to him, as his gelatinous gray matter spatters the lieutenant. He drops. McNeil, right behind him, peels off and dives behind a support beam. Yelling to the team, he spins up and starts firing above, "Get down!" The team scrambles for cover. Then there's the distinctive ping from an *M1 Garand's* clip being exhausted. The sergeant's thoughts scream, *That's an American weapon firing at us.*

Confused, McNeil ponders for a second, but shakes it off. Not wanting to waste the enemy's reload time, he bolts for Neuhaus, but it's too late. Within seconds, rifle fire rains down again from above. Neuhaus shudders and then his head slumps, as rounds tear into him. The lieutenant coughs no more. Dodging, McNeil spins away from the incoming gunfire.

"LT!" Enraged, Chorin repeatedly racks the shotgun and blasts indiscriminately at the hidden attacker. Although concealed in the shadows, the trench-gun is too far away and has no effect. The rest of the team can now see the muzzle flash from their attacker above, and they all return fire.

Up in the superstructure, on a catwalk covered behind a steel girder, a large, silhouetted shape fires off rounds at the men. The team answers. Their bullets clang against the metal around it. It volleys, unrelenting. *CHING...* the *M1's* clip empties again and the bolt locks back. This time it's out of ammo. The shape drops the rifle. Evading the continuous gunfire, it leaps across the catwalk and ducks behind another girder. It's cut off from an escape and unintentionally bathed in light. It's Siberian-Husky-colored bioluminescent eyes dilate from the brightness. Angered, it sneers at the men below and then scans for an escape. As it does, the alien beast becomes a large target. The men can fully see what was but a glimpse before. It stands nine feet tall, with a massive maw that possesses multiple rows of serrated teeth like a Great White. Its body is a muscular twelve-hundred-pounds, with thin but powerful legs and a striated barrel chest. The shaggy hide covering its head and shoulders tapers, as it traces down along its mottled leathery chest and back. Draped over its one shoulder and its lower half are the tattered remnants of an alien astronaut pressure suit. An Army ammo belt hangs around its waist. As rounds pound the wall around it, one connects. A *.45ACP* caliber projectile tears into its ribs. It's hit and roars out in pain! Ripping a *MKII grenade* from the ammo belt, it pulls the pin with the claw from its colossal hand and lets the spoon fly. The beast's lips quiver with hatred. It whips the grenade at the men. Hitting scaffolding, the explosive bounces from one level to another, clanging down the superstructure.

Down by the team Laskey watches in amazement. Mesmerized by the creature, he can't believe what he sees. All of a sudden the grenade passes by a service light as it drops. From his vantage point, he clearly sees what's coming at them and will explode in five seconds. For the first time this mission, he doesn't stammer. His voice rings out loud and clear, "Grenade!!" Instinctively, the team reacts and dives behind the air-handlers and pipes.

The grenade explodes in the air. Steel supports are snapped. Aluminum ducts are shredded. Metal flies through the air like shrapnel. And then calm.

DeVogler yells out, "Is it still up there!?"

Chorin peeks around a drainage pipe, "Holy shit that was close."

As the team starts looking for their attacker, there's a thundering twang. And then the groaning of bending failing steel. The weight on the missing supports starts straining the weakened superstructure. Platforms bend, braces snap and columns crumple. Suddenly... Busting pipes and ductwork start falling. Fragments and debris assault everything below.

The men dive for cover again. A twisting, falling amalgam of dirt, rock, and metal smash to the ground, with a crashing roar. The sound is deafening. The destruction piles like a grotesque asymmetric pyramid. The twenty-five-foot-high demolition mountain moans and gradually tips backwards, smashing against the east wall. A plume of dust bellows up engulfing the air. Then silence.

The *beast* roars triumphantly above. It quickly observes the men taking cover below and then scans what little remains of the superstructure for an escape. Holding its side in agony, it runs towards the busted missing end of a catwalk. Its feet make a resounding clang as it charges. In front of it, ending abruptly, there's nothing below but a thirty-foot drop to the floor. It strides forward unrelenting. As it reaches the end, it launches itself. It sails through the open air, soaring spreadeagle in a downward arc. Abruptly, the hulking creature slams against the I-beam on the other side. Screaming out in agony, it digs its claws into the joist, and scrambles up into the darkness. It's gone.

As the dust settles below, choking Chorin stands and scans where the beast previously stood. Getting up next to him, squinting for a better view, DeVogler peers upward, "Where'd it go?"

Laskey crawls out from cover, "Is… is… is it still there?"

Chorin, dusting himself off, shakes his head, "No, it's gone."

DeVogler kneels by the *M1 Garand* the alien dropped. He lifts it up and inspects it. It has the letters *MG* carved into the wooden stock. He knows those initials. “This is Groves' rifle. How'd an animal learn to shoot at us?”

Annoyed, Chorin scornfully quips, “It's an alien dipshit. If it can fly through space, I'm sure it could figure out a simple weapon.”

Pointing at Chorin, DeVogler stands and makes his displeasure known, “You know, I’m just about sick of your mouth.”

“Really…? Well, why don’t you let me know when you’re totally sick of it, that way maybe I can actually give two shits.”

Incensed, the corporal takes a threatening step towards him. As he does, the sound of metal clangs loudly. They all take notice and raise their weapons. *Is it there beyond the debris pyramid?* The sights of their weapons hang on the location from where the sound was emitted. Their fingers poised on the trigger; they wait for the next confrontation. Then, from behind the pile of debris, McNeil walks back with Neuhaus’ and Schaefer’s bloody dog-tags dangling from his hand. He says nothing as he heads towards the room’s control panels. The men ease up. Looking for any sort of comment, Chorin questions, “Sarge...?”

In no mood, McNeil responds curtly, “They’re both dead. Saddle up.”

“They're dead? That's all you have to say? Really…?”

McNeil stops in his tracks. He leers at the *PFC*, “Just what the hell would you like me to say, Jake?”

“I don't know, maybe a prayer... a moment of silence... somethin'! How ‘bout I'm sorry! Yeah, that'll work! I wanna hear you say you're sorry! Sorry that we're all gonna die down here in this shithole!"

"I am sorry!"

"Well, that's just great! You're sorry doesn't get us shit!"

"Why don't you give it a rest."

Trying to interrupt, Laskey calls from twenty feet away, "Um Sa… Sarge?"

Chorin shoots back at McNeil, "No, I won't give it a rest! We shoulda ran when we had a chance. You listened to Turner and dragged us down here when we –"

McNeil explodes, "I didn't have another choice damnit! What part of getting nuked don't you get, Jake!?"

"You didn't have to buy into Turner's bullshit! He may be smart, but he doesn't know everything! We could have outrun it!"

"And what if he was right!?"

Adamant, Laskey yells over both of them, "Guys!" They stop arguing and look over. "The… the… the door… the door's blocked!" He stands in front of a fallen three-foot-diameter cast-iron cooling pipe. It's lodged up against the entrance.

Chorin shakes his head in disbelief, "That's gotta be at least a couple thousand pounds. We're not movin' it." Above, gushing water pours from a ruptured transfer pipe coming from the water tower. He points to the damage, "And that ain't good either."

Seeing the predicament that they're in, McNeil laments, "Unbelievable…" He shoves the dog-tags in his pocket and shoulders his weapon. He glances down at the water starting to pool beneath their feet and then stares at the furnace. Turning back to the men he continues, "If this cold-water hits that hot furnace, it's gonna blow. Or at least scald us all to death. Either one, we gotta get the hell outta here… now."

CHAPTER 15 — THE MEZZANINE

In the other tributary where DeVogler and Groves were previously attacked, Lattanzi, Kowalczyk, Turner, Larson and Herrera move silently into the open mess hall. Only the emergency lights provide any visibility. Lattanzi leads the team with the *MG-42*, while Herrera brings up the rear with his *Browning Automatic Rifle*, prepared to unload suppressing fire. Stopping, the corporal sees the pile of denuded bone and discarded shredded Nazi uniforms, that DeVogler previously tripped over when searching with Groves. Although it has no effect on Lattanzi viscerally, Larson is visibly shaken. Terror grasps him. This isn't an army coming after them, it's a huge intelligent beast that tears flesh from its victims, before it snuffs out their lives. He doesn't want to end up like this. Frozen, the private doesn't move. From behind him, Turner places his hand on his shoulder. Larson jumps and snaps to look back. Motioning to ease down with his bad arm, Turner subtly points ahead with his *M1 Carbine* in the other, gesturing for the private to move on. Reluctant, Larson steps forward.

Stealthily the team moves around the industrial dining tables and cover the four access hatches that line the right wall. Without a word, Lattanzi turns to the team shakes his head no and waves them off from the corridors leading deeper down to the facilities depths. They need to systematically search every inch, that means starting here. They can't afford to miss something that may save them. The corporal points to the two metal staircases leading to the mezzanine above.

Furtively, they quickly cross the open space crouched and file in under the far staircase. Squatting, Lattanzi nods the go ahead to Herrera and Turner. They move. He then nods to Kowalczyk and Larson. It enrages the major to be taking orders from an enlisted, but he has to play along for now. They follow Herrera and Turner. Two by two they quietly ascend the stairs. Just as quietly, Lattanzi takes off to the far staircase unaccompanied, to protect the flank. It's a fool's errand, but it has to be done. Alone, he traverses the open space to the other flight of stairs. He'll be by himself if anyone or anything attacks.

Reaching the top, the four men spread out with their backs against the railing. Highly alert, their weapons' muzzles dance across the living quarters, that occupy the mezzanine. Suddenly a familiar stench hits them. It's not as potent as the others, but it's there just the same. Then they see it. They all frighteningly stare in disbelief at what lies before them. There on the floor in front of them lay thirty mangled bunks, which have been overturned and twisted by their unwanted alien acquaintance. Wool blankets and bedsheets stained from dried blood are intermingled with shredded corpses, appendages, and gore. Tossed footlockers are busted or flattened and their contents are scattered amongst the carnage. Everything was ferociously flung about during an unexpected and unrelenting attack. There is no sign of a gunfight nor weapons retrieved. None of the dead knew this was coming.

Not taking his eyes off the butchery, Larson silently leans over to Herrera and whispers, "That thing was able to do this? What the hell…?"

Always thinking and always observant Herrera quietly posits, "Who said there was just one mijo?" Astonished, Larson snaps to look at him. Herrera raises his eyebrow questioningly.

Kowalczyk interjects, "You two shut it." The two don't respond. The whole team waits.

Ascending the other stairs, Lattanzi arcs with the *machine-gun,* moving from front to back. He expects the creature to come from anywhere… above, below, even bust through the wall. Leaving nothing to chance, his eyes dart frantically looking for motion. He inhales and exhales deeply. Right now he'd take a charging Nazi platoon over being ambushed by that thing, but if something is going to happen, he'll find out soon enough. Still crouched against the rail, the team watches as the corporal reaches the top.

From the opposite staircase, Lattanzi visually assesses the situation… Nothing. *If it's here, it's waiting to attack. If it's not, where the hell is it?* Moving expeditiously, he rejoins the group. Ignoring the major, he speaks to Herrera, "That's one ugly hell of a mess, but we gotta keep going." Then the corporal addresses the whole team, looking across them all as he speaks, "Keep your eyes peeled. That thing could be anywhere. Let's move." He points to a heavy wooden door forty-feet past the massacre, where a faint glow emits from under the door. Every light in this section of the facility is out, except for the emergency lights and the light emitting from that lone room. It's a duty-hut next to the officer's quarters and something's amiss. They quietly look to each other, acknowledging the peculiar exception. The corporal motions for the team to move and treads towards the lit room. They all converge on the door.

Herrera levels his *BAR* in firing position, as Lattanzi slips up silently next to the doorjamb. Standing back, the other men assemble on either side of the door for cover. In angled descending lines, their weapons train on the closed doorway. The corporal leans in and places his ear against the wooden entrance. He listens. Kowalczyk mouths the words, "Hear anything?" Lattanzi shakes his head no, but not assuredly. He hears something faint, but it's undiscernible. Even though the door is now closed, he looks down to see that the door was forced open, and the jamb busted. With the *MG* clutched in his left hand, he moves the other gently downward reaching out for the doorknob. Grasping it, the mechanism clicks ever so slightly. He grits his teeth hoping that whatever's behind this door didn't hear. Herrera's finger tightens ever so slightly on his trigger. Lattanzi turns the knob and shoves. The door swings open.

The crackling sound of static emits from within.

Inside this small room is a large wooden desk, with a superheterodyne *Wehrmacht* command radio. They all see it. Elation runs over them. Salvation. However, seated in front of it with his back to the door is a *SS* communications specialist, blocked from full view by a tall leather-wrapped wood *Biedermeier* wingback chair. Just the top of his head, the headset he's wearing, and his elbows protrude from around the edges. A *Luger* pistol sits inches from his right wrist. Off to the side is a previously slept in bunk, with a swastika embroidered blanket tossed aside as if someone hurriedly jumped out. An ornately designed walnut storage-trunk is open and has been rummaged through hastily. Just from the well-appointed furniture and décor, it's obvious that to this base, this man is important. He is the eyes and ears to the outside world for the Nazi resistance. His accommodations reflect his significance accordingly. And now the team has to subdue him without them accidentally destroying the radio or letting him sabotage it.

Snapping the *MG* to aim at his head, Lattanzi quips, "*Sprechen Sie* English, asshole?" The Nazi doesn't respond.

As the team slowly files in with weapons raised, Herrera moves off to the right keeping the *SS* specialist locked in his sights. After purposely learning quite a bit of German during the war, he typically articulates all commands for the team. The rest of the men just picked up a couple of words or phrases to get by in combat. Herrera firmly commands, "*Heben Sie langsam Ihre Hände. Wer sich nicht daran hält, wird erschossen.*" Translated, he told the Nazi, "Raise your hands slowly. If you don't comply, you will be shot."

Again, there's no acknowledgement that the enemy soldier even heard him.

From separate sides, the two close in. They swiftly move and then they're upon him. Without breaking stride, Herrera knocks the *Luger* off the desk and shoves his automatic rifle in the Nazi's face. And then he sees. The SS specialist's throat has been torn out. Although dim and lifeless, his eyes are still frozen wide open. His mouth is agape, locked in the scream that was silenced by one swift tear. Eviscerated tendons, ligaments, fat, and skin hang from his lower jaw. Dried deep red is awash down his front. His headphones are only slightly askew. The front of the radio has been destroyed and electronic bits hang from the metal housing. And what should be running from the back of the radio, up the wall and out the ceiling is obviously missing. The hardwired transmission lines that lead up to the surface transmitter have been totally ripped from the retaining brackets and ceiling conduit. Suspecting the motive, Herrera turns and gazes at the wall directly behind. Around the door bullet impacts mar the wall. Visually taking in all the variables in the room, his mind plays through the possible scenarios. He thinks he knows how this went down. *The communications specialist fired at the creature breaking in but was subsequently overpowered and eviscerated. He never stood a chance.*

Lowering his weapon, Lattanzi pulls at the shattered pieces of the radio, "Holy hell." Asking Herrera, he questions despondently as he examines each sizeable fragment in his hand, "Why would he destroy their only means of communication?"

Also dejected but still professional, Herrera responds, "Maybe he didn't. Maybe that *beast* did… so no survivors could call for reinforcements. Cut off support and its own chances of survival got a whole lot better."

Shocked at the possibility of the creature being that advanced, Lattanzi doesn't even realize that he's speaking out loud, "Intelligent and calculating… that's frightening."

Herrera nods affirmingly.

A somber mood has fallen over the room. The team's hope of calling off the bombing run have been dashed.

Although they notice each other's body language, they are unaware of their own subconscious projections. They are all visually angry, unnerved, or crestfallen. Kowalczyk walks to the corpse and spins the chair around, "He's been dead for over a week. Late decomposition. The smell's almost gone. This area must have been one of its first kills."

Throwing the broken pieces of the radio back down on the desk, Lattanzi turns, "Well, that's real interesting Major, but it doesn't help us for shit now does it?"

The major studies the radio's pieces. The battery, speaker, internal diodes, transformer, amplifier, and the tuning coil are all smashed. Torn from the base unit, the microphone handset is nowhere to be found. With a look of delight, he retorts, "Actually… it does."

"Yeah, how's that?"

"Ask yourself. If you were this extraterrestrial being and knew that after this attack the rest of this armed installation would try to eliminate you, would you stay? Even if you were able to take them all out and destroyed their only means of communications, wouldn't you be thinking that reinforcements could possibly be coming at any moment? Why wouldn't you run?"

Annoyed, Lattanzi shrugs his shoulders, "You got me Major."

Continuing, Kowalczyk grins, "There's something here that it wants." The major is extremely pleased. He knows what it wants and it's what *he himself wants*. "And I guarantee you all that certain something is… its ship. We just need to –"

While scanning across the room, Lattanzi cuts him off questioning the whole team, "Where's Turner?"

Larson speaks up, "He was just next to me, not five minutes ago."

"Well, he ain't here now."

Not caring about Turner's current situation, Kowalczyk demands, "We can worry about Turner later. Right now we need to find that ship. If we can find it, it'll have technology. If it has technology, we can find a way to signal HQ?"

Ignoring him, Lattanzi walks by the team out into the mezzanine, "Nobody heard anything?" They all give rumbling denials, except Kowalczyk who's angered by the corporal's dismissiveness. All the answers are the same, no one has seen him. Nobody knows where he went. Looking back he gives directive with a determined poise, "Stay here and keep your eyes peeled. I'm gonna find Turner. And if it attacks…" He can't help himself and jests with a comedic tone, "…I guess you'll need another corporal." Grinning, he steps through the door.

Moving beyond the entrance, Lattanzi holds the *MG-42* ready to fire. The rest of the team fans out along the wall of the mezzanine, just outside the door behind him. Raising their sights, they scan the area, watching as he moves forward. The corporal calls out whispering, as he walks softly heel to toe, "Turner…? Turner…?" Step by step he calls out in a hushed voice. There's no reply at all, only the ringing silence from a huge room with no other motion. He calls out again, "Turner, where the hell are you?" Slowly and deliberately he scans left… then right… then above. Wearily, he moves further through the mezzanine away from the group. Taking another step, Lattanzi stops dead. There by his boot, obscured in shadow, is the answer. He squats down, reaches out and pulls back what his wishes he hadn't found. Turning back towards the team, he holds it up, "It's Turner's 'lucky' comb."

CHAPTER 16 — RISING WATERS

In the furnace room, McNeil sits on large, jagged piece of fallen concrete. Water is now up to his ankles. Another eleven inches and the cold liquid will rise above the furnace's cement pedestal, hit the steaming hot metal and result in a cataclysmic event. Removing the last of the cartridges from his ammo belt, he loads them into his *Thompson's* magazine. He pulls back on the charging handle and stands. DeVogler and Chorin run up to him. With a look of dread, Chorin gives an update, "We've checked everything. No hatches, no conduits large enough to fit through… nothin'. Not one point of egress. And the service ladder and scaffolding… gone. They both came down with the rest of it."

DeVogler adds to the heinousness, "There's a service tunnel for the minecars that leads outside, but we're not gettin' through the blast-door. The controls were completely destroyed."

Almost thirty feet from the group, kicking his way through the rising water like a frustrated toddler, Laskey wanders up sloshing from the other side of the large chamber. They all look over hoping for a positive response. McNeil calls over tentatively, "Anything?" The private regretfully shakes his head "no".

Weary yet unemotional, Chorin drops his head in his hands and sits on a pile of crumpled metal, "Well, I guess we can always just sit here and wait for this thing to blow. I'm tired anyway."

McNeil stands, "Knock it off with that shit. We're getting' outta here."

"Why…? So we can wait to get nuked?" The *PFC* looks at his watch, "Ya know, we have about sixty-three minutes left to find a radio. Let's face it… It's over."

"Until we're dead, it ain't over. So quit your bellyaching, get on your damned feet, and keep looking."

"This is bullshit and you know it."

McNeil cuts him a look and proceeds onward. He then starts following a coolant line, hoping to trace it back to some sort of an exit.

Not willing to give up, DeVogler beelines it to the base of the scrap-metal and concrete pyramid, "Well I gotta do somethin'." He starts to climb. Slipping on loose fragments, he expeditiously scrambles to the top and starts chucking debris to the floor. Large hunks splash, as they hit the rising water.

Chorin gazes up at DeVogler in amazement, "What the hell are ya doin'?"

The corporal continues to throw chunks of wreckage to the base below. Not stopping, Devogler yells down to him, "I'm digging us out!"

"Do you realize that we'll all be dead before you get through even five percent of that?"

"Not if everyone helped!"

Astonished at the well-intentioned hulking man's ignorance, Chorin shakes his head and waves him off dismissively. He doesn't even have the heart to insult him.

Almost back to the group, Laskey stops and watches DeVogler throw off massive pieces of wreckage that a normal man could never lift. The private knows the futility but has great respect for the man anyway. As he visually follows an enormous piece plunging to the ground, his eyes observe something peeking out from behind the leaning debris-pyramid's left side. He focuses and peers at it to see more clearly. There it is, almost obscured from sight… *hope.* Just an edge is showing, but it's enough. Where the asymmetric pyramid heap spreads at the bottom, the upper lefthand corner of a wooden doorjamb peeks out from behind collapsed concrete, rebar, and scaffolding. Mixed in with the destruction, just over the door jamb, an I-beam protrudes out from a crevice in the pile at a twenty-degree downward angle. Excited, he shouts, "I… I can… I can see part of… of a… of--" His stammering makes him fight to unsuccessfully expel the words he wants to say. Giving up, he just yells for their attention, "Over here! Over here!"

DeVogler hears and takes huge leaps down the pile towards Laskey. Turning quickly, McNeil rushes over. Fighting against his better judgment, Chorin gets up and heads for the private's pleas. As they gather around, Laskey vigorously and repeatedly directs their attention to the door with his finger, "A way… a way out."

DeVogler hurries to the fallen mass. He examines all around the rubble where the full door is covered by part of the pile. At about eye level, where the pyramid base is still flaring upwards, there's a small but evident gap. He stares at a five-inch-high opening, that tapers down into a two-inch fissure, which he can see stretches four feet horizontally between two abutting slabs of concrete. Getting his face within an inch away, his eyes peer through the jagged crevice. Although choking on dust, he doesn't move. His mind races. Suddenly, he looks back at the group with a smile and points to the crevice, "In there… just behind that crevice there's a hole with about seven inches of clearance between that girder and the bottom slab of concrete. It's maybe two feet wide going straight back through the pile, six or seven feet."

McNeil doesn't get the significance of an essentially seven-inch-high by two-foot-wide six-foot-long tube running back through the tons of wreckage, except ironically being the size of a really thin coffin. Skeptical, but wanting to be openminded due to their plight, "What does that do for us Corporal?"

DeVogler's huge mitt slaps the I-beam, "If we lift this just eight or ten inches, we can squeeze through. We can get out." The girder's resounding reverberation punctuates his statement.

Pissy as ever, Chorin remarks, "And what if everything above it gives way…? Then what genius? Whoever's going through will be crushed."

Losing his temper, DeVogler barks back, "You've got a better idea loudmouth!?" They all look at Chorin, as the sound of the rushing water continues unabated.

The *PFC* looks down at the rising water now up to their shins. Admitting defeat, Chorin just shakes his head no, "What do you want me to do?"

McNeil moves to the pile and looks in through the crevice, "There's an oak door on the other side of this, blocking the exit. We need to clear it or we're not getting through."

Determined, DeVogler puts his hand around the *MKII* hooked to his ammo belt, "Grenade?"

"No. That might shift everything in the pile… we can't chance it. I have an idea though. Step back." They all comply. McNeil strides up to the pile, shoves the barrel of the *Thompson* in the wider five-inch area of the crevice, turns his head away and fires. As the weapon bucks and jolts with each round, he cranks his wrist in a circular motion trying to blast through as much of the door as he can. The sound of the impenetrable wood starts to crack away and shatter inside. Not stopping, he pulls the weapon back and forth through the rest of the fissure. Wood splinters fly from the opening. The *Thompson's* bolt lock back empty. Expended, he drops it and looks in again through the pile. Pulling back, he retrieves a snapped short section of rebar from the ground, he slams it in the fissure and chips away at the remaining door fragments blocking the hole's exit. Final pieces of oak bust backwards. He looks again. Through the piled debris, the shadowed smashed door looks like the awaiting open mouth of a great white shark. The very top and bottom half of the door survive, but the at the five-foot level there's a gaping oval hole. *It's ugly, but it'll work.* "Okay, the door's clear enough for someone to get through." He holds up the rebar, "I'll keep this as a fulcrum to help lift when I get to the other side." With a good deal of force, he shoves it all the way through the pile. On the other side of the shattered door, the clang of metal echoes as it impacts the concrete floor in the blocked corridor. "DeVogler, grab something else to prop under the girder once we move it. We're only goin' to get one shot at this." The corporal gives the thumbs-up as an affirmative and starts scanning the debris.

Dubious, Chorin probes to see who the point-man fodder will be, "Who goin' first?"

"I am.", McNeil snaps back decisively.

Rummaging through different sized pipes and supports, DeVogler looks for the wedge object he'll use. Stopping, he challenges, "You can't be on point, Sarge. It's too risky. Let me go."

McNeil cuts off the discussion, "This isn't up for debate. I'm going through first." Moving into position, he presses his shoulder under the I-beam, "Laskey behind me, Chorin next, and Corporal... we need you on the end. Nobody can lift as much as you." DeVogler nods in agreement. McNeil turns back and looks at each man, "If that *thing*'s waitin' for me on the other side I'll do what I can, but if it takes me out... Whatever you do, just get through, start blazing and then find a damned radio. Don't die down here. Don't let it win." Gravely, the men all acknowledge. "Alright..." Unslinging the Nazi *MP40*, the sergeant pulls back its charging handle, "...let's do this." He holds the weapon in his left hand and places the right on the I-beam, beside his shoulder. Chorin and Laskey also position themselves under the girder.

DeVogler retrieves a downed section of conduit. He sets it vertically next to himself. It's about his height and four inches in diameter. He holds the cold rolled steel in his hands. He feels the weight. *This'll do,* he thinks to himself, as he walks back to the group. Shoving his neck and shoulders under the girder, DeVogler grabs the end with one hand and positions the conduit in the other. "I'm ready."

The sergeant responds, "Okay. You guys good?"

Hesitant, Laskey answers, "Rea… ready." Although responding with a confirmation that he's prepared, his face speaks otherwise. He watches as the waterline creeps up the furnace's concrete pedestal. Involuntarily, his facial tic begins twitching his eye and cheek in small spasms. He rubs his cheek trying to calm it.

At this point, Chorin thinks this is futile, but he's game. He may be willing to give up on this madness, but he won't turn his back on his team. He's a hardass, but he's dependable. Although less than enthused, he acknowledges that he's set, "Good to go."

McNeil knows he has to lift and then crawl as quickly as he can. He shifts under the I-beam trying to better his position. It's now or never. Composed, he starts, "Alright, on three. One... Two..." He inhales deeply and braces, "Three..." All of them heave. Their bodies strain against the punishing mass. Screaming like bodybuilders in a muscle gym, they growl out every ounce of force they can muster. The joist and the slab begin to shake violently, inching upwards. Cement crumbles. Calcified shards break free. Dust assaults them. Sluggishly, the I-beam lifts. The angled pile of destruction covering the door starts to move and its immense weight begins to shift further towards the rest of the wreckage. The crawlspace between the two slabs widens. Eight inches... nine... eleven... thirteen…

DeVogler savagely jams the conduit under the girders end. Yanking his hand away, he simultaneously grunts,

"Okay, drop it." The team tries to lower the weight slowly, but they're exhausted, and the beam abruptly drops with immense force. An audibly powerful *ga-chung* rings out, as the two pieces of metal slam down together. Not missing a beat, McNeil bolts out from joist and scrambles up into the crevice. He disappears through the opening. With the weight now being supported, the men ease up being both aching and drained. However, they still hold their hands securely around the propped-up I-beam, making sure that it doesn't slip off the conduit wedge. Catching their breath, they focus intently on listening. Not one of them is able to discern anything over the sound of the rushing water. They look at each other questioningly. Lost in the ambiguity of the situation, their thoughts run rabid. *Was he attacked? Was he killed before he could say anything? Why isn't he acknowledging?*

Chorin isn't going to wait through the uncertainty any longer. Yelling above the torrent, he calls out for some sort of response from the other side of the wall, "Sarge, you there!? You alright!? Sarge!?" They continue to listen. Nothing... He slaps Laskey on the shoulder and orders, "We can't wait any longer. You've gotta go now." Gripped in complete fear, the private looks back at him terrified. "Laskey, you've gotta move! Now!" Eyes wide with panic, the underling just shakes his head "no".

Then… the twanging sound of metal bending. The conduit is failing! As if in slow motion, the team all looks over to see the tube buckle slightly at a two-degree angle.

DeVogler yells, as he shoves his neck and shoulders back under the beam, "Move!"

Laskey still paralyzed, now contemplates the looming triad of death… get crushed in the hole, devoured by the beast, or engulfed by the impending furnace explosion. He won't move. Suddenly through the crawlspace, McNeil yells out distinctly, "We're all clear! Get your asses out of there!" His voice snaps the private out of his paralysis. Whipping around to see the furnace, the young man peers at the water about to break over the top edge of the concrete base. The furnace's searing-hot steel footings are only a half inch away from the lip. Feverishly, the private turns back and charges the escape. Another clang of metal echoes loudly as the conduit bends in the middle another five degrees. The I-beam drops two inches, shaking heavily as it comes to rest. The hole will collapse… but when? Still crawling inside, Laskey's face twists in the realization that this may be it.

"Shit!", Chorin shoves his shoulder under the I-beam, trying to hold back the collapse. His face strains against the weight. DeVogler shakes against the pressure already on him.

#

In a stark white corridor on the other side of the wall, McNeil has already ripped open the rest of the oak door. Bracing with the rebar thrust in the crawlspace, he shoves down on it using the debris and the bar as a fulcrum to try to hold up the I-beam inside. Laskey's head appears, as he scrambles through. With one hand, McNeil grabs him by the collar and helps yank him through the rest of the way. The sergeant yells into the now cleared hole, "Chorin, let's go!" While resetting his grip on the bar, the private jumps up to help.

#

Back in the furnace room, Chorin lets go of the joist and heads for the crawlspace. The conduit bends again, and the girder drops another inch. DeVogler winces and shoves with his legs, grunting to hold back the collapse. Stopping in his tracks, Chorin races it back to help support the I-beam.

Gritting through his teeth, DeVogler demands, "What the hell are you doin'!?"

Chorin counters, "I'm not going without you!"

"Don't be stupid! We'll both die!"

Then… rising up over the base, the water spills around the furnace legs. Scalding steam violently flares out from the clash, but it's nothing compared to what's coming. They both snap to look. When the water crawls up one more inch on the legs, it'll hit the main body of the furnace and that will be the end. Thermal shock will occur. The metal will expand at extreme rate. The furnace will explode. The fuel lines will fail. The resulting gas will hit the flames. And the whole foundry will erupt in an unimaginable fiery devastation.

Staring at each other, Chorin and DeVogler grunt and strain to keep the hole from ceasing to exist. The corporal eyes plead for Chorin to run. The *PFC* just shakes him off, as McNeil and Laskey yell from the other side for them to move. Exhausted, DeVogler barely gets the word out, "Go…" Again, Chorin shakes his head "no".

Steam envelopes the area. Rivet joints twang, as the metal stresses.

Digging in with everything he has, DeVogler yells to Chorin, "For the first time in your stubborned life, don't argue with me! Go!!" His face shakes with the words and sweat assaults the air.

Chorin shuts his eyes. Against every fiber in his being, his eyes snap open and he nods an affirmation to his previously adversarial friend. DeVogler nods back. Letting go, Chorin bolts for the hole and dives in. Again, the conduit bends, and the girder drops another inch. The *PFC* screams out as the joist slams against his back, pinning him. He's now wedged between the bottom slab and the I-beam. Clambering, he claws with his hands to pull himself forward. His fingernails snap and fingers bleed. Barely moving, he fights against the pressure and screams out, "DeVogler!"

The corporal sees him pinned and the water is only millimeters from starting the chain-event. Although wanting to give up, he can't. He won't. Like a Greek god or a mother lifting a car off her child, he lifts with everything he has... everything he ever will have… for just this one single moment. His hulking frame jerks upwards. The steel digs further down into his neck and shoulders. The weight is crushing. Forcing his body to exert an inhumanly amount of unbridled power, he roars his utter determination. His muscles sinew. Veins bulge from his neck and forehead. Every limb of his huge frame shakes. He is unrelenting to stand fully erect. Unexpectedly, the girder starts to move. A quarter inch… a half inch… an inch… two…

Chorin is freed. He crawls as fast as his arms and legs can propel him forward. He disappears fully into the crawlspace.

McNeil shouts from the other side, “He’s through! DeVogler, come on!” He doesn’t know the extent of what has transpired or the futility of his words.

Hearing him, DeVogler drops the beam and collapses to his knees. It crashes the hole closed. A rumble emerges from the pile. He bows his head and whispers, “I’m sorry mama. I’m not gonna make it home.”

#

In the corridor, dust spews from the collapsed hole showering McNeil, Laskey and Chorin lying on the floor with a gray chalky calcified layer. Getting to his feet, Chorin grabs McNeil, “We can’t save him! We gotta go!”

McNeil stares defiantly as he still tries to lift with the fulcrum, “We have to try!”

“It's gonna blow! Run!!” Ignoring him, McNeil fights with the rebar. “Frank, we are all going to die! We need to go now!” Not waiting any longer, Chorin grabs them both by the arms and starts pulling. A low pounding of metal rapidly expanding resounds through the wall. “Runnnnnn!!!”

Hearing the noise, McNeil doesn’t want to accept it, but he knows what’s coming, “Go! Move!” They all begin to run. Warping twangs echo from within. Tearing down the hallway, the soldiers hear the steel begin to fail. Thermal shock tears apart the machine’s structures. Welds crack. Rivets fly. The furnace’s failing metal explodes, throwing shrapnel through the air, rupturing the fuels tanks. As the men flee, vibrations shake the floor under their charging feet. Suddenly, an ear deafening blast. Cascading explosions rock the foundry. A shockwave permeates the air. It reverberates along the corridor’s tilework. As the team tears around a corner into another passageway, debris and rolling plumes blasts through the adjacent wall. Blazing flames eat away at the corridor where they just were, as a billowing cloud of metal shards and ash rush towards them.

CHAPTER 17 — WHAT WAS THAT?

As Lattanzi, Kowalczyk, Larson and Herrera move down the mezzanine stairs, looking for Turner, the entire facility shakes violently. Somewhere in the distance, loud rumblings bellow resonantly through the caverns and corridors. The walls tremor. The staircase yanks at its anchors in the rock wall. The team grabs onto the railings, trying to stay upright. And then, the shockwave slowly subsides.

Lattanzi rips, "What the hell was that?"

"One massive explosion," the major replies.

"I get that Major. I meant, what the hell caused it? It definitely wasn't a nuke because we're all still standin' here."

Herrera speaks plainly stating his position, "That could be the other team. We need to go."

"Right. Come on."

As Lattanzi readies to race off, Kowalczyk lobs cutting words that impede the corporal's hastened departure, "That's a mistake. We are running out of time Corporal, and we need to continue on, not look for corpses… because that's all we'll eventually find when we arrive at that devastation's aftermath." He points angrily at the explosion's location.

His words rattle around in Lattanzi's head, sparking a manic extemporized internal dialogue. *Are they all dead? Could they have survived? Was it even them? Do I chance it? If we continue to look for communications, they might die. If we help them, we may all die. What about Turner? Is it too late for him? Is it too late for any of us?* He knows that the right thing to do isn't always the smart thing, especially when seconds are ticking off the clock. For a moment he contemplates the correct way to proceed, but then he's suddenly sure. Like always, he'll go with his gut. "We're going to help them, Major. You can stay here if you'd like… I don't care. Forget them. Forget us. You just have to ask yourself one thing, what if that ship you want so badly is actually down there…" He points to the explosion, mocking Kowalczyk's gesture. "…in the wreckage… and you didn't take the chance to salvage it?" Without waiting for any acknowledgement, the corporal turns and runs off. Disgusted, Herrera cuts the major a dirty look and bolts after Lattanzi. Just as appalled, Larson follows.

The corporal's volley apparently hit home. Kowalczyk's nostrils flare. He breathes contempt, annoyed that the little "uneducated shit" was able to best him. Lattanzi was able to push his buttons. The major leans forward fighting the urge to stay, rocking back and forth in place with indecision. Resentful, but not willing to lose his prize, he begrudgingly begins to run after them.

#

The four men speed through the facility, with almost reckless abandon. Strategy is out the window. Their weapons face forward, and they only rapidly scan for danger, as they race towards the other team. Their footfalls are loud, and the pounding of their combat boots echo throughout the corridors. Generated by their running up and down motion, ammo mags clank in a quasi-synchronous rhythm against the metal weapons' magazine-wells. Strained sounds of inhalation and exhalation encompass the group. Although the beast could be waiting for them around any corner, they move as fast as they possibly can.

#

Back at the original 'T' where the teams split, Lattanzi, Herrera, Larson and Kowalczyk rush up upon the other hatch. Jumping through they enter a hallway of destruction. Broken pieces of tiles, boards, concrete, and metal litter the corridor. They all stop and stare at the ruination. Chorin and Laskey's arms and legs hang out from the debris. Jumping into action, the soldiers hastily descend upon their friends, ripping away the rubble in hopes that are bodies still attached to those appendages. Piece by piece they are uncovered. Both Chorin and Laskey are in one piece. They are covered in dust, scrapes, minor lacerations, and insignificant amounts of coagulated blood, but they are whole.

Worried, Lattanzi leans in and listens. Chorin still breathes. The corporal gives a sigh of relief that his friend is still alive, then shakes Chorin to wake him, "Come on man." Chorin doesn't move. Lattanzi starts to slap his face, expecting the abrupt sensation will shock him out of his state, "Wake up Jake. Wake up. Come on." A few feet away, Herrera gets Laskey to stir. Both men were knocked unconscious from the concussive blast.

Chorin abruptly wakes and barks in a gravelly weak voice, "Knock it off asshole. This isn't one of your fantasies." He coughs on the dust in his lungs.

Laughing at his friend's playfully condescending comment, Lattanzi beams, "Holy shit, I thought you were a goner."

"Yeah, you wish."

As Herrera and Larson tend to Laskey, Lattanzi helps Chorin to his feet. From behind them Kowalczyk posits a simple question, "Where's McNeil, DeVogler and Schaefer?" It dawns on them all. In their moment of elation, celebrating that their cohorts weren't dead, they didn't think about the others.

"Holy shit, where are they?" Lattanzi begins to step over scrap and again frantically pushes away wreckage, searching for them. The others join in clearing away the fragmentation.

Still woozy and not fully lucid, Chorin exerts himself to give a coherent commentary, "Schaefer and DeVogler they're… they're dead. DeVogler saved us, but he didn't make it." The others look at him expecting the worst about McNeil too. "The sarge… he shoved us ahead of him and away from the blast before the explosion hit, but…" Chorin gazes around trying to focus, "He was right behind us. I'm sure of it. I think."

They team starts digging through the wasteland of exploded construction material. Lattanzi calls out, "Sarge!? You under there!? Make some noise if you can hear me!"

An unsteady voice emanates from around the corner, "I'm here…" Hearing him, the team moves cautiously around the corner. McNeil sits on the floor amongst rubble, with a five inch long shard the size of a Bowie-knife sticking out from the side of his thigh. He's totally covered in white tile dust and looks like a powered donut in a confectionary dessert tray. He takes a long drag of a bent-broken Lucky Strike and looks up at them.

Lattanzi squats down and views the wound, "How deep is it?"

The sergeant responds humorously, "Deep enough."

"Can you walk?"

"It needs to come out."

"We don't have Schaefer's med-bag. All we can do is pour some sulfa over and dress it."

Indifferent to McNeil's injury, Kowalczyk frenetically interjects, "Is the ship back there? Did you see it? Did it survive? Can we get to it?"

Amused but not surprised, the sergeant smirks and responds, "There's no ship. There's no radio. There's nothing left. But no, I didn't see it."

Chorin who's now more clearheaded snaps at Kowalczyk, "Why don't you lay off Major. We almost just bought the farm back there."

Seeing McNeil wounded and now feeling a little backbone, Kowalczyk responds sardonically but with authority, "I know, Chorin… and it's such good fortune that you survived. Nevertheless… whether you like it or not, we need to keep searching. We find that ship or we find a radio because we are running out of time." He points to McNeil, "Now get that out of his leg and bandage him up. Most importantly, get him to his feet… We're moving out." The rest of the team all look to the sergeant for his approval.

Too tired and beaten, McNeil nods in agreement.

CHAPTER 18 — CLEARED FOR TAKEOFF

On the far side of the American zone in an undisclosed location, an *OSO* acquired clandestine airstrip is all quiet, except for a lone *B-17F Flying Fortress* heavy bomber being prepped for takeoff. American markings have been stripped away and the metal hull has been painted a flat black. Again, another aircraft has been wiped to hide its origins. However, it's still a sight to see. The tail, roof, and ventral machine-gunner's glass-canopies are equipped with belt fed *.50 caliber M2 Browning machine-guns*. Each is manned by a seasoned vet. The bombardier's nose glazing is armed with an equally powerful weapon, which is installed alongside the ordinance controls. Waist-guns reside on both the port and starboard flanks of the fuselage. Seated in the ordinance stowage rack of this mechanical monster dwells an atomic bomb. This warbird is armed to the teeth and is truly emblematic of its title... the "Flying Fortress". With the *OSO* being the precursor to the *Central Intelligence Agency*, this is the same aircraft used by the *CIA* to mount numerous nefarious covert operations throughout the world years later.

As a small maintenance team removes snow and ice off the *B-17's* four propellers, the whole flight crew sans pilot approaches the aircraft. Their faces are stoic, and their attitude is resolute. They have a job to do, orders will be followed unwaveringly, and the mission's payload will be delivered no matter the consequences.

#

Moving quickly through the halls of the barracks, Captain Blake Jeffers approaches a door to the officer's quarters. He is a loyal and ethical man, who earned a wartime reputation of being incredibly cool under fire. Most notably, the mission where he was promoted to the rank of Captain and was subsequently offered a position with the *OSO*. During one of his final sorties his bomber was decimated by squadron of swarming *Messerschmitts*, but he refused to leave the mission or his fellow Flying Fortresses. Three engines were blown apart, the fuselage was shredded, and the tail wing was nearly eradicated, but he persevered and dropped the plane's full payload delivering a devastating loss to the Nazis. And with only one functioning engine, he was able to land the aircraft on a controlled descent, saving the remaining crewmembers who survived the battle. Although the courageous *B-17* bombers' flight-crews only had a thirty-five percent survival rate during D-Day and the period leading up to it, he was one of the lucky ones to make it out alive. Like most of that generation, the stories told later don't do justice to the actual amazing acts of heroism that were performed. He stops and knocks at the door.

A familiar shrill voice calls back, "Enter Captain."

Without hesitation, Jeffers opens the door and walks in. The room is barely lit from a gooseneck desk-lamp deliberately placed on top of a davenport. From what's scarcely visible, it's evident that these quarters were finely decorated by someone with scrutinizing taste. Seated in shadows clutching a smoldering cigarette, the commanding officer doesn't speak. The captain salutes and breaks the silence, "You wanted to see me Sir?"

With a quick flip of his wrist, the superior officer takes a drag. The burning ember of his Chesterfield glows as he inhales, partly reflecting off his wire-rimmed glasses. Just as quickly, he fastidiously taps the short ash into a Tiffany Studios' bronze floor standing ashtray. Exhaling the smoke through his nostrils, he asks curtly, "Your team was briefed?"

"Yes Sir."

"Then you understand the importance of the cargo?"

"Yes Sir."

The superior officer waves him closer. The captain approaches. As Jeffers gets closer, his commanding officer's boney finger points to the folder on the davenport, "What does that read, Captain?"

Even though confused, Jeffers responds, "Top Secret..."

"Not that. Above it."

"Office of Special Operations only…?"

"Very good, Captain. Yes, Office of Special Operations only. And do you know what that means?"

It seems like a simple question, with an incredibly simple answer, but Jeffers knows that's not what he wants. Exceptionally confused by the unnecessary riddle, all the captain can do is question hoping the game will end, "Sir…?"

"It's quite cold in here. One second please.", the haughty brass quips, as he bends over to light a stack of wood in the fireplace. He places his gilded Colibri Stormgard lighter to the splintered wood accelerant. It ignites. As the fire grows, Colonel Tate's skeletal face and bald head are exposed in clear view. With the flames flickering across his spectacles, he looks back at the younger officer, "Better… yes?"

"Sir, we're supposed to doing a pre-flight check right now."

Irritated, the colonel probes more firmly, "*OSO* only Captain, what does it mean?"

He has absolutely no idea what the right answer may be. He gives up and tries the simple explanation, "What it says Sir? Nobody but the *OSO* is supposed to know."

"Wrong Captain. It means this mission never existed." Without ever taking his eyes off his underling, he leans forward, grabs the file, and tosses it into the fire, "From this day forward, we never speak of this, and you have no knowledge of what is about to transpire. Neither will anyone. No one will know Captain. Not the Allied Control Council, not the useless bureaucrats back home and not even President Truman himself. Is that understood?"

Shaken with the thought that not even the president would be told, Jeffers turns his head slightly to the side, as if to subconsciously deflect the alarming inquiry. Hesitant, he challenges the legitimacy of Tate's statement with a question, "It's… an atomic weapon Sir?"

"I know what it is Captain. You must understand that this installation's mission… No, all of the *OSO's* mission is to protect the interests of the United States above all else. And that's exactly what we'll do. And that's why you are going to deploy that sixty kiloton weapon over the target, whether their team contacts you or not. At this point, they are either dead or they're compromised, but either one is unacceptable. I will not allow that alien spacecraft nor its technology to fall into the hands of another foreign entity… enemy… or allied. That is what is in our country's best interest. Am I clear?"

"But Sir… shouldn't that call be made by a higher power?"

The words flare Tate's subdued temper, his eyes seer into Jeffers and he responds with venomous certainty, "We don't answer to a higher power Captain. We *are* the higher power."

CHAPTER 19 — WHEN DOES IT END?

Depressed, exhausted and with still no luck, the team moves down yet another endless tunnel. As they travel around a lengthy bend, the service lights abruptly end, and the visibility falls off. Straining to see, they tread forward. About ten feet ahead of the group, Lattanzi moves cautiously on point with the *MG-42.* Unexpectedly he stops and rhetorically quips, “What the hell? The Krauts just gave up building here?” The corridor is blocked off, ending in a solid rock wall barrier. But the Nazis didn’t just give up, there is a quintessential reason why the corridor ceases to go on. The end of the war, lead to the end of the money machine, which lead to the end of all expansion. Like the Third Reich’s thirst for dominance, construction was stopped dead in its tracks.

Still not being able to really see in the darkness, Chorin irksomely probes, “What now? What are you babbling about?”

Gesticulating up and down with his hand in front of the wall, Lattanzi simply states, “This…”

The rest of the group draws closer to see what he’s referencing. Chorin reaches him first and ignites a lighter. The small flame throws flickering amber hues against the stone. He stares at the now visible earthen impasse. A limping McNeil being helped by Laskey gathers behind them with Kowalczyk, Larson, and Herrera stopping in a slipshod semi-circle. They all gaze in disbelief. Valuable time has been squandered away on a dead-end. Annoyed, Chorin ribs his friend with an underlying taint of his true feelings, "Another waste of time… lovely. Good choice Joe."

The team is even more visually defeated. Without a word, McNeil turns back the other way. He starts walking with Laskey's help.

"I had to pick a door. It wasn't my fault. Any one of you coulda made the same choice." No one responds to Lattanzi's deflection. With all their glowering eyes focused on him, he's finally had enough, "Somebody else take point. I'm done!" Then to himself he mutters about the situation, "When does this shit end?"

Not missing the chance to take his frustrations out on his friend, Chorin adds insult to injury. Leaning his shotgun against his shoulder, he looks at his watch and acerbically retorts, "It ends in about forty-five minutes after that A-bomb lights us up. Any more thoughts on where we should go, or should we just stand around with our thumbs up our asses…? Cause the results would be about the same."

The corporal snipes back at Chorin, "You're so smart Jake, why don't you friggin' choose!?"

"Well, I couldn't do any worse!"

"Alright you two, that's enough… let's go." McNeil calls back.

"I'm giving the –" *CRACK! CRACK!* As Kowalczyk starts to assert himself again, the rip of semi-automatic rifle-fire rings out and a round whips past his head. The other projectile simultaneously pounds into Laskey's sternum, the force snapping him erect against McNeil. His fists involuntarily clench, and he crumples to the ground, pulling the sergeant with him. The team drops to their stomachs, scrambles to lock in on the attacker and returns fire.

At the end of the corridor, an unmistakable shape. Silhouetted by the last few service lights, the otherworldly *beast* unloads the rest of Turner's *M1 Carbine*. It snarls as .30 caliber death rocks from the front of the weapon. Its raging bioluminescent ice-blue eyes pierce the blackness. Then, as suddenly as the creature appeared, it's gone. In one swift leap its huge shadow disappears around the corridor's bend. The team's volley of bullets spark off the tile wall where it previously stood. Seconds later the random muzzle flashes subside, the clamor of gunfire wanes and the thick smoke from weapons' discharge dissipates.

Jumping up, Herrera hugs the wall for cover and speeds after the attacker. As the rest of the team stands and collects itself, he vanishes around the bend. Lattanzi helps McNeil to his feet, trying not to worsen his sergeant's bandaged leg. Chorin, still kneeling, feels the private's neck for a pulse. He looks back at the men and shakes his head "no". With sorrow in his voice McNeil laments, "He was gone before he hit the ground. Cover him with his poncho. We'll come back for him if we make it through this."

Chorin nods and starts digging the poncho out of Laskey's cargo-pants.

Kowalczyk states with some bit of shock, "That thing is picking us off one by one."

While wiping blood from his hands, Chorin stands and responds sarcastically, "Wow… brilliant observation Major. This is a bit obvious, but you do realize that wars are won by attrition?"

Leering at him, the major retorts, “I was commenting on its intelligence and its use of strategy Chorin.”

“Well, I feel much better now.” The two stare each other down. Their disdain for each other is palpable.

Herrera runs up to the group, “It’s gone Sergeant. It dropped a spent *M1 Carbine* back there. I think it’s Turner’s… but there’s no doubt, it’s been following our movements.”

McNeil comments on its tactics, “And using our own munitions against us.” He glances back to the group, “If any of us go down, don’t leave anything it can use.”

Larson unshoulders his sniper rifle, “Sergeant, if it’s following us, I can position here with my Enfield and take it out when it shows. You and the team could still go after the radio.”

“There’s no guarantee you’d kill it and I’m not willing to make you a sacrifice.”

Herrera questions, “Why hasn’t it hit us with something bigger? There must be more powerful weapons or better ordinance around here. It doesn’t make sense.”

McNeil can only speculate, “Maybe it used everything to take out most this facility’s compliment before we got here. I don’t know… But I’m pretty sure that *thing* didn’t do it with just claws and teeth. It doesn’t matter now. We have to deal with what is…” Again, he addresses the group, “We’re going to go back to the last convergence and head the other way. Hopefully that *thing* won’t be there. Everybody check magazines. Lattanzi… back on point. Herrera… back in the rear.” Although going to comply without question, Herrera’s body language nonverbally communicates that he’s not pleased. "Herrera, it's nothing personal. It's just that when we get further out, and I don't know where something's coming from... you're the one I'd want most covering our six."

Although it isn't military protocol and McNeil certainly wasn't obligated to give any reason, Herrera appreciates the words. "Thank you Sergeant." Honored, Herrera proudly responds and dutifully heads for the back of the pack.

"But Sarge I was -- ", Lattanzi starts to object.

McNeil cuts him off before he can start to spiral into a long winded protestation, "Save it Corporal. You've got the 'big' gun. You get the 'big' honors. Saddle up."

Kowalczyk approaches McNeil, looks down upon him from his two inches more height and states his displeasure, "I thought you relinquished your usurped command."

"Let's just say I was resting."

"Let's just say you have no authority."

Gritting his teeth in pain from his wound, McNeil leers back at him, "You're not in charge Major and you certainly won't be again. Court martial me. Hang me. Do whatever you want *if* we make it back alive, but you've made too many mistakes, cost too many lives, and told too many lies for any of us to roll the dice with you. So from now on, just shut the hell up and get back in line." The major just stares at him, thinking over his options. However, he knows without McNeil's blessing these men will never follow him again. Without a word, he steps aside and lets the sergeant pass.

#

Reaching the previous convergence, the team turns down the other tunnel. From the sewage pipes above, the sound of dripping water taps the concrete floor. With each drop it splatters, pools, and then trickles along the floor's grout channel turning into an upcoming ten foot wide by twenty foot deep opening. As they approach a gap, they tense up waiting for what may be lurking in the shadows. Being on point, Lattanzi's the first one on it. He shoves his back against the opposite wall and spins the *MG-42* at the opening. He scans the manmade grotto. His eyes dart, covering each inch of the opening. It's an exploratory adit, which is a test tunnel dug to gauge the soil and rock for tunneling viability, before extending in that direction. This one didn't prove sustainable for the Nazi builders and was utilized instead as a natural runoff sump to collect water leaks and condensation. In the middle of the adit's low point, the sump reflects back the service lights from its water filled oval reservoir. There's no sign of the creature. The corporal gives the okay, "All clear." Even though he's given the thumps-up, each man gazes in as he passes, wary that Lattanzi may have been wrong, and their lives are moments from over. They move on towards their new unknown destination.

As the team's footfalls fade in the distance, the sump's surface begins to ripple. Bubbles churn to the top. Suddenly, the water erupts from the sump in an explosive shower of spray. From within the *beast* bursts out, its heaving torso exposed above the waist. It gasps for breath and then sucks in slowly trying to suppress its noisy inhalations. It doesn't want to give away its position. It's vulnerable out in the open. It knows that a fully armed team is much harder to take out than picking off one at time. However, it must follow. Quietly and deliberately the creature crawls fully out of the sump that was much deeper than it appeared. The sewage's collected runoff drips from its matted hair. Its wet tattered flight-suit clings to the behemoth's soaked legs. Silently it moves to the corner and peers around. Its eyes scour the tunnel ahead for the enemy. It smells the air for their scent. The team is gone. Stealthily the creature treads towards their last position, following them quietly from a distance.

CHAPTER 20 — A GLIMMER OF HOPE

Lattanzi, McNeil, Larson, Kowalczyk, Chorin and Herrera emerge from the corridor. Before them stands a sixty foot diameter circular concourse. It is a hub where all the major activity converges from five passageways. Excluding the tunnel the team just left, there are four others that traverse this subterranean maze. One provides a roundabout connection to the rock stairwell leading up to the house. Another winds through the interior back to the mess hall and barracks. The remaining two passages are comprised of a walkway and a mining track that crosscut the concourse in opposite directions. One goes to the outside where raw materials were previously mined and carted in; the other meanders over a hundred yards back towards the now destroyed foundry. In awe, Lattanzi comments at what he sees that's more than just a room, "Holy shit. Someone's been decorating."

Here the architects put aside the basic need for mere functionality, and they classically designed this chamber for sheer veneration, reminiscent of the Roman Empire's Golden Age. Corinthian columns line the perimeter. Limestone facias with carved garland festoons stretch between each corridor. Portraitures, sculptures, mosaics, and tapestries proudly hang throughout, flaunting the Third Reich's grandeur during the war and inspiring confidence during upper echelon *Reichsleiter's* impromptu inspections. Amidst the architectural beauty, a demolished glass display case lies in the center, with shards and its contents strewn about the floor. Directly behind that mess is a circular-shaped bronze bank-like vault door, which has been pounded by gunfire and explosions. Copious amounts of dried reddish-brown coagulant decorates parts of the vault door and the floor. On the vault face, under the layers of blood and weapons damage, marred but surviving are a spoke turning wheel, a release mechanism, a four number rotating dial lock and a lever for opening it. Unlike most vaults of the period, this one's design is quite unique; its hinges are on the inside. The bronze housing is framed by a concrete triumphal arch, with an undiscernible inscription which has been partially blasted away by an explosion. High above, recently invented in 1941, *Siemens AG CCTV cameras* are suspended from multiple points in the concourse… some watch the vault, others watch the approach.

"What the hell are those things? They look like cameras.", Larson questions pointing at the cameras.

Kowalczyk answers boastfully, "They are… They're close circuit cameras for monitoring….. We have those at *OSO* headquarters too. A rather recent invention I might add."

McNeil noticed the cameras' slight movements and the discreet sound of their servos turning as they entered. He states matter-of-factly, "And someone's watching us."

"If they have that tech, then they should have some form of communication."

"Well, I don't think they're just going to invite us in Major. Chorin, can you rig something?"

Suddenly the vault lock snaps, the internal thirty-two security locking bars retract from the housing with a violent clang, the spoke turning wheel spins and the vault door creeps slightly open. A gap a little more than a foot wide allows entrance. Between the weight of the door and not knowing what's on the other side, they don't attempt to open it any wider.

The major throws a glance at McNeil, following up with a sarcastic remark, "You were saying?"

Dubious, McNeil raises his weapon and treads closer limping. The team follows. As each man passes the wrecked glass case, they can now clearly see the contents scattered across the floor. There are Nazi medals, citations, and black & white photos. One photograph is of this facility's base commander Klaus Albrecht dressed in a leather slicker, a black Hugo Boss uniform and *SS* officer's field cap seated in front of an unfurled swastika. Another is a photo taken at a concentration camp, which ceremoniously exhibits the assistant commander Diedrich Schwab gleefully smiling with pride. Next to him are his psychotic cohorts, all admiring the mass grave of victims that they've just created. Viewing this Chorin rages inside, with the thought of how his Jewish brethren have perished at the hands of this sociopath. Seething, he crunches the glass frames and photos under his boot as he passes.

All are ready to engage what could be an awaiting ambush on the other side. One by one, the team hastily slides through the vault opening with their weapons raised. There's no sound of gunfire and there's no initial engagement, but what waits further inside?

After the first three, it's now the major's turn to enter. As Kowalczyk disappears through the vault door, the sounds of huge pounding footfalls echo from the tunnel behind, resounding throughout the concourse. *It's* coming. Now being the only two left outside, Chorin looks back and exclaims to Herrera, "Get in! Move! Get in and close the damned door! Now!" Charging on all fours from the passageway, the *beast* bears down on them with unrelenting determination in its deathly cold eyes. It snarls in rage. It's maw is agape, razor-sharp teeth exposed, spittle flies through the air and its fur ruffles as its sinew stiffens with each bound. Without time to turn and fire, both Chorin and Herrera struggle inside and yank on the unwieldy vault door. The massive bronze ingress slowly swings on its internal hinges. The *thing* descends upon the door. With it only inches away, the vault door slams shut, and the security bars snap into the locking position. The creature impacts with immense force. The clang of brute force against the metal is thunderous. With a guttural roar, it pounds the vault's entrance with unimaginable ferocity.

#

Inside the vault, the men crouch in an antechamber, facing an unlocked closed hatch that leads to whomever opened the vault's access. They listen behind to the barrage of fists and jaws colliding repeatedly with the metal. Then… there's silence. Giving up in frustration, the creature walks off, its footsteps fading into the distance.

Bent over catching his breath, Chorin gives a rhetorical comment, "Bloody hell, that thing wanted us bad."

Kowalczyk posits another idea, “Or it just wanted in… And what’s behind that door.” He points to the unopened hatch.

Trying to relieve some of the tension, Lattanzi jokes with Chorin, “Bloody hell…? Since when are you a Brit?”

Throwing his friend a sarcastic glance, Chorin responds, “Funny… You spend a war fighting alongside them you tend to pick a few things up.”

Lattanzi strings a bunch of incoherent British words and idioms together in a strained English dialect, “Smashing. You’re a cheeky fellow. Bob’s your uncle. Cheers mate.”

“Do you even know what the hell you’re saying?”

“No, but it’s fun. You oughta try it.”

McNeil glances at his watch and speaks up, “Okay… if Abbott and Costello are through, we need to get in there and get on with it.”

Larson inquires, “How much time Sarge?” They all know what looms over their heads, but he’s the only one who really wants to know how much of their lives are left ticking away on a timepiece.

“Thirty-six minutes maybe, but who knows. We could be out of time in twenty.”

With a healthy amount of acerbic vim, Chorin chimes in, “At least we’ll never know when it hits us.”

The sergeant gestures acknowledgingly and then ardently emphasizes, “No time to waste.” Wincing, McNeil limps to the unlocked hatch. He’s so sick of doing this and doesn’t want to charge blindly into one more surprise. Holding the *MP40* at the ready, he places his other hand around the hatch release. He waits. The men file into apposing echelon formations around the door. Muzzles lock on the entrance. Looking at each individual in the group, McNeil impresses, “Don’t fire unless you actually see something. We can’t afford even one round to hit a radio if there’s one in there.”

Chorin opines, “This could be suicide.”

McNeil retorts, “What’s the alternative?” Chorin shrugs in agreement. Fiercely, McNeil yanks the hatch open, "Okay, let's do this." They all charge in.

CHAPTER 21 — CLOSING IN

Cruising at 28,000 ft, the *B17* pierces the billowy cirrocumulus clouds that fill the dusky sky. The *Flying Fortress*'s wings undulate from the air temperature change, as the vaporized ice particles pass over the warm steel. The four turbocharged radial engines rock from the turbulence, making the hum of the props sound like warbling waves of buzzing bees. Even at this altitude, the four propellers churning is audibly noticeable from the ground. To lower the possibility of being detected, the aircraft's flightpath has been plotted along the most sparsely populated if not an almost uninhabited route.

#

Inside the cockpit, Captain Jeffers pilots the huge bird, pensively tapping his fingers on the control-wheel. He and the copilot exchange glances in-between staring out the glass in silent contemplation. Not able to bear the trepidation swirling around in his head any longer, the co-pilot reaches down and engages the inter-communication phone's operational switch. At this altitude, the only way to communicate is through the headsets attached to their oxygen masks. And every crew member is able to hear what is said over the open line. There is no privacy on a *B-17*. Through his headset co-pilot Lieutenant John Fitzgibbons questions, "Are we really doing this Captain?" Fitzgibbons is a very good pilot in his own right and has flown with Jeffers for the majority of the war. Midflight during a raid, his first pilot was cut in half by a German *BF109 Messerschmidt's 20mm* mounted canon. Although he misses him, he's still extremely proud of two facts… One, that his Irish family has descended from medieval nobility, who served in the Knights of Glin. And the other is that he currently serves with his very best friend, Blake Jeffers.

Jeffers answers pragmatically, "We have our orders."

Looking over at his friend, his green eyes flare above his oxygen mask, "We're not even going to give them a chance?" The captain doesn't respond; he just inhales deeply through his oxygen mask and stares back out the cockpit windshield. What is ethical in his head severely clashes with the orders given him. He is torn. Fitzgibbons continues, "Those are our men down there, Captain. Our soldiers." Difficult as it is Jeffers ignores his copilot's plea. Angered that he can't get through to him, Fitzgibbons blurts out anything in his frustration, "Ya know, Tate's an asshole right!? He is an out of control megalomaniac who only cares about his career and he's always out for himself … I don't trust him. And who knows if this mission was even authorized by Allied Command!" He still receives no response and explodes. "It's a damned A-bomb they want us to drop, Blake! An atomic bomb! Do you get that!? You can't just follow the whims of some unhinged egomaniac!" His fury has turned his ruddy complexion even more red.

Annoyed with the copilot's persistence and wracked with the guilt from knowing the truth, he barks back, "Yes! Tate's an asshole! But he's also our commanding officer and he gave us explicit orders! And those orders are to drop the payload no matter what… and that's what we're going to do!

So I'm telling you, let it go, John! *That's* an order!" Fitzgibbons' anger doesn't subside, but he obeys his captain's command. He doesn't say another word. The two men sit in strained silence. Jeffers finally speaks to his friend with an apologetic subtext in his voice, "John… let it go. We have a job to do. Just… let it go."

The copilot nods and responds in defeat, "Alright…" He glances at his watch, "Thirty-two minutes."

Jeffers nods back, "Thirty-two."

Unbeknownst to McNeil's team, Tate's surreptitious meeting with Jeffers provided them a few more minutes than they thought… but will it be enough?

CHAPTER 22 — INCONCEIVABLE

Prepared to take incoming fire and possible casualties, the team charges in through the hatch crouching to make smaller targets. Swiftly they fan out to both sides of the door, weapons trained and ready to blast away. But there's no one. No resistance. No gunfire. So who opened the door? Moments pass and their minds start taking notice of where they're actually squatting. They stand and stare in awe.

This is a massive aircraft hangar, converted from an atomic research and development lab. This hardened shelter reaches three stories high and occupies seventeen-thousand square feet. High above in the ceiling, hydraulic cylinders hold forty-foot wide steel doors closed to the surface. Hanging from rails on both sides of the doors are two overhead bridge cranes, with hoists and hooks. On the floor below, this space is filled with Nazis' failed experimental aircraft and conventional weaponry prototypes. Chalk boards with physics equations and metallurgy formulas are grouped about the floor. Diagnostic equipment is scattered amongst lab tables. Huge metal lathes with partially turned shafts are anchored on iron platforms. Acetenyl tanks and welding apparatus stand next to stacks of forged and refined metal parts. Oscilloscopes and radiological instruments are perched on a desk above three uranium-235 encased lead chests, that have been conspicuously labeled with radioactive warnings in German.

Kowalczyk takes a step forward and words of astoundment subconsciously escape from his lips, “Sweet fancy Moses…” He stares at his inexorable quest’s trophy. Before him stands what he’s been waiting to gaze upon… longing to touch… yearning to possess. In full glorious view stands the *alien spacecraft.*

At eyelevel, positioned directly below the hydraulic doors is the creature’s ship, strapped to an aviation maintenance platform. After it crashed due to a core failure, the Nazis seized it, hauled it in and sited it for research. Significant damage from the crashlanding marred its surface, but it cannot veil its unique artisanal beauty. The otherworldly vehicle is an impressive thirty-two feet in diameter and brilliantly designed. Although built for interstellar flight, it’s been finely crafted by a culture that embraces aesthetics, exhibiting quite a contradiction to the ferocious creature that they’ve encountered. The mangled fuselage was originally fabricated into an elegant semicircular body with contoured exhaust channels and framed by in-atmospheric ogival delta-wings, which are now shattered. A cracked ribbed canopy, smashed weapon ports and severely crushed longitudinal chines make up the rest of the horizontal profile. A sophisticated radio-transponder has been torn from the keel, leaving a gaping hole in the underbelly. The bent and buckled hull is a silvery-gray alloy tinted by blue-green asymmetrical wavelike patterns, created from the alien’s unknown manufacturing process. Remnants of reverse engineered propulsion technology litter the floor alongside. In their quest to attain the superior technology, both the thrusters and flight drive had been hastily extracted by the Nazis.

Still captivated by the sight, Kowalczyk utters, “Inconceivable… It’s more magnificent than I could have imagined. Absolutely breathtaking.”

Lightly nudging McNeil with his elbow, Lattanzi asks rhetorically, “Can you believe that shit, Sarge?” Straight-faced the corporal asserts, “I don’t know what’s more the conspiracy… that fact that they’re willing to blow us up to keep this hush-hush or that they weren’t willing to tell us it existed. Either way, I knew something stunk to high Heaven. But I can see now why the Major was so worried. I wouldn't want the bad guys havin' that thing either.”

He’s a few feet away, but Kowalczyk overhears. Leaning forward past McNeil to see Lattanzi the major counters, “I’m glad to hear you say that Corporal… However, our objective wasn’t to keep this hush-hush. It was to keep the future of America from being decimated.”

“That’s what the government always says to justify the evil things they do.”

Insulted, the major starts to retort, but McNeil interjects, “We don’t have time for this shit. Everybody spread out and find a damned radio. There’s gotta be --”

Cutting him off midsentence, a throat clears loudly and then a robust voice yells from behind a workstation in muddled English with a heavy German dialect, “We surrender Americans! We surrender!” All weapons snap in that direction, except Larson who’s been scoping the high areas for a possible sniper. The team watches with their fingers poised on their triggers. Rising from the workstation's tabletop, chubby hands extend up over the edge. Then arms reach upward. Finally a rotund Nazi officer fully reveals himself with his hands raised in a signal of surrender. Although disheveled from lack of shower and hygiene, he is still dressed in his best black *Waffen-SS* uniform. His features are distorted from his weight, but there is no mistaking he is the assistant commander from the photos. "Good day Americans. I am Colonel Diedrich Schwab… the last surviving officer and acting commander of this facility. And these are --"

CRACK! A .45 caliber round rips through his face, blasting his head backwards. In a burst of gelatinous meat, the back of his skull blasts apart in fragments from the exit wound. He shudders and drops to the floor with a thud. The whole team looks to where the bullet was fired. Standing with his *Colt M1911* sidearm drawn, Chorin peers down a smoking barrel.

Enraged, McNeil yells out, "What the hell Jake!?"

Holstering his pistol, Chorin responds bluntly, "He was a murderous Nazi thug, and he got what he deserved."

"Son-of-a-bitch! We need answers! Not more dead bodies!"

"You're sticking up for that piece of shit!?"

"No! But that 'piece of shit' might have known where there was a radio! You could have killed him at any time! What the hell were you thinking!?" Burning, McNeil leers at the results of Chorin's pure stupidity and recklessness lying on the floor and then casts his infuriated gaze back upon the *PFC*.

A careless hothead in a critical situation is never a good thing and Chorin's impetuousness may have just screwed them in the worst of ways. McNeil's words hit home and a wave of logic rushes over him. He realizes what he's done. Ashamed and embarrassed Chorin backs off, but he can't find the words for his regret, he just softly voices, "I'm… sorry."

Enraged or not, McNeil understands there's nothing that can be done now and that Chorin was only acting out of frustration and rage. His thoughts vacillate between admonishing the man further or forgiving him his impulsive stupidity? Not wanting to extend this argument any longer, he shakes his head in disbelief, but doesn't respond. Collecting himself, McNeil cools off and thinks. *There's gotta be something here for a radio… please God.*

During McNeil and Chorin's back and forth, one distinct set of probing eyes have been fixated on another subject. When the pistol was fired, there was slight movement on the other side of three inch opening under the workstation's legs. Always aware and searching, Herrera was the only one to spot two sets of shoes shuffle and recoil from the sound. Holding the *Browning Automatic Rifle* focused on that area, he speaks up, "Sergeant… there are two more hiding behind that table." Without a word, Lattanzi begins slowly arcing around the counter to flank them. All of the team grips their weapons tensely.

McNeil yells one of the few German phrases he picked up during the war, "*Komm jetzt raus*!" He tells them to "Come out here now!" There is no movement. In no mood for games, he angrily barks his stern directives, "*Jetzt! Schnell!!!*" His spoken German is verbally askew, but his words and intent are unmistakable. His orders translate to a forcefully authoritative, "Now! Quickly!"

From behind the workstation, a flinty female voice with a French dialect responds indignantly almost commanding, "Don't shoot." Standing up with her hands raised, a ninety-five pound, five-foot nothing, brassy-blonde French woman obstinately submits. Her face is youthful and angular, her bobbed hair is exceedingly matted, and her lab-coat is filthy. During the war her skill was in high demand, which led to her being placed as the lead scientist for radiological operations. Now she has more important duties… extraterrestrial research. Dignified, she stands unafraid. However, she scornfully stares down on her male associate, ashamed of his cowardice. She motions her head for him to stand up.

Frightened by Schwab's execution, her companion hesitantly rises from behind the workstation. He too is dressed in a soiled lab-coat. He's a six-foot-two blonde, with a slightly muscular build and a messy receding hairline that's graying at the temples. Except for the minor balding he appears too physically intimidating for a stereotypical scientist, but he's always been one his whole adult life. He was a physics professor before the war and has been the lead science research engineer since coming to this facility. They slowly advance towards the team.

Now behind them, Lattanzi gives his orders in an American dialect since the woman responded in English, "That's far enough. Hands behind you heads." Without argument she complies. However, the German scientist doesn't understand what he said and keeps moving forward with his arms raised yielding. Realizing the peril that he's in, she quickly puts her hand on him to stop and tells him in German, "*Folgen Sie dem, was ich tue.*" Ardently, she tells him to follow what she does. He looks over and places his hands behind his head. Lattanzi hastily descends upon them and pats them down. While checking for weapons, he questions, "Anyone else here? And don't lie to me." She forcefully shakes her head no and indignantly reinforces with a one word curt answer, "No." The corporal assures the sergeant, "Sarge, they're clean."

McNeil just wants to stop the impending bombing run and gets straight to the point, "Miss, is there a radio here?"

She responds unassuredly, "No, only in the communication officer's room… I think." McNeil closes his eyes in frustration, knowing that one was destroyed. "Well, we need to be sure." Pointing to the other captive, "Do you thing he might know where we can find one?"

Before she can answer, Chorin cuts in asking McNeil, "Why are you wastin' you time with this lyin' Nazi bitch? She's not gonna give anything up." Even though she has a French dialect, Chorin's attention was instantly honed in on her German response to her colleague. It was too natural… too innate. He has her pinned in his mind. He knows in his bones she's a Nazi.

Staunchly brave, the woman glares at him with unmitigated contempt. With a venomous tone she sneeringly retorts, "My name is Lisette Allard, and I am very much one-hundred-percent French… not a Nazi."

“Yeah… Well, if you're not one of them, how do you know German and how'd you end up being on of their lackeys?”

“One… Unlike you Americans, Europeans teach their children multiple languages, which is why I can speak your English and why you probably can’t read above an eighth grade school level. And two… How does anyone end up in the hands of these monsters...? You do their bidding, or you end up dead in a mass grave.”

“Really…?” He points to his team, “We didn’t.”

“You have guns with which to fight. Hitler took all the guns… for the ‘good of the people’… before he slaughtered them. Where would you be without your guns American?”

“I wouldn’t have been over here saving France’s ass.”

She snickers at his attempt to give her a shot and responds in kind, “I’m surprised you were able to find France on a map to ‘save our asses’. Besides, we’re even now… we just saved you from that thing.”

Pissed, he wants to verbally unload, “You didn’t --”

McNeil jumps in, “Chorin… enough.” He repeats his question to her, “Miss, does your associate know where we can find a radio? This is imperative.”

Ignoring the question Lisette quips, “Instead of your men insulting me Sergeant, you should all be thanking me for letting you in. If it were up to Schwab he would have left you out there to be torn apart by that thing. He didn’t trust you. He said you would kill us all, but I was the one to convince him otherwise and that you may be able to save us.”

McNeil is losing his cool as each moment ticks by, "Yeah, we're all grateful. Now answer my damned question!"

He gets her attention. Lisette thinks for a moment trying to remember any other communications herself, but to no avail she's blank. She nods to McNeil that she'll ask. Unconcerned with being shot, she pulls her hands from her head and holds up one finger gesturing, "Give me a minute." Leaning over, she questions her associate in his native German. As he responds, they have a lively back and forth. Finally he shrugs and gives her his last thought. She turns back to McNeil, "Dr. Eckehart asserts that he could fashion together a working radio from parts we have available here." Delighted, the sergeant lets his emotions show. He's ecstatic with her response. A slight grin rolls up his face and his gray-blue eyes reflect hope. Hesitating only a second, she notices and continues with the bad news, "However…"

Chorin scoffs, "What'd I tell ya? Can't trust her." McNeil cuts him a look to shut it and motions for Lisette to continue.

Making a circle in the air with her finger, she points to the chamber. "Sergeant, this is all solid rock, concrete, and steel… basically an acoustic impedance. We could never transmit from here. Even if we opened the bay doors above, we'd still have a line-of-sight propagation issue. Electromagnetic radiation travels in a rather direct path from source to receiver. Unfortunately, your team will still need to make it to the surface to transmit."

Rolling his eyes, Chorin purposely glances over at McNeil. The sergeant's expression of happiness fades. He knew it was too good to be true, but at least there's still a chance. Peering down at his watch, McNeil questions her, "Okay... Can he cobble something together in less than ten minutes?"

Shocked, she suspiciously asks, "Ten..? Why only ten?"

Although he doesn't want to say the words out loud, he knows he must. Staring into her with as much honesty his eyes can project, he utters, "In less than thirty minutes this facility is going to be wiped off the map. You, me, everyone... dead. And the only way to stop that is to transmit a cancellation code into the ether and pray that our pilot hears it. If not, we won't have to worry about that *thing* out there. It's game over..." His words strike fear in her. For the first time since they've encountered her, Lisette seems vulnerable. The sergeant can see she's shaken, but he doesn't have time to waste on anything but their survival. "That's the reason for the radio. So if he's able to build it and we still need to make it to the surface, then we'll need that extra cushion time... I need to know now." McNeil motions towards Eckehart and tells her, "Ten minutes is all he has... Ask him."

Still visibly upset, Lisette fully flustered turns to Eckehart, communicates what McNeil just said to her and impresses their perilous situation. Horror fills her associate's eyes. His arms slowly lower to his side and he stares at McNeil almost to visually ask "is this true?" Grabbing his wrist, she snaps him out of his frozen gaze and questions him again more forcefully. He shakes his head "no" repeatedly, until she yells, "*Du musst*!". In defeat, he thinks for a moment, wavers, and then answers in a semi-confident tone.

The team watches the two scientists interaction, praying for hope. She turns back to McNeil, "In such a short amount of time, he can only assemble something very crude that may work." The faces of the men enliven… there's hope.

McNeil follows up, "All we need it do is to send a code. Nothing fancy."

She once again translates. Eckehart nods to her and then addresses McNeil, "*Ja. Ja.*"

Elated, the sergeant understands what "yes" is in German. He yells to the team, "Herrera… Larson… help the professor get what he needs. Lattanzi… Chorin… see if you can find any weaponry in here." They follow orders and move with purpose.

All this time, Kowalczyk has been admiring the alien spacecraft. And although he's been uncharacteristically quiet, Kowalczyk finally speaks, "Mademoiselle, there are two seats in that cockpit…" He points to the ship, "How many of them are there?"

Lisette regrettably laments, "Five."

Shocked, both McNeil and Kowalczyk ask at the same time, "Five…?"

"There were five. All catatonic when they were brought in from the crash. Two from the cockpit. Two from the fuselage. One died upon impact."

The major inquires apprehensively, "McNeil, if we only encountered one, where the hell are the others?"

Lisette adds, "Another died during experimentation."

Still not enamored with her answer, McNeil clarifies, "So there's three?"

"One is trapped inside an environmental chamber, where we were testing their ability to survive extreme temperatures. It is very angry and hostile, but that one won't be an issue. The walls in the chamber are three feet thick concrete. It would take a bomb going off for it to escape. So two."

"One's bad enough." McNeil tightens the bandage around his wound and laments, "Two's a nightmare."

CHAPTER 23 — WATCHING

From the shadows, deep trilling breaths seethe across multiple rows of pale-white serrated incisors. Intermittent snorts break its shallow rhythmic respiration. Beneath a heavy furrowed brow, determined bioluminescent crystal-blue eyes scan intently ahead. In the corridor leading to the concourse the *beast* patiently waits… watching.

CHAPTER 24 — TIME TO MOVE

Eight minutes have past. Eckehart feverishly continues to work with scraps of technology to craft some sort of communications device.

Across the room, Lisette tends to McNeil's wounded leg. His pants are half off and his exposed wounded leg rests in her lap. She holds a needle from a first-aid kit poised above the laceration, "Hold still… this will hurt. I'm sorry there isn't a local anesthetic."

The sergeant grabs his chair's edge and inhales, "Do what you gotta do."

She pours antiseptic over the wound. He grits his teeth. Giving him a second to recover, she inquires, "Are you ready?" He nods. She sticks the needle through the laceration's two flaps of skin and pulls it through. She repeats. The wound begins to close. With each stich he winces slightly from the pressure, as the sutures tighten. After finishing one pass, she heads back the other way giving him a double stich. With what they still have to face, she doesn't want to chance the wound reopening.

Through the pain, he expresses his appreciation, "Miss Allard… Thank you, by the way."

Momentarily looking up from her work, she looks him in the eyes, "Lisette..."

"My name's Frank."

"Okay Sergeant." Teasing, she smiles warmly and then continues stitching.

For just a moment she seemed gentle and caring to him, unlike the harsh woman she first presented. He wonders which one is the real personality, even though it's completely irrelevant and soon won't matter. However, her act of kindness flooded him with memories of his loving, nurturing wife back home. He misses her so much. He wants to see Ginny again…. If only for a second. McNeil's thoughts wander to the past where he held her in his arms and remembers the smell of her hair, the touch of her skin and her breath on his cheek. For a second he's happy. While dreaming of their embrace, reality hits him like a hammer. Dreams don't keep you alive. The only way to stay amongst the living is to focus on the here and now. He shakes the thoughts of her from his mind and observes Lisette again. While she finishes patching him up, he anxiously glances at his watch. Trying to ignore the countdown, he asks, "So, did the Nazis shoot that thing down or were you lucky enough that it just fell out of the sky?"

Lisette chuckles, "Amazingly, that's pretty close to how it happened?"

With a confused look, McNeil inquires, "Meaning…?"

She stops suturing, looks at him and responds, "That ship started showing up right after this facility began trying to enrich uranium-235 and dumping the depleted waste in a nearby mine."

"What were they looking for?"

"I have no idea Sergeant. We weren't able to ask them, so your guess is good as mine. Maybe they were intrigued by our weapons capabilities or looking for a fuel source they needed or to simply see if we were destroying the planet. But somewhere during their observations, something went drastically wrong. One of the returning *Wehrwolf* squads reported hearing a deafening explosion and then watched as the vehicle careened uncontrollably from the sky. The crash site was immediately surrounded and secured by almost every soldier available. Then they chained it up and it was ultimately dragged in here. Every scientist was promptly forced to switch to this facility's new objective, and there it sits in all its glory. Dropped out of the sky just for the whims of madmen." Ending with a bit of sarcasm, she unenthusiastically gestures with her hand towards the ship. Without another word, she goes back to tending to his wound.

"Where's the rest of them?"

"Who?"

"The other scientists working here."

"Dead I would assume." She doesn't elaborate. McNeil's eyes implore her for the story. She ties the last of his sutures and cuts off the excess thread. McNeil eases his foot to the floor, slowly pulls his pants back on and then watches her. She stares down at the first-aid kit, silent and sullen. Her hands are still. Her eyes are fixated on a moment of time. Her thoughts weigh heavily upon her.

"Are you alright?"

Suddenly awash in sorrow, Lisette closes up the first-aid kit and softly confides, "No..." McNeil's face is a cross between concern and questioning. Looking over at him, she explains, "It was 3 a.m. when the creatures escaped from their cages in the medical center. I don't know how they did it... I wasn't there. But they are highly intelligent, incredibly calculating and obsessively observant, so I'm sure they found a weakness in the makeshift prison-cells, or they exploited our human fallibility… either way, it doesn't matter… They were free. And I assume that they tore their way through the med-staff because not one of them ever came to warn us. We all slept in complete peace… totally unaware. And when they attacked, it was a violent collision of unmitigated ferocity and utter chaos. Until the first screams, no one even had any idea what was happening. The room was suddenly awash with red and high pitched blood curdling screams that pierced the air. Flailing appendages reached out for help amidst the flashes of their fierce brutality. Most of the science staff and soldiers were eviscerated in seconds. Those of us who survived the initial attacks ran and didn't look back. Some ran for the surface… some down here… most didn't make it. Only Eckehart, Schwab and I made it inside the vault before they hit again. The others who were locked out screamed and pleaded for us to let them in. We didn't. We feared that the creatures would make it in and..." Her voice trails off. Guilt and pain overtake her and sorrow trembles from her lips. "We could hear the sound of the carnage, the gunfire, the screams that were silenced… one by one. We never opened the vault again until your team showed." Her eyes well and she hangs her head. "We have all these emergency supplies… food, water, fuel, medical supplies, and we didn't let them in. We didn't give them a chance. We just waited for the slaughter to stop." Tears stream from her eyes. She's riddled with grief, guilt, and shame. Lisette looks up at him, "Before you assume anything, my tears aren't for the Nazis. I hate them. I cry for my scientist friends who were in the same position as me… broken prisoners and useful tools of the Third Reich."

"I wasn't thinking anything… except if you were alright?" Believing it's what she needs, he leans in to comfort her.

Forcefully, she recoils. Throwing up her hand she once again assumes her harsh façade. She sniffs repeatedly, wipes away her tears and composes herself. Standing, she starts to walk away, "I'm perfectly fine Sergeant."

"Wait. Lisette, I'm sorry. I was just –" He stops midsentence. He's not going to explain himself for what he felt was right, but he's glad he apologized for making her feel uncomfortable. Changing the subject, he probes, "You mentioned that you experimented on these things… Is there anything we should know that could help us?"

She stops dead in her tracks and turns back to him, "Make sure you kill them Sergeant. Make sure they're dead."

Unamused, he gets up from his seat and sarcastically replies, "Great advice. Thanks."

The fact is that she wasn't joking. She was absolutely serious. With great fervor she explains, "That was not sarcasm Sergeant, that was a sincere warning. Those creatures do not die easily. Although I studied their intellect, the Nazis studied their ability to survive at great lengths. They beat them, burned them, froze them, starved them, shot them and they still would not die."

"No wonder they're so pissed off."

"Quite understandably. And it's a shame because they are truly magnificent creatures…" With every word her temper flares and her blood slowly boils until she's ready for bear, "…but the Nazis were incredibly stupid and shortsighted. Instead of trying to understand these more advanced beings, they wanted to punish and subjugate them… like every race they feel is superior to them. The Fuhrer's 'Master Race'…" With venom in her voice, she gives a snort of derision and remarks, "…a bunch of sociopaths with inferiority complexes. And now their idiocy has left us with no alternatives, but to kill those great beings at any cost." Pausing, she exhales attempting to lower her anger, "Please excuse me, I digressed…" Returning to her original point, she attempts to further impress upon him her concerns, "Sergeant, don't take what I'm saying lightly. Those creatures have an unfathomable tolerance for pain and their cellular physiology is staggering at an evolutionary level. Their ability to make themselves whole is on par with Earth's lower order planarians or cnidarians, but at a scale that's unimaginable. Lacerations and gunshots heal within seconds. Gaping wounds mend within minutes. They spontaneously regenerate limbs, organs, and large tissue masses within hours. They are as close to an indestructible animal as I've ever seen. Shockingly, the Nazis were only able to neutralize one during experimentation by strapping explosives to its head and chest and blowing it to pieces. As you well know the creatures are vicious, unrelenting, and pretty much impervious to your weapons… unless you destroy the whole entity at once. Everything must die Sergeant." Her intense gaze lingers on him along with her words.

"I'll try to remember that."

"Good. Then what's your plan going forward?"

"Survive."

"That's not much of a plan."

"It's all I got." McNeil turns to leave.

Lisette calls, "Sergeant…" He stops and looks her way. She continues, "The Nazis underestimated the aliens, and their arrogance was their undoing. Don't let that happen to your team." She smiles warmly, "…or you." A slight approving grin appears on McNeil's face. He nods, then heads off towards Eckehart and the rest of the team. With a platonic fondness, she feels a confused affection for this man. Something in his eyes provides her comfort, but she doesn't know why. Without trying, he disarmed her… something with which she's not accustomed. A stranger she just met made her feel just like someone she's known her whole life and it unnerves her greatly. She walks over to the first-aid station and tucks away the first-aid kit in the cabinet next to the oak apothecary.

#

Across the hangar over by Eckehart, the team impatiently waits for him to complete his laborious task. Lattanzi, Herrera, Larson and Chorin all anxiously watch the engineer fumble with pilfered components from surrounding prototype aircraft's electronic devices and machinery. Although doing his best to calm himself, Eckehart's hands nervously shake as he rapidly solders wires together on the improvised radio's circuit board. The communication device is an amalgam of cobbled together machined aircraft parts, a wavelength tuner, transistors, vacuum tubes, rudimental batteries, wires, a speaker, a headset, and other gadgets to finish the job.

McNeil shuffles over to the group. His limp has become more of a walk-drag since the sutures. Quietly sideling up, he whispers to Herrera, "Eleven minutes… What's the status?"

Herrera subtly points to Eckehart and unobtrusively replies, "He seems to be making headway Sergeant, but I'm not sure. We didn't want to slow him down by asking. As for weaponry… there's nothing down here, except what's on the aircraft. There's not enough time to strip them off and make them usable. And the alien weaponry we found; we don't even know how to turn them on. You touch the trigger, and it glows, but the weapon won't fire. I don't know what they shoot, but it's not bullets. From the schematics over there, it looks like the Nazis were trying to figure them out and they didn't have any success either."

McNeil questions in astonishment, "Think they're rayguns?"

"Right out of a Flash Gordon comic... maybe? But we'll never know." Herrera raises his eyebrows in a completely puzzled expression. McNeil nods acknowledgingly.

Eckehart abruptly stops and apprehensively looks up at the men surrounding him, "*Das ist das Beste, was ich in so kurzer Zeit tun kann*." As the scientist awaits a response, blank faces fall over the squad members. They exchange bewildered glances with each other. That was incomprehensible. And then they all look over at Herrera for some sort of translation.

The sergeant outright asks, "What did he say Herrera?"

Somewhat shrugged, Herrera totters his head back and forth in a "maybe" motion, "I'm pretty sure he said that this is the best he can do in such short time." Unsure and knowing his German isn't going to get any better in a matter of seconds, he at least clarifies with the scientist if he's done, "*Bist du fertig*?"

With uncertainty and complete lack of faith in what he's just constructed, the German answers, "*Ja*."

Herrera looks at McNeil, "He's done."

Relieved, McNeil follows up, "Ask him the fastest way to the surface."

Acknowledging the sergeant's request, the soldier pivots, and questions Eckehart. The German provides what seems like a long explanation and an equivocating response. Herrera tells McNeil the engineer's response, "He thinks the rightmost tunnel, but he's not sure. He hasn't been to the surface since he arrived. And something about the blueprints for the base's floorplans being in the maintenance room… I think."

Although not pleased with the answer, McNeil knows they need to go. He looks across his team, "Alright, time to move." Chorin glances over with questioning suspicion at Lattanzi, with a look that says, *do you believe this shit?* The corporal shrugs, crosses himself, points to God and grins back at his friend. Larson grabs the makeshift radio, shoves it in a leather satchel and slings it over his head. Before leaving, Herrera tells Eckehart to come with them. The German's face and hands gesture, *why am I going?* Herrera forcefully nods to move. Reluctantly the scientist stands and awkwardly follows them. Edgy and uneasy, the team heads towards the vault door.

As they walk away from him, McNeil turns around and yells to their other new cohort, "Lisette… Do you know the fastest way to the surface?"

Her face questioningly twists into one of dubious repudiation. Not saying a word, she saunters over to him. Stopping in front, Lisette peers into his eyes and levels her statement at him, "I won't tell you Sergeant, but I will show you. I'm getting out of here now."

"That's not advisable. We may all die."

Indignant, she retorts undeterred, "If you do, the code won't be transmitted, and we'll all be dead anyway. I'm going."

He can't argue with her logic, he nods in agreement. Yelling over his shoulder, he calls to his team's sniper, "Larson… How's your *Enfield* set for ammo?"

The private examines the magazines in his ammo pouch. With four magazines containing ten cartridges each, he feels his sniper rifle's in pretty good condition compared to the rest of his team, who have exhausted much of their ammo due to their higher rate-of-fire weapons. Shouting back to McNeil, he speculates, "Probably better than most."

"Good. Bring me that *MP40* you're carrying."

Obeying the order, Larson unslings the Nazi submachine-gun that he previously lifted and runs over to the sergeant, handing it to him.

Although he doesn't have to ask, but knowing what they must face, McNeil kindly inquires, "You alright with this?"

Seeming unaffected, Larson downplays McNeil's concern, "I never carried a backup before, why start now? Besides, it was weighing me down."

McNeil okays with a nonverbal "Thank you". Larson acknowledges and runs back to the group. Turning back, the sergeant holds the weapon out for Lisette to take, "Do you know how to use this?"

"I can manage." She takes the weapon, yanks back the charging handle, grabs the forward stick-magazine for stability and folds her fingers around the pistol-grip, with her trigger finger poised on the trigger guard.

To McNeil she appears to be a natural, like she's been holding weapons in her hands her whole life. With her posed stance, tiny frame, angular face, bobbed hairstyle and steely eyes he thinks to himself that if it were thirteen years earlier one could possibly mistake her for the notorious gangster Bonnie Parker. He chuckles to himself and responds, "I guess you can. Come on." The sergeant heads for the team. She follows.

From over at the vault door, Chorin's gaze cuts a frigid stare directly at her. He doesn't trust her, and he certainly doesn't like that she's armed. While walking over, she notices. Amused, she winks at him. The *PFC* fumes. As she joins the group, McNeil shouts to Kowalczyk, "Major, you gonna join us?"

Pulling his head out of the hole in the hull of the alien ship, he yells back, "I'm staying here."

The sergeant walks towards the major. He responds in a shocked tone, "You're what?"

"I'm staying here."

“We need every man we –”

Kowalczyk cuts him off, “McNeil, you’ll need someone to open that vault door very quickly in the event you need to fall back.” The sergeant looks at him dubiously. The major adds to his rationale, “What are you going to do…? Fumble with the combination? Or the lock release? When that thing’s bearing down on you, you’ll need me in here. Besides, I’m not as good as any of your team with a weapon. You know that as well as I do. I’m made for combat in the sky… not on the ground.”

McNeil mulls Kowalczyk’s words over in his head. Reticently, he agrees, “Alright Major. Just make sure you keep your eyes on the cameras…” As he walks away, he points to the alien’s vessel, “…and not that ship.” With actual sincerity, the officer nods back an essential and absolute understanding, “Count on it.”

CHAPTER 25 — RUN!

In the concourse there is calm. A foreboding peace lingers throughout the hub, extending back into the five corridors. Nothing moves amidst the ominous quiet.

Then a violent clang of the security locking bars retracting shatters the silence and the vault door sluggishly swings open. From inside, the *MG-42's* muzzle appears, scanning back and forth. Moving with solicitude, Lattanzi fully emerges with the large enemy suppressing machine-gun. He squats and covers the five corridors the best he's able. Swiftly following behind, Lisette, McNeil, Larson, and Chorin join him. Right behind, Herrera exits the vault pushing a reluctant Eckehart who's now holding one of the previously retrieved gas/bolt-action *Gewehr-41s*. Without a word, Lisette points to the second most right tunnel with mining car tracks. The team runs for it. As they disappear inside, Herrera stops at the mouth of the passage, turns around, and squats just inside the shadows. He watches the vault door… waiting.

From inside the vault, Kowalczyk starts to pull the massive twelve-hundred-pound door shut. Slowly it lurches backward. The vault door swings on its hinges, with a foot or more to close completely. Moving only a quarter inch at a time, it still has a long way to go.

Herrera scans all of the concourse's tributaries, not sure of where the creature may be hiding. Leaning the *BAR* against the wall, he removes the last two *MKII* fragmentation grenades from his ammo-belt, pulls their pins and holds.

Suddenly, the *beast's* footfalls charge down the corridor towards the vault. It's been silently observing, waiting patiently for the vault door to open again. And now it's coming… determined. It wants in.

Herrera's gaze darts wildly trying to determine which passageway holds the rushing death. He closes his eyes and listens intently to focus. Raising the grenades, he readies to throw, with his fingers barely holding the spoons.

The creature's raging blitz draws closer. The pounding of its feet resound through the corridor. It doesn't growl or verbalize, but its forced breaths pulsate ever more loudly with its rapidly approaching pace. A steadily increasing tremor in the floor gives away its position.

The soldier knows where it is and from where it's coming. He lets the spoons fly from the frag grenades and begins to cook them. Their four-to-five second fuses tick off the impending explosions. One… Two… Herrera hurls them as the *beast* breaks the cusp of the tunnel. He shields his ears and dives to the floor, with his feet facing the impending blast. The creature covers a huge distance at an amazing speed. It closes on the vault door in seconds. As its claws clutch the vault door's handle to yank it back open, it sees the coming attack. Reactively it raises its arms to deflect the blast. The fuse ends, the nitrates ignite, and the hurtling weapons explode mid-air. The cast-iron grenades' bodies splinter into scalding metal fragments, throwing shrapnel in every direction. The double blast is substantial, and the sound is deafening. The animal's one hand is shredded, leaving only three fingers. Chunks of its arms are torn from the bone. The skin on one side its face is ripped clean, where it's exposed beneath its arms. Shrapnel tears into its side and the thing is blown back from the concussion. Slamming against the wall, its bloody mass slides down the wall. It lets out a guttural roar in pain. Not wasting any time, Herrera uncovers his ringing ears, grabs his automatic rifle, and begins to unload. At first the rounds smash tile around the *beast*, but then find their mark. Searing projectiles slam into the creature. It roars again. Extremely hurt, still being hit, it struggles into self-defense mode. As fast as its able, it stands and stumbles to get back into the cover of the corridor. The already half empty twenty-round-magazine in Herrera's rifle drains. Exhausted and smoking, the bolt locks back on the *BAR*.

The door to the vault slams against the housing. The locking wheel spins. It's shut.

Herrera thinks over the situation. The plan was locked in. No matter how many of these things they would encounter, do only what was necessary to buy them enough time to transmit the code… but this proud man has other plans. He's going to give his friends a fighting shot. He's going to kill this thing.

Slapping in his last full magazine, he charges after it. There ahead in the tunnel, it staggers as some of its wounds start to heal under a purplish foam, trying to get back to health. Herrera will not let that happen. With the *BAR* unloading, rounds chew through the creature inflicting heavy damage. It smashes against the wall, as the rifle's action locks back once again. Its steps are labored. Its coughs blood and its breaths wheeze from a punctured lung. It hardly moves forward, sliding against the cold wall's tile. Tossing the automatic rifle aside, Herrera unslings the backup *Gewehr-41* that he'd been carrying. Bolting in a round, he fires. It hits. Then another. Then another. It writhes in pain. Each round tears in the animal's flesh, damaging organs and spilling out more of its life, until the weapon is empty. Herrera discards that one, draws his *Colt M1911 pistol* and closes on the thing. He levels in. As he goes to fire, the *beast* drops and crumples into a mass on the floor. It doesn't move. Sounds gurgle up through its throat. Not chancing that it's still alive, the soldier starts firing .45 caliber rounds into the alien's body lying on the floor. Thigh, hip, stomach, chest… each grows closer to its head as Herrera draws nearer. Within a foot from the alien, he goes to unload the last three bullets into the *beast's* head. As the *1911* starts to spit death, its eyes snap open and it suddenly raises its arm. *CRACK!!* The barrel jumps and the projectile flies, blowing off a hunk of sinew.

Before Herrera has a chance to fire again, the thing counters! With every ounce of strength left, the creature sweeps around kicking with its foot. The soldier is knocked off his feet by the almost two hundred pound leg. The pistol fires astray and he crashes to the floor. It seizes the moment and immediately throws all of its weight on top of Herrera, pinning him. With great ferocity, the thing chomps down on the soldier's arm with the weapon, biting it off at the joint. He screeches in agony. Coughing up blood, the *beast* stares him in the eyes and roars a joyful resolve. Herrera's eyes fill with terror. Slowly and deliberately, it slides the claws from its good hand into Herrera's gut. The skin rips, the cavity spreads and the soldier's wail turns to a high pitched scream. It eviscerates organs, as it digs under the chest cavity, locking on the ribs. In one swift motion, the creature yanks the ribcage from Herrera's body, silencing him forever. Still choking on its own blood, the creature's lips curl back from its massive maw and it sneers in delight.

The beast's pleasure quickly wanes, and it succumbs. Dropping on what's left of Herrera's gelatinous meat remains, it exhales heavily. It lays frozen… motionless.

CHAPTER 26 — UNTIL THE LAST MAN STANDING

Depending on unknown variables and where the *Flying Fortress* is currently in the sky, McNeil knows only fourteen minutes are potentially left on the clock. They all know.

As they expeditiously race for the exit, the team runs along mine-car tracks, trying not to stumble on the rail ties in the floor. The passageway is at a steady incline in a curved configuration up to the surface. They pass lesser channels that route into other mining veins. Above them, interior lights pass every twenty feet providing the only illumination in the shaft, except for the slivers of light that will be emitted from the surface access when they reach the guard hut, a few hundred yards up around the next bend. The support beams and tiles that make up the corridor abruptly end, turning into a solid tunnel of magnetite iron and bituminous coal. In these tunnels lie what was once the Nazi's major source of operational fuel and processing ore for metallurgy. Due to the peak maturation of the organic material, the smell of methane hangs in the air. McNeil notices it, "What the hell is that smell!?"

Lattanzi smells it too, "Yeah, what is that?"

A winded Lisette yells back ignoring them both, "We're almost there! A few hundred yards ahead… just around that bend!"

Not stopping to contemplate, they press forward faster knowing that salvation is so close. As they round the bend, the rock walls become black with residue and the wooden rail ties turn charred. The interior lights flicker and then totally cease twenty yards further down the tracks, but what's there is still visible from the faint light behind them. One by one they stop running and look in disbelief and horror. A wall of destruction blocks their path and rocks of varying sizes are scattered about the floor. The surface is now unreachable from this tunnel.

Hanging his head, Lattanzi laments, "Holy shit, were screwed."

McNeil eases forward a few steps for a better view. Remnants of two scorched Nazi guards lay strewn within the fallen rubble. Their bodies are burnt beyond recognition. If it weren't for the unmistakable *Waffen SS* helmets lying next to them, there would be no discernable markings attesting to the fact that they were once *SS* soldiers. Two others are crushed in the collapse, only their arms and crushed skulls stick out between the rocks. Across from the corpses, in the debris lies another alien. It too is severely burnt. Its head, torso and one arm are all mashed under a two ton boulder. A severed hand and its two twisted legs stick out from underneath.

McNeil wipes his hand against the wall, quickly studies the color and then smells it, "This is burnt gas residue. That's the smell. Looks like they got one with a grenade and took themselves out with it... stupid bastards. Lucky for us though, one less to deal with." A Nazi grenade meant for the creature ignited a methane blast that caused the massive cave-in to happen. The lingering smell is the highly flammable hydrocarbon gas still leeching from cracks in the coal's strata.

Knowing they can't get through, he orders, "We gotta go back."

Leering at Lisette, Chorin snidely derides her, "Great job Frenchie. Was this your plan all along?"

She barks back sarcastically acerbic, "Yes, I wanted us to all die… imbecilic."

Looking at her askew with a partial leer, he irreverently jests to the rest of the group, "Well I guess, smoke 'em if you got 'em."

Moving quickly, McNeil cuts Chorin a look, as he passes. Grabbing Lisette by the arm, the sergeant motions for her to lead the way back, "Please…"

Although her words talk about the distance, they actually provide the subtext about the futility they face. The trembling alarm in her voice speaks volumes to her actual meaning, "Sergeant, the surface is a long… *long* way back there."

He understands what she's saying, but he's not willing to give up, "I know. Please just lead the way." Shaken, she nods.

Before she can move, Larson yells out, "Where's Herrera?" They all feverishly look across the faces of the group. McNeil, Chorin, Lattanzi, Lisette, Eckehart, Larson… but no Herrera.

Incensed, Chorin snaps at the private, "He was supposed to be with you!"

Larson retorts, "With me? I was just doin' what we all talked about. We were running. I heard the explosions. I just figured he was behind us like the plan."

"You figured!"

McNeil cuts in, "We'll find him after! Now move!" Again, he nudges Lisette to lead. She bolts off and he follows. Not willing to let this go, Chorin glares at Larson with a stare that could kill and storms after the two. The rest of the group follows.

#

The team charges through the tunnels hoping to make it in time. They race through the concourse choosing another passageway. They bolt through the subterranean corridors, barely sparing a wary second to look for the *beast*. They have no idea if Herrera rendered it wounded, killed it or if it waits somewhere in the shadows ready to finish them off… but there isn't a moment to consider those variables. They rush onward. Dashing up the limestone stairs, they compete with the clock that ticks off precious seconds between life and desolation. A light from above still shines through the blasted hole in the limestone wall, that leads to inside the farmhouse facade.

#

Finally reaching the surface, the team breaks from the blast hole in the bedroom's closet. Exhausted and weary, they want to embrace the solitude and safety, but there's no time to stop. They rush through the house, out the back door where the team's initial incursion took place. Outside in the open they now have a clear line-of-sight for the electronic transmission. Freezing, they spread out into a relaxed circle. Even with the elements, fatigue, preoccupation with the *beast* and being minutes or even seconds from death, all that's on their minds is the weapon of mass destruction hanging above their heads and sending this code. Their military training isn't even on their radar; there's no guard, no one sets a perimeter, it's an undisciplined free-for-all and no one cares. While trying to catch their breath, all eyes instantly lock on Larson, as he whips the satchel from his shoulder and sets the radio on the snowy ground. Their silent exhalation mists from their mouths, looking like sheep awaiting the slaughter. Dispersing the makeshift radio's assembled parts and extending the connecting wires to their fullest extent, Larson scans the mechanism and despairingly questions, "Where's the microphone?"

Forcefully whipping through the trees, only a bitter-cold wind groans an ironic response of hollow emptiness, as it cuts between the farmhouse and the barn. The team has no response.

Frantically, the private starts scouring over each piece carefully examining them like he missed something. Watching from the side, McNeil can clearly see that there isn't a mic. The sergeant doesn't say a word, he just subtly and quietly shuts his eyes in frustration. Looking back and forth at the two of them, Larson yells directly at the scientists repeating himself, "Where the hell's the damned microphone!?"

Shivering, the team anxiously turns their gaze upon the two, awaiting an acceptable reply. Not knowing the answer, Lisette queries Eckhardt in German. He responds candidly. She asks another and he shakes his head "no". Turning back to the group, she translates with a concerned delivery, "He built it in the time you gave him. You said you just needed to send a code."

"So where's the damned mic?"

Chilled to the bone and deathly serious, Lisette reveals to unfortunate truth, "The rocking lever on the circuit board is for Morse code, not speaking. There is… no microphone. He thought you being soldiers, you would know Morse code."

McNeil laments, "Of course… And from your tone, I assume the good professor doesn't know it?"

She shakes her head "no" and sadly responds, "Neither do I."

"Does anyone remember Morse? I only remember friggin' *SOS*. Larson, tell me you know it?"

Like deer in the headlights, Larson gazes up at him clueless, "Not me Sarge."

Pulling his lighter and another bent cigarette from the pack in his cargo pocket, McNeil lights up hoping the smoke will calm his nerves and warm him a bit. The flame glows on his frigid cheeks as he asks, "Chorin… you?" He slaps his lighter closed.

Chorin quips, "I'm not a code-talker and I'm not in the Navy, so why would I remember that shit? No. Absolutely not." Before McNeil can ask, Chorin looks to his best friend Lattanzi and follows up, "How 'bout you Joe?"

The corporal eyes give away his answer before he even speaks, "We're doomed. Herrera was the radio guy Sarge, not me."

Those words ignite Chorin's fuse. Pointing, he moves aggressively towards Larson, accusing him of failing Herrera, "You were supposed to have his back!" McNeil grabs him by the collar, stopping him.

Larson yells back, "I was just following the plan!"

Wanting to punch the kid, Chorin pulls menacingly forward against McNeil's grip, "Plan my ass! Cause of you we're all dead!"

"Screw you! You coulda done somethin'!"

"You little shit!" Even more forceful, the *PFC* tries to get his hands around the young man's neck.

Still firmly holding his collar, the sergeant shakes him forcefully, "Back off Jake! That's enough... We don't need this shit." Although still enraged, Chorin stops pulling and raises his hands in submission. McNeil lets go. The *PFC* turns away, but his vicious stare could still put Larson in the dirt. McNeil takes another drag and exhales. Shouldering his weapon, he places his hands on his hips and drops his head back. Defeated, he peers into the open sky, "I can't believe this. I can't friggin' believe this."

With the machine-gun leaning against a tree, Lattanzi rubs his hands together for warmth and tries to add a positive spin on the conversation, "Well, if we gotta bite it this way, you gotta say it's better than being torn apart by that *thing*. At least it'll be quick."

Chorin anger fades away. He starts smiling and chuckles in cynical amusement, "It'll be quick alright. Incinerated in seconds. Like that..." He snaps his fingers. "Accentuate the positive, right Joe?" He starts mildly laughing at the absurdity. "We make it through everything.... all the way back here with a radio and nobody knows friggin' Morse Code... how the hell is that possible? Could we possibly have any worse luck?" He laughs even harder and then rests himself on the frozen ground. "I guess we just sit here and die."

Larson speaks up, "The major might know it Sarge."

Inhaling deeply, McNeil disparages himself, "You idiot… I knew I should have made him come with us." Frustrated McNeil growls to the team, "Alright… maybe we have a few seconds left on the clock. Maybe not, but we gotta try. Lattanzi and Larson, you two get the major and bring him back here ASAP."

In a very nonconfrontational voice, Larson softly objects just out of logic, "Sarge, there ain't enough time. That's at least another ten minutes in just one direction. We won't make it there and back before… you know."

The mental picture of reality hits like a spike in McNeil's brain. It's like watching a Superbowl with two minutes left on the clock and knowing your team needs three touchdowns… *it's over*. McNeil loses it! His face twists in rage. Up to now he's tried to be the voice of reason but confronted with what he knows to be the inevitable truth, he explodes. His piercing grey-blue eyes drill into Larson, "So, what do we do… just sit here on our asses and wait for it!? We have no idea if we could be gone in the next five seconds or the next five minutes, but we also have no idea if that plane took off on time! They could have been grounded by snow… or by ice on the wings… or mechanical issues… We don't friggin' know where they are or when we're gonna bite it! But I know this… we don't give up ever! Not 'til the last man standing! You got that!?" Seething with frustration, McNeil accentuates one word, "We don't *ever* give up!"

Embarrassed that he brought anything up and didn't just follow the order, Larson contritely answers, "Yes, Sergeant."

Lattanzi speaks up, “No need to chance anyone else with that thing down there Sarge. I’m the fastest one here, I’ll go by myself and –"

A familiar voice with superfluous verbosity interrupts from the farmhouse’s doorway, “Samuel Morse’s telegraphy cipher isn’t as ubiquitous in the service as many would believe. However… I am profoundly knowledgeable.” All eyes snap towards his voice. There in the doorway, a disheveled Private Turner stands alone with a smile on his face and a *Colt 1911* gripped in his hand. His hair is a wet stringy mess, his face is covered with dirt and his uniform is rumpled under his winter-gear. For the first time ever, they see him completely unkempt.

A shocked and extremely pleased Lattanzi can’t believe he survived, “Holy shit. You’re alive?”

“Fortunately. I was able to evade the attack by sliding under an industrial drainage grate, but I lost my rifle. It was viciously chomping at –”

With his anger instantly melted away, an elated McNeil cuts off Turner and hurriedly orders him to move, “Save the story for later. Get your ass over here and start transmitting.” Losing his smile, the private gives a thumb-up affirmation and runs towards the radio. As he starts to pass Lattanzi, the corporal hands him his “lucky comb” and jokes, “You’re gonna need this.”

With a somewhat terse tone, Turner quickly replies, “Making it down there alone showed me that I really don’t… but thank you anyway Corporal.” Lattanzi’s a bit surprised by his reaction but nods an understanding. Without another word, the private darts off to the communication device without his "lucky comb". Kneeling in the snow, he looks up at McNeil and slightly shrugs as if to ask, "What do I message?"

Thinking for a moment, McNeil remembers what Kowalczyk handed him before they left. He reaches into his chest pocket and pulls out a piece of paper containing the major's writing. With a Lucky Strike bouncing between his lips again, he speaks, "This is what we need to do. Hopefully the major wrote down the right info or this is all gonna be for nothin'. Okay… first set the transmitter to five hundred kilohertz." Turner complies. With all the words in German, he can only guess what may be correct He moves the only dial with markings on it to the indicator reading the number 500. He nods that its done. McNeil takes a quick drag and throws the cigarette to the ground. This is too important. Speaking slowly and clearly he instructs, "Now transmit our callsign. Sierra, Whiskey, Zero, Seven, November…"

CHAPTER 27 — SILENCE

High above, the *Flying Fortress* cruises on towards its final destination, with the drop-zone drawing ever closer.

#

In the cockpit, silence fills the cabin like a choking stench. Jeffers and Fitzgibbons sit in uncomfortable reticence, each locked into their own view of the situation and mentally clinging to their own motivations. As they watch through the cabin's glass, a bluish-gray haze streams by them as the horizon rushes beneath.

Suddenly, the command radio crackles and comes to life. Broken and sporadic Morse code begins sparking through their headset speakers. The reception frequency was set to receive, but a few millihertz off. Leaning over, the copilot fine tunes the calibrated frequency dial, so a clearer signal emanates forth. Then a full uninterrupted message transmits through the command radio. Dot dot dot… Dot dash dash… Dash dash dash dash dash… Dash dash dot dot dot… Dash dot. It repeats. And then again.

Ignoring it, the pilot doesn't avert his gaze from face forward. With his hands still effortlessly manipulating the flight controls, he steadily reaches over and readies his hand above the throttle, anticipating the moment when they must descend to a bombing altitude.

Fitzgibbons holds the one headphone pressed firmly against his ear and listens closely. He verbally translates,

"Sierra, Whiskey, Zero, Seven, November…" Pulling back, he stares over at Jeffers, "That's them. That's their callsign." Passive, the pilot is unemotionally indifferent. Turning to look overhead, the copilot slaps the transmitter's toggle switch on the control box above them.

Jeffers breaks his silence, "What are you doing?"

"Responding."

"Turn it off."

"We have to respond."

The pilot shouts back, "We don't have to do anything, except follow orders! Now turn it off!" As they continue to argue, the callsign continues its torrential blast across the radio-waves. It's almost as if you can hear the deserted team's desperation through the mechanically-driven sound's repetition.

Fitzgibbons flips the tone selector to "MCW" Modulated Continuous Wave, to transmit Morse code telegraphy. He responds to Jeffers at the same time, "That's their callsign Blake! They're trying to stop the bombing! We can't ignore them! I'm answering."

Seething, not from being disobeyed but due to the turmoil his friend has put in his head, Jeffers reiterates angrily, "Shut it off… now!"

The copilot explodes, "We can't do this! We can't just wipe a bunch of our men off the face of the earth! What the hell is wrong with you!?"

"Tate could be right! They could be compromised!"

"And what if they're not!? Can you live with that!? I know I can't!" He implores with his pronounced glower and emphasizes the question “Can you live with that?” to Jeffers with the subtext of just one utterance, “Blake…?”

Even though Jeffers cognitively grapples with Fitzgibbons pithy retort, he ignores him and yells back to the bombardier through the inter-communication system, “Rosetti, open the bomb-bay doors.” Within seconds, the sound of servos engage, hydraulics squeal and a rush of air whooshes into the cavity of the plane. The aircraft jostles, as the steel bomb-bay doors spread open and drop into position. With a clang, they lock fully clear of the payload. The atomic bomb hangs above the earth, held back only by its retaining rack.

The bombardier Staff Sergeant Jack Rosetti calls back, “All set Captain.”

Jeffers slides down the throttle levers, cutting the rpms on the engines. The *B-17* starts rapidly descending. The hulking aircraft bucks and shakes vigorously while it passes through changes in temperature and air pressure.

Incredulous, the copilot can’t let it go… or won’t let it go. He knows this isn’t the honorable man with whom he spent years cheating death amidst multiple bombing sorties. This isn’t his friend who saved countless lives at the risk of his own. He knows he can reach him. He knows there’s hope of changing his mind. Shifting tactics, Fitzgibbons lowers his voice and calmly speaks in an unassailable tone, “They have lives to live Blake… families to go home to… celebrations to be had... Against all odds, they made it through the damned hells of war and now it’s just over for them? This way…? By us..? That isn’t right. It’s not fair for them to have gone through all that, just to have their ‘brothers in arms’ take it all away. We have to give them the benefit of the doubt. They've earned that. We have to respond." Jeffers eyes his friend indignantly, as Fitzgibbons continues his impassioned plea, "Blake, you've always done the right thing…" He imploringly presses the quintessential point, "…Don't throw that away now."

CHAPTER 28 — NEVER SAY NEVER

The wind swells and a frigid chill slowly creeps up over the mountains. A storm is coming.

Gusts assail the weary group. Weapons slung; they tightly huddle around Turner. Listening intently for anything that could even be remotely construed as a response, they wait and pray. Except Chorin, who sits on a log contemplating where they are now and staring out over the precipice from whence they came. *All this for a lie.* Almost amused, he chuckles to himself. He can't believe this is how it's going to end, with his temper gone and being truly accepting of his fate. Behind, sporadic pops of radio static disrupt his thoughts. For a moment he has hope. But then he clearly hears the unending repetitive hiss emitting from the analogue monophonic speaker. No one's coming. No one will save them. He breaks the team's silence and glibly states the obvious, "They're not answerin'." McNeil shoots him a look of annoyance. Catching the sergeant's gaze in his peripheral vision, the *PFC* adds, "Well, they're not..."

Lattanzi gives his two cents, "I'm just happy we're not goin' back down there. Like I said… better to go quick up here than end up as a hot lunch down there."

McNeil chooses to vocalize his displeasure this time, "You have to add something too?"

"I'm just sayin'."

Chorin jokingly supports his friend's current optimism, "You tell 'em Joe."

Shivering, Lisette steps closer to McNeil. Leaning in, she subtly asks a question to which she already knows the answer, but is actually hoping he's willing to lie to her, "So, was this all for nothing Sergeant? Are we too late?"

"Probably…" Catching what he said, McNeil restates his answer, "Maybe… I hope not. I don't know." Trying to make up for his words, he puts his arms around her reassuringly. This time she doesn't back away from his kindness. She squeezes him tightly.

Chorin looks up in the sky, waiting for the inevitable end and grouses in response, "You're wasting your time. This is never gonna work." Although subdued, his words are still loud enough for the others to visually react to his mockingly dour comment. The body language of those surrounding him screams that they didn't appreciate it.

With hearing the dire remark, Turner stops hitting the telegraph key, looks up at him and snaps back incredulously angered, "Are you saying this a futile endeavor *PFC!*? Would you like us to just cease our actions and give up!? What is wrong with you!?"

McNeil interjects, "It doesn't matter what the hell he's saying. Ignore him." He points directly at Chorin, "And you shut it." Addressing Turner again, "Chorin may be right and none of this may matter soon, but until then… keep at it." Turner acknowledges, doesn't say another word, and gets straight back to his work. He starts tapping off their callsign once again.

Unmoved by the sergeant's command, Chorin repeats himself slower and louder just to tweak McNeil, "No Turner… I'm just saying that this is *never gonna work*!"

"Son-of-a-bitch..." Enraged, McNeil starts to pull from Lisette's embrace.

Suddenly Morse code dits and dahs, better known as dots and dashes, begin clambering through the speaker. It's the *Flying Fortress*. They're responding.

The group erupts into cheers. Even Chorin shouts out what could be considered a noise of delight. Elated, Lisette joyously throws her arms back around McNeil and firmly hugs him. With salvation in sight the sergeant's anger subsides, and he instantly forgets about the altercation with Chorin in which he was about to engage. He gives Lisette a cheerful grin and hugs her back. Eckhardt looks around, deduces it has to be good news and smiles, shaking his fists in triumph. The celebratory fervor continues until Turner swiftly raises his hand and sternly shushes them, "Quiet please! I need to hear!"

The team instantly goes silent. Maybe they celebrated too soon. Their faces twist with sudden anguish. Turner focuses, concentrating on the sounds of the streaming code clattering through in semirhythmic tones. Mouthing the alpha-phonetic translation of the code, his lips purse and release repeatedly as he commits the incoming letters to memory. His face grows from one of deep deliberate focus to one of complete understanding. He has the message. Nodding his head, he starts tapping back feverishly, then stops. Purposely paused again, he listens to the *B-17's* response. Every person surrounding him holds their breath, hoping that this will be the end.

Lattanzi speaks in a hushed tone, "Come on Turner… give us some good news."

Lifting his head with a smile from ear to ear, Turner looks across the group and states, "Never say never..." They stare at him just waiting for the actual words. The private speaks slowly and deliberately, "They're calling off the strike. Now, you can celebrate." They all explode into boisterous cheers again. Larson and Lattanzi dance an impromptu comical jig in the snow, Lisette and McNeil embrace one last time and the rest just scream howls of joy into the air. With their spontaneous reveling, they've all forgotten what threats may still be lurking.

Letting go of Lisette, McNeil faces Turner and orders, "Tell them that we took the base and have the objective." He quickly follows up, "And Turner... nice job. You saved our asses." The private humbly nods, smiles an acknowledgement, and goes back to transmitting the new message. The sergeant then addresses the group, "Alright... let's all wait inside for the cavalry where it's a little warmer. Lattanzi and Chorin... first watch. Turner and Larson switch off with them in a half hour. I'm gonna cover 'The Hole'." With his commands given, the group's celebration slowly subsides. He starts walking towards the backdoor.

Starting to follow, Larson reluctantly asks, "Hey Sarge... What about the Major?"

Not stopping, McNeil yells back, "He can wait there until the reinforcements arrive. He's safe. No need to risk anybody else to tell him the good news."

Chorin harshly objects, "Screw him. We oughta leave his ass down there." Then he directly questions the sergeant's statement, "And what the hell would make you believe that those bastards are gonna send reinforcements? They were going to nuke us for shit's sake."

As McNeil crosses the door's threshold, he stops, faces him, and responds deathly cold, "I don't believe anything… I know for a fact that they'll send them. They'll send them because we have the only thing that's important to them… the only thing that ever mattered…" He points to what's below, "…that ship."

"And what if they decide to mop up and finish this because of what we've seen?"

Lattanzi throws in his two cents too, backing up his friend from his conspiratorial point of view, "That's a good point Sarge. This thing's been rigged since the beginning. Maybe we weren't ever supposed to know. Maybe they have other plans now."

McNeil glances at Lattanzi and then over to Chorin. He briefly considers their point. Although he hadn't thought about that angle, he knows they may be right. Tilting his head to convey the thought "Good point", he takes a step, but then stops. He wasn't going to speak. He honestly didn't think it required an answer. But then his own wavering trust and dwindling faith compels him to posit, "Let's just hope General Buchwald's still one of the 'good guys'." Checking his *MP40's* magazine, he slaps in a fresh one, pulls back the charging handle and promptly enters the farmhouse. He's loading up for a fight, but which one… those around him are unsure. The mood just went from celebratory to somber within minutes. With only a jaded look amongst each other, Larson, Lisette and Eckhardt follow him inside.

However, Chorin is quite satisfied that he made his point and rhetorically responds, “Right…” He stands, stretches and readies to start his watch. Gripping his trench shotgun, he leans into the blustery gale and walks forward. Looking over at Lattanzi, he points to himself and then to the west. Lattanzi acknowledges and motions to the opposite direction. Giving the subtle thumbs-up, Chorin heads off.

As Turner finishes with the communications and begins packing up the makeshift radio, Lattanzi walks up next to him on the way to his watch, “Hey…” The young man looks up at him waiting for a wiseass remark or a condescending comment. Neither happens. Lattanzi states sincerely, “Good job Turner. Thank you.”

The young private answers with a bit of snark, “Turner…? I’m Turner now? No Goldilocks or some other witty epithet you can muster up to amuse yourself?” Although Lattanzi doesn’t understand the word epithet, he gets Turner’s meaning. A little miffed and confused why the kid isn’t just accepting his expression of gratitude, he stands there momentarily speechless. Dusting off his hands, Turner throws the satchel with the radio over his shoulder, stands and crossly inquires, “Corporal, may I ask you something… personally?”

Lattanzi doesn’t know where this is going and reluctantly responds, “Okay...”

“Since I’ve joined this squad, Chorin and you both have shared the need to continuously denigrate me… why? Have I done something to offend you? Is it because I was in the Marine Corps before joining the Army? Or do you just not like me? The two of you have been tenacious. Why? Please explain this to me."

Once again the corporal is confused by a few other words, but he can read the context. Being called out and thinking about his interactions with Turner in the past, Lattanzi gets a little irate. Indignant, he explains himself, "Truthfully… We thought you believed you were better than us." Turner gives him a puzzled glance as if to ask *what are you talking about?* Lattanzi clarifies, "You're always actin' so prim and proper. Then you speak all hoity-toity, like you don't want us to understand what the hell you're talkin' about. Like right now… denigrate… tenacious… who talks like that? It's like you're talkin' down to us or somethin'. Then with your perfect posture and your perfect hair, it's like you were puttin' on airs. We don't like it. And worst of all, since you joined our team you've completely avoided us… never even a hello. So who's really been rude to *whom*?" The corporal emphasizes the word whom, with a sanctimonious smirk. "See, I can be all condescending too."

Turner irksomely counters with aplomb, "Those characteristics you find so easy to ridicule and dismiss Corporal have absolutely nothing to do with you. And they certainly weren't intended to project any conceit nor disparage anyone. I carry myself as I do because I want to better myself, personally. People measure you by your words, actions, and appearance… that's just a cold hard fact. An unfortunate one, but one that this poor white-trash kid learned by the time he was twelve and I decided right then to change. I knew I couldn't afford new clothes nor go to college, but I could afford a stupid comb for my appearance and immerse myself in free library books. Was the comb lucky…? Did I become an educated man…? No, but it made me feel that way. I wanted to be appreciated and respected, so I presented, spoke, and acted accordingly. I don't know why you'd mock me." His eyes lock onto Lattanzi's to impress the point. The private scornfully continues, "As for looking down on you… You wouldn't know this Corporal, because you never cared enough to ask, but I came from nothing. I have hardly a tenth grade education… My mother and seven siblings barely got by on the measly pittance that my father's job provided, when he wasn't blowing it all at the track… And the only things that I owned on the day I was drafted were the soiled clothes on my back, so believe me… I know all about people looking down on others. I've had to endure it my whole life. So let me assure you unequivocally, I would never proliferate that repugnant behavior with anyone else… not even with a smart-mouthed know-it-all corporal." Lattanzi is stunned. That response wasn't anything he was expecting. He thought he was going to get some ridiculous verbal tap-dance and then a pathetically insincere apology. He was wrong on both accounts. And now he knows he was wrong with his initial judgment of Turner. With his temper subsiding, Turner adds softly, almost sadly and without being verbose, "And as for me being standoffish… you do realize that the two of you haven't been very pleasant with me, don't you? You realize that, right?"

Feeling like a complete heel, the corporal agrees without reservation, "You're right. You're absolutely right. We've been a couple of idiots and totally out of line. I'm sorry. Can you forgive us?" The corporal offers his hand to shake.

Taking a second, the private mulls his sincerity. Then thinking of the biggest Thesaurus word in place of 'certainly', Turner jokes with a smile, "Indubitably… " He extends his hand.

CRACK!! A searing projectile slams Turner in the temple. With the smile still on his unexpecting face, an exit hole bursts from the other side of his head in a shower of skull fragments and gore. He is dead upon impact. His lifeless body slumps to the ground. Yanking his hand away, Lattanzi instantaneously snaps to look over at where the round was fired and moves. More gunfire whips past his head. Although somewhat obscured by the falling snow, he can still see between the farmhouse and barn, as he races for cover. A hundred and fifty yards past the front of the property, coming up over the hill, a Soviet soldier runs through the deep snow firing off repeated 7.62 caliber rounds with his semi-automatic *Tokarev SVT-40.* Another soldier comes up over the crest and then another. A full frontal assault is beginning! Leveling in with the *MG-42,* the corporal screams to his team, whether they can hear him or not, "Soviets!! They found us!" He squeezes the trigger unloading a volley of hot lead. As his machine-gun chugs death, he charges the farmhouse's corner for cover while firing.

#

Inside the farmhouse's bedroom, in front of 'The Hole' McNeil sits in a wooden chair guarding against the *beast,* just as the Nazis did a few short hours ago. The room is silent, until the pounding salvo outside breaks the calm. Hearing the gunfire, he jumps to his feet and bolts down the hall.

MP40 in hand, he storms into the living-room to see Lisette and Eckhardt braced with their backs against the wall, holding weapons in their hands. The two stand between the boarded up windows waiting for a chance to fire. As rounds pound the wall behind them, wood splinters and dust cracks away from boards filling the air with debris. Cascading rays of light pierce through the busted slats, dousing the room in jagged illuminated segments. Cold and snow rush in assaulting the room. Their breaths instantly morph into a crystalized vapor cloud.

Across the room, Larson is already sniping through the slats at the Communist soldiers. He fires, cycles through the bolt action and fires again. McNeil races up next to him, gets cover and peers through the nailed planks. He sees the enemy. Spreading out across the fallen snow, a platoon of Soviet ground forces spill over the ridge attempting to set up a double flanking maneuver. He knows that the only thing helping their cause is the fact that deep snow is slowing down the charging thirty-five-plus soldiers. “Larson get upstairs! Don’t let them flank us!”

Larson pulls back from a snipe and stares at McNeil. With a panicked look on his face, Larson yells over the incoming fire, “I’ll try Sarge, but there’s so many of them!”

“Do what you can! We have to hold them off ‘til help arrives!” McNeil cracks off rounds at the invaders. The young private nods and tears off out of the room. His feet pound up the stairs and then across the ceiling above. Glass shatters and *Enfield* fire starts echoing above. The sergeant blasts a few more volleys of lead and points to Lisette and Eckhardt, “Shoot damnit!!” Although terrified Lisette grits her teeth, sneers with determination, spins to face the window and fires her *MP40* unrelenting. Not knowing what to do, Eckhardt follows her lead and nervously starts shooting the *Gewehr.* While blasting McNeil yells over, “Short bursts only! Save your ammo!”

Hearing him, Lisette consciously stops firing. Flustered, she momentarily squeezes the trigger and releases it. But then she swiftly changes her line of fire and repeats this time with resolve. Automatic submachine-gun fire spits short blasts from her muzzle. And although striving to make the ammo last, her thirty-two round magazine will soon be spent.

As both scientists do their best to help stem the tide of the rushing platoon, a board shatters inward, partially impaling Eckhardt’s chest. Lisette glances over at him and the wound appears superficial; she’s relieved. In shock, he gazes back at her. Still firing, she screams to him in German, “Are you alright!?” Silently, he falls backward on the floor. Thudding like a slab of beef dropped on a butcher’s block, his chest exposes the entrance wound of the 7.62 caliber projectile that caused the wood to splinter. The wound was much worse. Seeing this, Lisette turns to McNeil with a horrified expression.

There’s no time to mourn the dead in combat. The sergeant commands, “Keep firing!”

#

On the east side on the farmhouse, Lattanzi’s machine-gun blazes from an open unprotected position and then he immediately recoils back behind the stonewall corner. As he does, enemy bullets ting off the cornerstone next to him and chew at the ground in front of him. Withdrawing back behind the wall, he reactively spews venom, "Holy hell… I'm gonna friggin' kill you!" With a momentary break in the pounding gunfire aimed at him, he levels again. Even more determined to pay them back, he locks his jaw and blasts with unrelenting fortitude. As he does, a round pings off the brim of his helmet. Stunned, he quickly pulls back. Resting against the wall, he briefly thinks *That was close… a little too close.* He knows he has to slow their advance. Reaching down on his ammo belt, he unfortunately realizes that he used his two grenades on the original assault of the barn. To make matters worse, the *MG-42* is running out of ammo. His mind races. He has to give his team more time. He won't give up. Screaming with defiance, he spins the muzzle around the corner again and lays down a stream of suppressing fire. Ninety yards away, two Russian soldiers violently shake and drop.

#

On the other side of the dwelling, Chorin stealthily peers around the corner of the building and sees the onslaught approaching. It's a staggered charge with ten or so feet between each rushing enemy soldier and almost ten men split between each flank and fifteen pushing the frontal attack. They're now seventy yards away and closing quickly. He doesn't fire. Quietly he removes the remaining grenade from his belt. Kneeling, the munitions expert takes a tripwire from his parka and ties it around the shrubbery next to the house. With great care, he unfurls it across the snow until it reaches the building's foundation. Testing for length, he pulls it taught and cuts off the excess. Quickly twisting the new end around the grenade's pin, he ties it off. All through the air, the sound of gunfire rages. It draws ever closer. Up against the house, he frantically uses his fighting knife to dig out some of the soft mortar surrounding two rocks in the stone foundation. Raking it back and forth, he digs in further. With enough material gone, he pulls the tripwire tight and wedges the grenade's spoon in the crevice between the two stones. With the whipping snow he doesn't even have to camouflage the wire, it won't be seen. Easing away backwards, he turns with his shotgun to engage the enemy with Lattanzi. He races off.

#

Up in the second floor bedroom, huddled below the window, Larson cranks his scope down to 75 yards. Battlesight zero doesn't work on a sniper rifle. To be more effective, one has to adjust for the collapsing target distance. Kneeling up, he levels the *Enfield* on the enemy soldiers swarming in on the right flank. Peering through his scope, the cross-hairs flowingly dance. Moving steadily clockwise, the reticle covers all white until it lands on a Soviet *RP-46* machine-gunner who's unloading with the belt-fed 250 round brute. Larson squeezes the *Enfield's* trigger. *CRACK*! Red erupts from the Russian's chest. He staggers and falls. Not pulling back from the scope's eye relief, Larson racks back the bolt again, and chambers another round. His sight rapidly searches. There… A Soviet private charges screaming and firing at Lattanzi's position. As the Russian closes within sixty yards of the perimeter, Larson fires. It misses. He whispers to himself, "Shit…" Not having time to adjust the scope again, he mentally compensates for the shorter distance, cycles the bolt and shoots again. The young Soviet's head snaps back in a crimson wake. The dying soldier is snapped erect, becomes momentarily rigid and then drops. Pivoting towards the left flank, Larson fires again… then again. Two more targets cease to breathe. There's no getting around it now, the swarm is drawing closer more rapidly and he has to adjust for distance. He drops below the window and cranks the scope down to 50 yards.

#

In the living-room, McNeil fires back and forth through the slats, concentrating on the middle. Then his *MP40* empties. Grabbing for another magazine, there isn't one. He knows they're outgunned, outmanned and soon they will all be dead or captured. He scans the floor where DeVogler and Groves were once loading magazines but weren't able to finish. Diving at the pile, he starts shaking them to find the ones with actual ammo left in them. As he finds magazines with the 7.92 *Mauser* cartridges that matches the *Gewehr*, he tosses them over by dead Eckhardt's rifle. Still rummaging, he finds four that are still partly filled with the 9mm cartridges that match his weapon. Quickly emptying them, he shoves them into the *MP40s* stick mag. There's only twenty-three, but it's better than nothing.

A barrage of projectiles pound the wall and windows where Lisette is firing, narrowly missing her. She screams out in frustrated fear and drops below the window for cover. Splintering debris falls down upon her. Yelling to McNeil, "What are you doing!?"

Sliding over to the *Gewehr* he starts loading the left over cartridges into its ten round magazine. There are only eight. Suddenly, he stops dead and listens. The distinct sound of metal tracks clanging, and a rumbling diesel engine resounds through the air. Slinging the Gewehr over his shoulder, he clutches the *MP40* and yells back, "We have to move!?" Ducking, he squat runs over to her, grabbing her by the hand and yanks her up, "Run!" Bullets whizz by them impacting the interior walls behind. As he pulls her towards the hallway running, a thundering explosion erupts, followed by a whistling large projectile. With a violently massive impact, the bottom side of the house explodes in a shower of rock, wood shards, and cement dust. McNeil and Lisette are thrown to the floor from the concussive blast. With a gaping hole to the outside behind them, they lay motionless under rubble and dust.

#

Above them, Larson is shaken off a snipe as the building forcefully quakes. Knocked teetering from a kneeling position, he stops himself from completely falling over with one hand. Steading, he stares out the window at the *T-44* medium tank baring down on them. The turret turns slightly, the gun mantlet whines and its barrel raises locking on the second floor. He sees what's coming. It fires! Reacting, Larson runs from the room and dives for the stairs. His body hits hard, banging and flailing down the staircase as the projectile hits. A massive explosion decimates the room and a plume of smoke billows down the stairwell, engulfing him.

#

Still utilizing the farmhouse corner as cover, Lattanzi hip-shoots and Chorin fires squatting, as the shell explodes on the side wall above them. They instinctively both pull back as remnants of destruction rain down. Holding their ears from the artillery blast, they hunch over trying to protect themselves from anything still falling. They are battered by shattered wood and cement powder, while large chunks slam to the ground narrowly missing them. Chorin yells, "This is insane! We have to go! They're bringing the damned place down around us!" Recovering, they indiscriminately fire streams of lead and buckshot around the corner trying to slow the Soviets' advance, but the wave is too great. They can no longer hold his position. Lattanzi is steadfast and won't budge, "No, we hold the line!" Chorin barks back, "There's too many! We have to go!" Suddenly, Chorin's trip-line on the other end of the house explodes! The Russians have reached the house on the other flank. Multiple Soviet soldiers scream out in pain. Chorin knows if they don't move they're done. Solidifying that fact, the ground erupts forty feet from them where they stand, as a poorly thrown Soviet *RG-42* grenade detonates. They're just out of shrapnel range but are still showered with falling dirt. Grabbing his friend, the *PFC* pulls Lattanzi towards the back door, "We have to go… now!" Enemy fire swarms the air around them and they are now clearly within grenade distance. Running for the back door, they blast suppressing fire to keep anyone from rounding the building till they can get inside. But it's too late.

Two Soviets turn the west corner and fire their rifles. Simultaneously, Chorin blasts them with buckshot from the trench-gun, catching one squarely in the face and the other in the shoulder, spinning him. Still depressing the trigger, he racks another round ending the other one. A stray bullet from the encroaching enemy found its mark… Lattanzi was hit. Limping behind, the corporal holds his thigh as he grinds out the word, "Shit!" Before they even has a chance to turn and react, a soldier rushes from the east and unloads. The searing lead tears into Lattanzi's back, riddling him with holes and dropping him face first into the snow. Winded and coughing up blood, Lattanzi rolls back over and watches the destruction around him. Chorin spins firing, catching the enemy in the chest with *double-ought* fury, shredding him. Running over, Chorin kneels at his friend's side and looks down upon a severely wounded Lattanzi. The corporal touches his sizable exit wounds and then looks at his bloody hand, stunned. He never thought he'd go like this… he always thought he could outrun death. With a frothy crimson spewing up from his collapsed lung and red churning over his lips, the corporal barely gets out only one word, "Go…" Lattanzi's eyes plead with his pal to move. There's only mere seconds until another Soviet will round the corner. Chorin's eyes well, and grief ridden he shakes with the obvious visceral reality. Against every fiber in his being, Chorin grabs his friend's hand, squeezes it, and then runs off. Just as he enters the back door, a Russian speeds around the west corner. Straining to lift the *MG-42,* Lattanzi blasts wildly, as he struggles to hold it steady. Just the ferocity of the weapon streaming a spray of fire is enough to silence the enemy soldier. It empties and he drops it utterly fatigued. Cold and exhausted, the corporal draws his *1911 Colt* pistol from its holster, rests it on his leg and waits for another attacker. Lattanzi's eyes haze over, and his upheaving chest goes still.

#

As Chorin enters the farmhouse he sees McNeil helping Lisette to her feet. He slams the door shut. Reacting, the sergeant snaps the *MP40's* muzzle at him. The *PFC* exclaims, "Don't shoot!"

McNeil had already backed off the trigger as soon as he noticed it was Chorin. Holding up his hand in acknowledgment, he asks, "Lattanzi…?" Chorin shakes his head. Another shell hits the dwelling shaking it. They all steady themselves. The ringing in their ears is still deafening, but the sound of gunfire pounding the house can still be dreadfully heard. Trying desperately to regain his cognitive faculties, McNeil steadies himself and prepares to lead them back into hell. The sergeant motions with his head, "Down the hole!" He moves swiftly towards the bedroom. Lisette follows closely behind watching the shattered windows. Just then, Larson staggers from the stairwell. Chorin sees him. With all his previous anger and resentment towards Larson melted away by this impossible situation, Chorin just yells to him, "We're going kid!" Before moving, the *PFC* notices that Larson has both his grenades left; being a sniper he didn't use them on either combat engagement. Shifting past him Chorin swiftly grabs a cracked ceiling timber, hurries back and shoves it crossways between the door and the hallway's opposite wall, blocking the door from opening. Just as quickly, he snatches up two bricks and two wooden boards laying on the floor.

Coughing and clearing his head, Larson asks, “What’s that for?”

“You’ll see. Come on.” Not hesitating, they run off.

Outside, the sound of Soviet gunfire whizzes through the air and slams into the heavy wooden farmhouse door. As the two charge from the room, a grenade flies through the window landing in the hallway. It explodes!

#

In the bedroom, McNeil rips the filthy covers and soiled mattress from the bedframe and tosses it on the floor. He reaches down and flips the frame up against the wall. Confused, Lisette watches with absolutely no clue what he’s doing. As Chorin and Larson hurriedly enter, McNeil yanks clothes from a dust covered meager looking dresser.

Concerned by what he sees, Chorin yells to McNeil, “Whatever you’re doin’, you better hurry up! What I rigged out there isn’t gonna hold for long.”

As the sergeant pulls the bureau over, he yells, “I’m making this look like it’s been ransacked… maybe it’ll buy us some time. Into the ‘Hole’ now!” Both Lisette and Larson follow his order and move into the closet, through the blasted steel hatch and into the limestone staircase.

Pointing at the strewn mess, Chorin questions skeptically, “You think this is gonna buy us some time?” He sees the plan but doesn’t think it’ll help too much. The Soviets are outside right now, pounding away at the door to get inside. It’ll give way soon.”

“Even if it only slows them down and makes them think for thirty seconds, that’s still thirty seconds further we’ll be away than we are now… right? Let’s move.” Finishing his statement, McNeil picks up the mattress. Chorin shrugs and enters the closet. As he does, McNeil yanks the mattress inside the closet and shuts the door. Entering the blast hole, he pulls it behind him upright against the busted hanging steel hatch, covering it. With the closet light out and if someone wasn't focusing on the darkness, one might actually miss what's further behind… but they might question why it's in there. For now, the slightly slanted vertically standing mattress covers 'The Hole'. It's hidden.

CHAPTER 29 — FIRE IN THE HOLE

With McNeil's team no longer returning fire, the Russians have now completely surrounded the farmhouse. Through combat attrition only twenty-two remain, but it's still too large a force for the survivors to overcome. Unabated, the Soviet soldiers blast away at the dwelling. The slowly encroaching *T-44* tank holds its fire, as the ground-troops ready to storm the building. Exiting the tank's hatch, the commander resonantly yells, ordering them to enter and engage. They close in and charge. Simultaneously smashing through the bullet-ridden decimated front and back door, they unload a fierce torrent of lead. The interior walls on the other side of the entries are shredded.

Swarming through the house, the soldiers look for McNeil's group, ready to crush them with one final swift blow.

#

Rushing down the limestone spiral stairwell, Chorin briefs McNeil, Lisette, and Larson of his plan. His breathing and words grunt a rhythmic cadence as each foot hits another stair, "We have to try to collapse the corridor to buy us time. If we don't and we run into that thing… no matter how it ends, the Commies will still have enough time to wipe us out. If we don't run into that thing, they'll eventually make it to the vault and who knows how long it'll take them to get it open. We have to slow them down until our men arrive."

Hustling down the stairs in front of the group, McNeil calls back, "What do you have in mind?"

Chorin motions to Larson, "Junior here, still has two grenades… it's not true demolitions, but they contain close to four ounces of *TNT* together. That should be enough to blow the supports and collapse the tunnel… maybe."

"You can throw them that accurately?"

"No…"

"Then what are you proposing."

"Nothing good."

#

As the Soviets move through the house, they arbitrarily blast each closed door to take out any enemy hidden behind. Cautiously, they then shove it open with the muzzle of their rifles. Each room is checked, one by one, until they reach the bedroom. Seeing the closet door, the corporal motions the group with forward. Their weapons are trained on the closed closet access. He hold up his fingers and counts down silently. Three… two… one… Suddenly seven muzzles spit a barrage of searing lead, unloading on where they think the survivors are hiding. The closet door splinters and cracks, blown apart on its hinges. There are no screams of pain. There is no sign of anyone hiding in there. They stop. Smoking barrels stay locked on the target. As the commander enters, the men make way and snap to attention. This strategically cunning officer made his mark while leading a rifle division that helped hold off and subsequently expel the invading German *Wehrmacht* forces at the brutal Siege of Leningrad. He's a well-respected man who commands the room as soon as he enters and not because of his rank. He eyes each man, as if to individually ask what have they done? A terse tone of displeasure hisses from his lips as he ask's what's going on, *"Chto proiskhodit?"*

The corporal answers that the survivors are gone, and they must have escaped, *"Vyzhivshiye ushli. Dolzhno byt', oni sbezhali, ser."*

With a snort of derision, the commander shrewdly eyes the room and considers the staged pieces. His thoughts mull that it doesn't look random enough. Looking further he locks onto the closet that the soldiers were assaulting. The mattress is chewed apart exposing its goose feather stuffing. The floor surrounding it is littered with the same. Snatching the corporal's *PPS-43 submachine-gun,* he whips it around and strafes the closet. As he arcs, the bullets pierce the wall and then the mattress again. The sound of wood cracking is interrupted by chipping rock and then a distinct metallic pinging. Leering at the corporal, he shoves the weapon back in the inexperienced young man's chest. He walks into the closet and yanks down the mattress. The busted steel hatch and blast hole are exposed. Turning to the men, he barks for them to engage and to move now, *"Privlekat'! Dvigaytes' seychas!"* Without a response, the soldiers pour into 'The Hole'.

#

Three stories below, while standing around the first set of supports in the tunnel, McNeil, Chorin, Lisette and Larson hear the machine-gun fire echo through the stairwell from above. It's not going to take long for those forces to be on their position. McNeil snaps, "Okay, what's the plan. We gotta move."

Squatting, Chorin places a brick on the concrete floor. He sticks the bottom end of the board behind it as a brace and the other end he leans up at an angle against the vertical support timber running up the wall. He speaks quickly to the private, "Hand me your grenades." Not asking any questions, Larson complies and hands them over. Chorin places one on top of the board with the spoon in the crook between the small plank and the timber. "Larson can you hit this board from down there." He points to the end where the 'T' intersection branches off into the right and left tunnels.

Proudly, the young man retorts, "*PFC*, you buy me enough time, I can blow the ass off a gnat at five hundred yards."

"Good, then go get set."

McNeil asks, "What do you want us to do?"

Chorin looks up, "Give him cover and buy him some time."

"What about you?"

"I gotta set these. I'll be there… just go."

McNeil knows just how dangerous it is for Chorin to set these live grenades lodged into the wedge with the pins pulled. One mistaken move or an accidental roll and they go off. Acknowledging his brave effort the sergeant nods a nervous thank you. The *PFC* nods back with a look that it'll be okay. McNeil then looks to Lisette and whispers, "Come on". They both run off. Chorin watches as Larson hurriedly kneels on the right corner of the 'T', using the wall as bone support. McNeil and Lisette split. She takes position kneeling on the left side with her *MP40,* and McNeil stands with his above Larson ready to provide cover. Making sure the grenade's spoon is adequately shoved in the crook, Chorin pulls the pin. Making a face of "please don't move or blow up", he slowly backs off. Hastily, he moves to the timber on the other side and repeats the process. He can hear the resounding enemy footfalls pounding down the limestone stairs. Backing away, he turns and runs towards Lisette's corner. McNeil, Larson, and Lisette watch as he runs, waiting for him to get far enough away from the potential blast radius. Ten feet.... Twenty... Thirty... Their faces determined. Their weapons trained. The echoing of the compounding Russian soldiers boots sound like a division instead of a platoon. Chorin reaches forty feet away from the grenades, "Fire in the hole!"

The Soviets breach the stairwell's arch and start to spill into the tunnel. They fire unrelenting. Savagely, McNeil and Lisette return fire blasting, as Chorin hugs the wall swinging in by Lisette. As he does, he's hit in the shoulder and dropped to the floor. Lisette yells out, "Chorin!?"

On the other end of the corridor, the first Soviet through is caught in the neck, staggering he drops. Whizzing projectiles fill the air.

With his sighting eye fixed on the board through the scope, Larson squeezes gently on the *Enfield's* trigger. Although the ringing of automatic gunfire all around them is deafening, it's almost as if sound disappears as his rifle goes off. Time momentarily stops. It kicks and as the bullet blasts from the muzzle... it finds its mark. The *.303 Mk VII cartridge* slams into the right board, knocking it out from under the grenade. The spoon flies and the grenade explodes. The concussion blast jolts the other grenade from its perch setting off the other rigged detonation. The doubled massive explosion shatters both supports, violently fragmenting brick, and shredding the first two lines of the encroaching enemy. As they scream out, parts of the ceiling tumble in on them. Rolling plumes of smoke and debris engulf the corridor on both ends, rocketing through like a blast from a canon barrel. For a moment, the remaining enemy onslaught is slowed as they attempt to take cover behind the stairwell arch. McNeil, Larson, Lisette and Chorin are showered in smoldering wreckage and sediment. The corridor groans and more debris falls sporadically. As the dust clears there is a four foot 'V' left open between two huge piles of rubble that block the sides of the passageway… The tunnel didn't completely collapse. Larson hangs his head. McNeil sighs in disbelief. Even with stubborn resolve, Lisette's eyes well up knowing their fate. Holding his shoulder, Chorin struggles across the floor to get to cover of the corner. The group knows they're done for, but they won't quit fighting. Maybe the cavalry will arrive… maybe they will die. Reluctantly raising their weapons, McNeil, Larson, and Lisette check their fields of fire and await any motion near the 'V'. Although bleeding, Chorin draws his sidearm; he can't lift the shotgun.

Suddenly, the Soviets start climbing up the rubble into the 'V' and fire. The volleys of lead begin again.

Lisette and Chorin on the left, McNeil and Larson on the right fight for their very existence. Bullets pound the back wall at the 'T' intersection. As rounds hum by his head, McNeil's *MP40* locks back empty. Immediately dropping it, he unslings Eckhardt's *Gewehr* and returns fire. Then Lisette's *MP40* is done. Scrambling, she retrieves Chorin's trench-gun and cracks off blasts. Larson snipes each soldier's head he can as he sees it appear through pile of the rubble. He shudders for a moment, feeling a jarring sting but ignores it and keeps cycling through snipes.

Stacks of Russian soldiers start piling up, but they won't be stopped forever. They have the larger force, innumerable munitions and time. Rushing into the breach, a Soviet specialist has had enough. He will end this American trash once and for all. He drops a *41mm grenade* into his *Dyakonov rifle-propelled grenade launcher*. Unwavering, he jumps on the rubble pile, pulls away the bodies blocking his advance, crawls to the crotch of the 'V' and fires! The streaming projectile rises quickly. Leaving a trail of smoke it rushes towards the group.

With all his might, Chorin grabs Lisette around the collar and pulls her into the left tunnel of the 'T', behind the corridor wall. McNeil and Larson dive at the right passage. The rifle-propelled grenade impacts with the last top support joist. A brutal eruption of wood and brick engulf the 'T'. The force is enough to unleash the natural physics held back by the intersection's retaining structures. The massive weight gives way and the whole end of the tunnel collapses. The Soviet specialist inadvertently achieved the survivors' goal. The Russians' path is blocked. There's no getting through the tons of wreckage without immense time spent digging through.

As the enemy soldiers look in shock at the situation before them, the commander makes his way up to the specialist. Roiled with anger, his rigid eyes study the unfortunate aftermath and sneers at the specialist. As the soldier gives his most sincere apology, the commander slowly and deliberately peels off his leather tank gloves. The young man watches. With a vicious stinging slap across the face with the gloves, the commander barks, *"Idiot!"* Surprisingly, it's the same word in English. Turning to the rest of his men, he yells that no matter what it takes he wants them now and to dig, *"Chego by eto ni stoilo, ya khochu ikh pryamo seychas! Kopat'!"*

CHAPTER 30 — THE LAST STAND

Although they are beyond the Soviets' reach for the moment, McNeil and Larson are also cut off from Lisette and Chorin.

In the right tunnel McNeil and Larson shake off the debris and struggle to stand. Their ears ring from the blast and they are disoriented. Gray dust is caked on them. Trying to focus, McNeil looks at the collapsed tunnel. With a staggered steadying step, he motions a "right on" as if to assure himself. He looks back at Larson, who's leaning against the wall. Walking towards him, he speaks, "We can't reach Lisette and Chorin… we gotta go."

Not even able to lift his *Enfield*, Larson concurs, "Right Sarge…" As he takes two stutter steps, he drops. Falling back, he collapses with his legs underneath him.

The sergeant runs over and kneels by the private's side, "Larson…?"

Deep thick red coughs up out of his mouth. Its severity is accentuated by the extreme contrast to his pearly white teeth. The blood is from deep within his chest, spilling into his trachea. Gazing at McNeil holding his head, he speaks with a susurrating gurgle, "I caught one back there. I guess it was worse than –" Larson's light green eyes freeze open and haze over… Dead.

#

Recovering slowly in the left tunnel, Chorin still lays on top of Lisette from trying to shield her from the blast.

They two are both covered in wreckage and dust. His shoulder wound is now accompanied by fresh shrapnel lacerations. He's pretty bloody. As she stirs, she pushes up with her hands, but can't move. Pinned by his weight, Lisette speaks up, "Get off of me please." The *PFC* doesn't move nor respond. She tries to shimmy under him to shake him off, "Get off please."

Finally, he rolls over off of her. He lies on his back in pain and answers sarcastically, "There's some gratitude for you."

"I am very grateful. I just can't stand feeling trapped."

He breathes out in pain and then jokingly retorts, "Well, as long as you're grateful... That makes me real happy Frenchie." He puts his one foot flat on the ground, shifting to try to relieve some of his pain.

She stands and reaches out her hand, "We have to go."

"Go where...?"

"We can still meet them at the vault. I know this facility. I can get us there."

"Go without me. I'm good. I need a rest anyway."

Indignant, she stands over him with insistent body language, "If you think I'm going to let you save my life and then not return the favor, you are incredibly mistaken."

Begrudgingly, he reaches up with his hand, "Maybe you ain't so bad after all Frenchie." As she starts to pull him up, his Star of David falls out of his shirt over his parka. It hangs outside, a gleaming shimmering silver.

She looks stunned, "You're Jewish?"

Almost amused he sardonically responds, "Well, there's that charming Nazi quality I was expecting to eventually show up. That change your mind? Gonna leave me to die now?"

Although irked by his comment, she yanks him to his feet, "You're a moron Chorin." She throws his arm over her shoulder, supporting his weight. He gives a grunt of pain. As she begins to drag him down the tunnel, she emphatically states, "My mother's maiden name was Aronowicz. I'm half-Jewish. It would seem that we have more in common than you thought… Sometimes you have to hide who you are to survive." She slyly smiles, "And I hate Nazis too."

Still staggering, he looks over at her in shock.

#

Alone with Larson's *Enfield* slung over his shoulder, McNeil moves cautiously through the subterranean base, armed with the *Gewehr.* Only that rifle's four remaining rounds provide any semiautomatic protection and then he'd have to switch to the much slower bolt action. His odds don't look good. His chances are dwindling, but he only has to make it another roughly ten minutes until the vault door. Silently he prays that he won't encounter the *beast.* Steadfast, he treads further on through the overwhelming labyrinth.

#

In the collapsed corridor, the Soviet commander keenly observes the bucket brigade that he has ordered the Russian soldiers to create. The nineteen remaining fighters are broken out almost evenly amongst three rows of human chains and face the sizeable barrier of rubble and wreckage. The first of each formation approaches the pile, grabs a fallen rock or brick, and hands it to the soldier directly behind. This continues man by man until that piece of debris is tossed way in the back and no longer an impediment. Although the process is slow and arduous, the commander is patient because he will have the Americans.... At any cost.

#

From out of one of the side tunnel spokes, McNeil appears in the shadows at the ridge of the concourse hub. Although it hasn't changed at all since they've been here, everything looks changed to him... everything looks suspect. His breathing becomes shallower. His eyes dilate. His heart pounds. He's so close, yet so far. Pulling the *Gewehr* in tight, he levels it across the concourse. His finger tightens ever so slightly on the trigger, ready to fire. Scanning the open area through the iron sights, his eyes dance over every object, sculpture and silhouette looking for any sign of the creature. His rifle's front-sight-post purposely lands on every curve and every mishappen item checking its validity as manmade, and not some organic behemoth hiding within or behind. He can't be too careful. If it's there, he'll have no chance.

With a deep breath, he steps from the side tunnel and races up to the vault door. Staring at the closed-circuit-camera he waits to hear the vault's locks snap back. Nothing happens. There is no sound, but his own breathing. The lingering hush of the expanse starts creeping into his mind. He silently, but wildly spins around looking at all five tunnels' openings expecting the worst. He knows that now out in the open, he's a sitting duck. There's nowhere to run. There's nowhere to hide. Losing his cool, he starts waving feverishly at the camera. No response comes from within. Either the major isn't watching, or he just won't open the door to let him in. Enraged, McNeil screams at him, "Kowalczyk!

Open the damned door!" Drawing his sidearm, the frustrated sergeant cracks off a few rounds, trying to elicit his attention. Again, nothing… Losing it, McNeil starts violently kicking the vault door, making absolutely no effort to contain himself. He pounds at the bronze frame. "Major! Open the damned door, you son-of-a-bitch! Open it!" Suddenly… there's a metallic squink, followed by the heavy snap of retracting safety bars. The vault door shudders slowly open.

#

In an adjacent tunnel, lying face down in a percolating foaming violet-colored mass of self-regeneration, the *beast's* right eye snaps open… *It's alive.*

#

Trudging down yet another tunnel, Lisette helps a bloody Chorin to keep moving forward. His weight leaning against her has her slightly hunched, as they attempt to walk. As he staggers, she attempts to give him positive reinforcements, "Just a little further. We'll get you in the vault and get you patched up. Everything's gonna be fine." Within a few steps Chorin goes limp and drops to the ground, pulling her over. They both lay prostrate hung up in one another. Quickly regaining her footing, she pulls his arms from around her and squats at his side. Tapping his face she pleads, "Wake up Chorin. Come on… Wake up. You can't do this to me… you're gonna survive." Her eyes dart back and forth into the darkness ahead. Right now, she wants to be anywhere but here. "Come on… wake up." He won't move. With a forceful slap, she racks him good across the face. His eyelids flutter, his eyes roll, and he finally responds. He stares at her. She whispers, "You have to get up. It's only a few hundred feet… I swear. Please get up." Knowing that she needs this more than he does, he nods that he'll try. Once again, she yanks him up and they start heading for the concourse.

#

Entering through the vault door, McNeil sees Kowalczyk at the inner release lever. The major speaks immediately, "I'm sorry. I've been watching back and forth, but I needed to gather as much of their documents and data I could." Only leering, the sergeant doesn't respond, he just starts pulling the vault door closed. As Kowalczyk moves to help, he asks, "The strike was called off?"

"Obviously…"

"Where's the rest of the team?"

McNeil curtly responds, "They're all dead." The vault door slams shut with a resounding thud and the safety bars snap back into place.

The major's eyes grow wide in disbelief. When they left they were still a decent sized squad. He hesitantly inquires, "What happened?"

"That thing happened! And then the Soviets found us and finished us off Major." There's no mistake that his tone is blatantly referencing Kowalczyk's blunder with the drop-zone that brought about the Soviets attack.

"I'm sorry Sergeant… truly I am."

"Save that shit, it's too late now. They're all dead, alright?" McNeil can see in the major's eyes that he honestly regrets what he's done and the choices that he's made. In the slightest attempt to give him some solace, McNeil offers, "But maybe… I don't know… Lisette and Chorin could still be alive. We were cut off. Right now we have bigger issues." The sergeant rushes by him and starts frantically looking around the test facility.

Kowalczyk moves up next to him and carefully questions, "What are you looking for Sergeant?"

McNeil whips around, "We have to bring this whole place down to the ground!"

"What are you talking about?"

"The Soviets are temporarily blocked, but as soon they're through they're going to march on this place, and they will get in… and then they'll have that ship!" He points at the alien's vessel. "They will make your worst fear a reality Major."

Kowalczyk is hit with a verbal gut-punch. That's the most terrifying thing that he's faced since they've gotten here. More terrifying than the gunfights. More terrifying than the deaths. More terrifying than the *beast*. The realization that they will lose. He can't believe that through all this an enemy force will eventually end up with the ultimate weapon and the unique ability to cripple America. "What about reinforcements?"

"They won't make it in time."

"What do we do?"

Driving home the point, McNeil stares him directly in the eyes and emphatically states, "We blow it up. We blow that friggin' thing up and make sure that the Commies can't get their hands on it… right?"

Kowalczyk's thoughts of rapid promotion, exclusive elite officer parties and unending adulation evaporates. He hangs his head. His mind races. *Are we giving up too easy?*

What if he's wrong? What if we blow it up and they could have made it here on time? This vault is pretty impenetrable. Maybe we should try. He's indecisive.

McNeil barks with urgency, "We don't have much time!" The major stares at him as if in a trance. "Major, I need your damned help!"

Suddenly, clarity washes over Kowalczyk. He knows what must be done. Asshole or not, he's always wanted the best for his country. For the first time in his career, he's decisive and unwavering… the ship must go. He nods back at McNeil, "What's the plan?"

McNeil points to the immense elongated steel cylinders set back behind the aircraft dais. There in the shadows sit the backup diesel generator's five 50,000 gallon fuel tanks and the prototype aircrafts' two 1000 gallon fueling tanks. With a grit of purpose, he explains, "You have at least 250,000 gallons of diesel and jet fuel sitting there. We cut the fuel lines on two, let them spill out on the floor and then light it. When the explosion hits the rest… good night nurse. There won't be anything left."

Kowalczyk is not willing to back down because he is committed, but his question has the twinge of fear in it, "How do we survive?"

"I haven't figured that one out yet. There's gotta be something." McNeil quickly scans the area. Nothing immediately comes to him. He needs to concentrate, but right now they have a job to do. He continues, "Then again…. maybe not. Either way, they won't have that ship." He slaps the major's shoulder and runs off towards the emergency rack, that holds the fire extinguishers and axes. Grabbing two axes, he holds them up to show Kowalczyk who's still standing across the aircraft hangar. With a deathly cold timbre McNeil yells, "Let's do this."

#

Surprisingly, Lisette and Chorin reach the concourse hub with him still on his feet. His whole right side is drenched in a dark crimson. His skin is pale and his eyes sallow. His breaths are labored. He's only made it this far out of sheer will. Only a short distance stands between them and the vault. Lisette is exhausted. Although her resolve is great, his bodyweight on her diminutive size has taken its toll. She doesn't feel as if she can take another step, but she knows she has to move. Drained, Chorin still leans against her shoulder for support. Unable to carry his shotgun and Chorin too, his trench-gun is slung over her other shoulder. Stopping, she pulls the shotgun down and wields it against the open expanse. Still hugging the tunnel's shadow for concealment, she whispers to him, "We've made it." His eyes droop and he doesn't speak, but he's able to nod an affirmation.

As she drags him towards the vault door, a familiar sound reverberates through the concourse. Over and over, there's a dragging scrape followed by a thunderous thud. It's the punishing crash of approaching huge heavy footsteps against steel. Then the cadenced snorts of breath resonate through rightmost darkened tunnel. Lisette's eyes fill with terror… It's here. Not waiting to see if McNeil or Kowalczyk see them on camera, she pulls Chorin faster towards the lock.

#

McNeil and Kowalczyk now stand in front of the fuel storage about ten feet apart, each with an axe in their hand. As the sergeant pulls back the axe to swing on the first fuel line, his peripheral vision catches the radioactive material storage boxes stowed under one of the lab tables. He freezes. Getting ready himself, Kowalczyk notices and stops, "What's wrong?"

Pointing at the cases, McNeil replies, "I forgot about those! What about that radioactive material?"

The major isn't sure. He hesitates and thinks back to the minimal thermal radiation and nuclear physics training he received from the *OSO* when he joined the intelligence agency. "I'm not sure… If those cases are carbon steel alloy with lead cores, maybe they can withstand up to twenty-eight-hundred degrees Fahrenheit."

"And how hot does diesel burn?"

"If I remember correctly… Roughly 3000 degrees plus."

"Son-of-a-bitch…" That's not what McNeil wanted to hear. They can't catch a break. "Okay, so we may be irradiated. Will the boxes at least survive the initial blast?"

Kowalczyk shrugs and motions with his hand maybe, "Aside from *OSO* training, my college major was engineering… I'm not a scientist, so your guess is as good as mine. But I'm pretty sure that if this place collapses in and encapsulates the containers before they melt, the radiation should be contained. If we can escape the blast, we have a shot."

"Then let's make sure we escape the blast." Although it's a statement, McNeil raises his eyebrow as if to question what he just said. The major nods in agreement.

#

In the concourse, huddled next to the vault controls, Lisette attempts to spin the lock combination on the dial while staring back at death. Her eyes are locked in horror at what approaches. Still partially healing, the *beast* lumbers forward with its jaws agape. Then it snaps its threatening displeasure. Although the menacing bites are to strike fear in her, it's eyes aren't locked on her, they're locked on her hand and it's watching very astutely. It snarls a deathly growl and then bellows an ear-shattering roar, as it limps directly for her. Struggling for consciousness, Chorin leans against the wall. The ferocious sound snaps him back to lucidity, if only for a moment. Exerting everything he has, he grabs the trench-gun from Lisette, racks it, and holds it against his hip to fire. Struggling to steady it, he yells back to her, "Run!"

In utter fear, Lisette's hands shake as she tries to turn to the last combination digit on the dial. She yells back, "I won't leave you." With the lock's combo set, she freezes.

He barks at her one last time, "Lisette… run!!!!!" Facing his oncoming demise, he's prepared for the ultimate sacrifice. He focuses with fortitude, inhales with grit, fights to raise the muzzle of the shotgun and takes faltering steps towards death. Hearing him call her by her actual name for the first time snaps her out of fixed suspension and into action. Trembling, she hurriedly rushes over to the lock release and yanks it. As she does, the *beast* focuses in on the new threat… Chorin with the shotgun.

#

Kowalczyk sets down two flares on a lab table to get a better grip on the axe. He chokes up on the wooden handle and gives the okay. Across from him, McNeil readies with his steel edge hovering over the fuel-line. With a nod, the sergeant rears back and then brings down his axe with incredible force. The fuel-line is cleaved in two and 50,000 gallons of diesel starts pouring onto the floor. Simultaneously, the major swings down and chops a jet fuel line in half. In a gushing stream of amber, the 1000 gallons of refined kerosene clashes with spilling diesel on the deck. The swirling liquids release an extremely volatile flammable gas into the air, with a very dangerous flashpoint. The two step back cautiously hoping the diffusing vapor dissipates quickly and something doesn't accidentally ignite a blaze. Suddenly, there's the unmistakable clang of the vault's security rods snapping back in the unlocked position. The two look at each other and run for the closed-circuit-cameras' monitors.

Charging up to the desk with the three monitors, they gaze down upon what's unfolding just beyond the vault door. As they watch in flickering black and white images, they see Chorin fire the shotgun at the creature. It writhes in pain as the blast strikes it center mass. Howling, it attacks. Chorin tries to rack the shotgun again, but it's too late. Striking with brutal speed and accuracy, the beast clamps its jaws down on his collarbone, severing his left arm at the shoulder. An eruption of arterial spray marks the end of Chorin's life. Screaming, Lisette tugs at the pull bar straining to pry open the huge stronghold's access. McNeil yells to Kowalczyk,

"We have to help!" The two bolt for the vault door. Both slamming into it at the same time, it lurches forward.

#

On the other side of the door, with panic in her eyes, Lisette pulls with all her might. The vault entrance moves slowly wider. Inches of an opening appear. The pushing grunts of McNeil and Kowalczyk rush through the newly opened sliver of space. Then a few more inches, but not enough. Lisette screams in frustration.

Behind, the *beast* tosses Chorin's carcass aside like a ragdoll. Searing from under its furrowed brow, the creature's bioluminescent eyes stare down upon the fresh foaming violet wounds in its peritoneal cavity. It's brutally injured again and still recovering from before, but it knows it doesn't have time to waste waiting to heal. It lumbers forward again. It's either going to get in or tear Lisette apart trying. Closing steadily, it gets ready to strike.

Blindly, McNeil sticks his *1911* sidearm through the vault opening and unloads indiscriminately. Instinctively, Lisette recoils to the side. The hail of bullets blasts past her through the air, three finding their mark… they slam into the *thing's* hide. It roars in defiance. As the sergeant pulls back the empty weapon, Lisette shoves her body at the vault opening. Barely slipping through, she runs past them and joins the effort on the other side of Kowalczyk. All three frantically pull together to shut the door. The hulking creature snatches the release lever and throws its weight backwards. The door lurches. McNeil, Lisette and Kowalczyk are yanked back in the other direction. Forcefully, they dig their heels in and fiercely exert to pull it back the other way. The vault door tug of war goes back and forth only inches due to its immense weight. Knowing that they're going to die if they lose, McNeil swings both his legs up on the housing next to the vault door and shoves with all his might. Although the 1600 pound *beast* has the weight advantage against the three, the weakened monster starts losing the battle. The massive portal moves closer to shutting completely. McNeil, Lisette and Kowalczyk grunt, spit and scream as they move the almost unmovable force. The creature's grip slips, and it's claws rake across the bronze, with a metallic screech. The vault door suddenly slams shut. The sound of temporary safety reverberates throughout the hangar. Fatigued, the three momentarily rest with their backs against the door.

Lisette begins to sob, "I didn't save him. I didn't even try." The loss of another person outside this vault haunts her deeply and tears at her thoughts. It's too much. Her body heaves and she mourns those she let die and Chorin who she feels she failed.

Stepping away from the door, McNeil touches her shoulder, "There's nothing that you could have done."

Again, she forcefully jerks away from his attempt at a comforting touch, "He saved me.... Twice. And I did nothing."

Trying not to push, McNeil states gently but firmly, "Lisette, we have to go. We don't have a lot of time." She doesn't move, just continues to emotionally crumble. The guilt gnaws at her guts. She feels broken.

Subtly so she doesn't see, Kowalczyk motions for McNeil to leave them and continue to find a way out. The sergeant strides off to look for an escape. As he leaves, the major steps softly next to her, takes a moment and searches for the right words to convey what he thinks she needs based upon his own demons. Empathetically he offers, “Miss Allard… I can’t tell you how to feel or how you’ll deal with this for the rest of your life, but you need to let this go and deal with the here and now. And right now you need to live. We all do. Let me tell you… you were out there trying to survive that thing, just like everyone else and no one blames you for anything… you shouldn’t blame yourself either. Remember, you did what you could to get us here. We’d all be dead now if it weren’t for you. And what happened to Chorin… that isn’t on you. It’s on me.” Still weeping she lifts her eyes to him inquiring, almost hoping he has some sort of absolution, because inside she’s ready to give up. He continues assuredly, “It’s my fault he’s dead... and everyone else. Out of stupidity and arrogance, I killed every man on this mission… indirectly. I made huge mistakes. Trust me… mistakes are a hard thing to deal with, but this one isn’t your fault. I have to live with the repercussions of my choices and Chorin is one of them. So, let it go. Live today and leave tomorrow to mourn mistakes.” As the tears stream down her face, she sniffles and nods an understanding. She steps away from the wall, wipes her face and breathes deeply. Looking him in the eyes as she walks by him, she utters two words very faintly, “Thank you…” With new resolve, she runs over to McNeil. The major follows.

Almost directly under the forty-foot-wide massive steel overhead doors, McNeil stands staring up above. As Lisette reaches him, he looks over to see if she’s okay. She nonverbally motions that she has it together and she's ready to do what it takes. Smelling the fumes and seeing the fuel on the floor, she asks, "You're going to blow this place up?"

The sergeant responds with uncertainty, "That's the plan."

"We all make it out alive?"

"God willing."

"Leave nothing left?"

"Yep… Nothing left."

"Good."

As they finish their little repartee, Kowalczyk sidles up to them. Looking back up, the sergeant hopefully solicits, "What'dya think Major?" He points to the overhead bridge cranes with the hoists and hooks above, "We could get out on those… but as soon as we drop those huge doors open, that *T-44* outside is gonna hear and it's game over. Thoughts…?"

The major offers his opinion, "Maybe we can hang below, wait till they blast the barn a few times and then try to time our escape in-between reloads."

"That tank already fired three or four from its ammo stack… I don't remember. They may have around six left, but that thing has a total fifty-eight projectile capacity. If their gunner's good he can change out stacks in less than a minute. I don't see much of a window. That doesn't even account for the mounted machine-gun."

"Maybe we could –"

Lisette cuts Kowalczyk off midsentence, "Men…" Scornfully she peers at them both. "…and their weapons. Always thinking militarily. Did you ever think about asking a woman's opinion… especially one that's been here at this facility? How about we try a little bit of stealth and avoid enemy engagements altogether?" McNeil and Kowalczyk both stare at each other like they just stepped in it. Indignant, she points above next to the hydraulic doors, "There is a maintenance hatch up there, next to the suspended catwalk. We ride the cranes up, open the hatch and then slip silently out of the barn undetected. The last one through drops the flame and blows this place up."

McNeil turn to Lisette and states directly, "My apologies..." And then turning to Kowalczyk he adds, "Looks like she has a valid point. I'm gonna grab rations."

The major replies, "I'll grab the flares."

Lisette starts to speak, "You'll need --"

Once again the vault's safety bars snap open. *Clang*!! They slam a booming alert that someone is coming. The three momentarily freeze and watch the vault door begin to move ever so slightly. McNeil rhetorically asks, "The Soviets couldn't have made it through that fast...?"

Lisette laments, "No. It watched me dial in the combination."

"It what? Shit..." With concern rushing over his face, McNeil sees that they won't get to the door in time to stop it from opening. He draws his sidearm and hands it to Lisette, "Take this, drop the cranes and get out! Don't wait for us! Head West... that's where our reinforcements will be. Go!" Fear briefly grips her, but she's not going to be afraid again. She's going to do this. She grits her teeth, nods an affirmation and rushes off towards the crane controls. The sergeant yells to Kowalczyk as he runs for the *Gewehr* that's leaning against a table a few feet away, "Major, get the flares… I'll cover you!"

Kowalczyk peels off in the direction where he left the flares.

Lisette rushes up to the bridge cranes' controls and slaps a levers on each. There's a squeal of hydraulics and the chug of a motor. Both crane hooks begin dropping. As the gear-motors turn and the drive-pullies spin, the two hooks' descension pace seems like an eternity, even though it's only about 40 seconds in reality. She impatiently awaits, as she stares at the ever widening space between the vault door and the housing. Its wounded huffing exertion echoes through with a chilling tone.

McNeil pulls the *Gewehr* in tightly. His eyes glower at the hulking shadow that slowly creeps through the open space. He's ready, "Come on you son-of-a-bitch…" Suddenly it leaps through the vault opening, crashing down on lab tables, flattening them. It roars its shaking jaws with protruding rows of serrated teeth. McNeil fires! Unloading the rifle, the *beast* bellows as the rounds impact. Snatching up a lab table, it retaliates and flings the eighty pound oak furniture like a frisbee. It slams into McNeil knocking him flying and spinning to deck. He lies unconscious.

The *beast* scans over the area… It sees its ship. Noticing that the propulsion system has been removed and the vessel is too damaged to fly, it snorts and growls its displeasure. It knows it needs time to repair it, that means ending the enemy… any human standing in the way must die. Feeling the freshly incurred wounds, it looks at its own blood on its hand. Angered, it begins to move towards its attacker…

McNeil. As it does, it sees Lisette now standing on one of the crane's hooks, clinging to the lift-cable being hoisted and ascending up to the catwalk. The thing quickly accesses. It ignores her, calculating that she's not an immediate threat. It closes on the blacked-out sergeant who's starting to finally stir. As McNeil opens his eyes, the bright lights from above silhouettes the huge behemoth baring down on him. It rears up ready to strike.

CRACK! CRACK! The *beast* is struck in the upper trapezius of its back, by two heavy rounds blasting from the major's sidearm. Grabbing over its shoulder at the wounds it falters and staggers sideways, slamming its other hand down to catch itself from falling. It's weakened. Its wounds aren't healing at the rate that they're being inflicted. In the creature's moment of weakness, McNeil scrambles to get away. The alien brute's eyes track his path and quickly scan the area for danger. The *Gewehr* is empty. The *Enfield* sniper rifle sits at the closed-circuit-camera desk, and it isn't near enough to the human quarry scuffling away to be a risk. McNeil is no longer an issue. It needs to address the immediate threat and cranks its head around to find its attacker. It sees him. Across the way, now with the retrieved flares in his right hand, Kowalczyk holds a smoking *1911* in his left. The weapon is still leveled at the creature. Slowly it turns, squaring up with its prey. It charges! Leaping side to side, zig-zagging back and forth the creature levels in to take out Kowalczyk. The major's pistol kicks, as it unloads. Rounds whiz by the *beast,* but some connect. It's slowed but not stopping.

No matter what, McNeil doesn't want that thing to win. At this point, he doesn't care if he dies. Bring the whole pace down. He yells to Kowalczyk, "Light the flares!"

While firing the major screams back, "No!" He won't let another man die on his watch. He won't sacrifice McNeil. They are going to do this. The enraged *beast* closes the distance… thirty feet… twenty… ten… Heaving the unlit flares, Kowalczyk tosses the pyrotechnic sticks in the sergeant's direction and then unwaveringly aims at the rushing colossus to bring it down. As he blasts off the last of the pistol's rounds, they tear into the *beast* one after another. Impact after impact, the searing bullets do their damage. Mid-step it loses motor function. Tripping, it spins wildly and crashes to floor, sliding from momentum just inches away from Kowalczyk. It lies slumped on its side motionless. The major look across the way to McNeil and makes an "oh shit" expression to McNeil and yells, "That was close!"

Standing, McNeil answers back as he walks towards the flares lying on the floor, "No, that wasn't close… that was stupid! But I appreciate what you did! Come on, let's get the hell outta here!" Suddenly, from the depths of his mind, Lisette's words come rushing back to him, *Make sure it's completely dead.* He freezes still. Clutched by dread, his eyes lock on Kowalczyk and he shouts out, "Get away from it!"

With a smile, the major takes his first step and yells, "What…?" Too late… It attacks! Lashing out, it rakes its claws across his legs dropping him to the floor. As he slams down, it spins on top of him. With unbridled ferocity it clamps its jaws down on Kowalczyk's chest. A guttural scream explodes from the major's throat and then quickly silenced. It tears into him. Bones snap, blood erupts, and organs are decimated. Ripping with its maw, it snaps over and over and tears flesh from sinew, eviscerating him. Sinking its claws into his sides, with a vile cracking sound, it yanks ferociously pulling his ribcage clear in half. Kowalczyk's shaking husk jerks and spasms. He moves no more. It turns for its next kill. There's only one left in its way.

Helplessly watching the few seconds of horror that transpired, McNeil stood unable to stop the slaughter with the *Gewehr* exhausted, his sidearm empty, and the *Enfield* too far away to reach in time. Now he faces the *beast* unarmed. Ready to run, his eyes snap towards the sniper rifle. Acutely aware, the creature sees, cocks its head as if to say *try it* and takes a menacing step in that direction. McNeil stops. He sees his only choice is the flares and bolts off. As he races for the pyrotechnic sticks, the heavily bleeding behemoth summons all its strength and makes two huge leaps. With a thunderous crash it lands a foot behind the flares. Steadying itself, it guards against what it can only perceive as a threat, hovering over them with purpose. Although drained and weakened, it won't give up without a fight. And it knows that even in its critically injured condition, in a physical battle with a human it will end bloodily in its favor.

With his path blocked and suddenly no chance of retrieving them, McNeil skids to a stop about twenty feet away. It watches his every move… calculating and evaluating the potential threat. The sergeant is trapped. Try to retrieve the flares and die or run and the ship falls into the hands of his alien foe or the Soviets. His thoughts roil for a momentary eternity. He knows he needs to survive to at least come up with a plan.

Spinning abruptly, McNeil tears off towards the bridge crane's controls. Trying to hide its frail condition, the creature rears back, raises it fists and roars its superiority. Then it charges! It's now a race for life. McNeil continues running as fast as he can with his one sutured leg. Storming after him, it pushes itself past its limits. Rushing up to the bridge crane's control, without stopping McNeil slaps a lever, as he rushes past. Fifteen feet away, the other hoist cranks to life and the second hook starts to rise from the deck, where Lisette left it retrieved. He beelines for it, with his muscles straining every inch of him. Out of sheer self-preservation, the thing knows it can't let him escape and bring back more humans… It must stop him. Dropping on all fours it fiercely gallops behind trying to close the gap. Still racing, McNeil sprints for the hook and jumps at it just as it lifts above his head height. His hands slam hard against the drop forged steel and inertia swings him forward. Grasping tightly, both he and the hook quickly climb upwards, swinging like a pendulum. The floor pulls away… 11 feet… 15 feet… 18 feet… McNeil watches as the raging creature hits its last stride like an equestrian horse ready to jump a course-fence. It's muscles undulate and contract, then spring back. Using the returning force, the beast launches itself through the air diving at him. Fully outstretched, it reaches spreadeagle. Fearful of what's coming, McNeil yanks his legs up, pulling his knees into his chest. Its claws rake by just barely grazing his boots. It falls with great velocity, crashing back down onto the dais' retaining rail. Flipping over it slams to the deck. It stands angrily and leers up at him.

Looking down upon it, McNeil quips, "Too bad asshole… you lose." As the hoist continues to pull him higher, a thought hits him. This isn't over. With only twelve feet left 'til the top, he pulls himself up and shoves his one arm through the center of the hook. Securing the crook of his one arm around the hook supporting his weight, he digs into his cargo pocket with his other hand while hanging.

Suddenly the beast remembers… marching over to the bridge cranes' control panel, it smacks all the levers mimicking the human. A deafening screech of huge moving hydraulics reverberates from the floor. The dais with the spaceship starts to ascend and with a sudden jerk McNeil's hook stops and starts back down. A fortuitous accident by flipping switches. The *beast's* lips curl back from its serrated teeth in a triumphant smile. It has him now. Swiftly, the creature strides forward, making it way to the dais. As the platform continues to rise, it jumps on. Going up, it rests trying to regain some strength all the while keeping its eyes fixated on McNeil. With tons of metal lurching upwards the ride is slow, but it knows it'll have him soon.

Realizing his newly unfortunate predicament, the sergeant lets go of the object in his pocket and rapidly scrambles to climb up the crane wire. He moves very slowly compared to the wire dropping. Hand over hand he struggles to escape. For just a second, his eyes dart downward to look… Although still thirty feet below, the creature draws ever closer. With all his strength he moves as swiftly as he can. He climbs within a foot of the catwalk and hurls himself into the air. His fingers stretch for the railing. His hands contact the metal cross-rail. Catching it, he clutches with all his might and hangs on for dear life.

#

On the surface, occupying the front entrance driveway of the farmhouse, the *T-44* medium tank sits in the snow awaiting anything. Then the echoing sound of the hydraulic doors opening resound clearly from the barn. Seconds pass and then the gun mantlet whines to life. The treads spin in reverse, backing the steel armored vehicle rearward. Swiveling, the turret turns and the barrel raises.

#

With the maintenance hatch open above him, McNeil now stands on the catwalk. He glances over to the side where the hydraulic doors are still opening, then looks down upon the *beast* steadily rising. Its wet hide and the dais floor beneath are covered in its oozing regenerative violet foam blood. It has become more pronounced as its healing has expedited. Rising up from kneeling, it stands fully erect and stares him straight in the eyes, with a look of *I'm coming for you.* It's now only nineteen feet away. At full strength it may have been able to jump up high enough to grab the catwalk, but for now it needs just a few more feet. Breaking their locked gaze, McNeil peers across the floor below to the fuel covered deck where Kowalczyk's disemboweled remains lay. The volatile mix of diesel and jet fuel continues to spread everywhere on the hangar floor. Reaching into his cargo-pocket again, he pulls out his pack of cigarettes. In a frenzied motion, he yanks his chrome plated cigarette lighter out of the pack's wrapper. Slapping open the hinged metal cover, he rolls the spark wheel. It flashes... He rolls it again. It sparks... It ignites!

An ear-piercing blast shatters the quiet above! McNeil is startled almost dropping the lighter. There's a sounds of a whistling projectile. And then an explosion rocks the air above them! The *T-44* tank is attacking. Boards crack and wood splinters from the barn above, then rain down through the open hydraulic doors. Flying past McNeil as he ducks, the barn's debris cascades down upon the *beast*. The creature holds its arms up defensively and tries to sidestep the assault. After the boards have sailed by, snapping barn ceiling joists and load bearing beams follow falling all around it. They slam into the disabled alien ship and pile up on the dais. One slams into the huge brute knocking it back.

Not wasting a moment, McNeil grabs the catwalk ladder that leads out of the maintenance hatch and whips the lighter over the rail. He scurries up through. The chrome casing of the cigarette lighter glistens as it spins on an arcing descent to the floor. The blue-yellow flame flickers, as it licks in and out of the vented wind guard.

The *beast* sees it and instantly realizes what's happening. Now only fourteen feet away, it takes three huge steps towards the edge of the dais and launches its nine foot frame upwards and out at the catwalk. Sailing, it falls and misses the railing, but its claws slam into the catwalk's floor edge. It seizes so desperately the force crunches the edge. As it yanks itself up on the gangplank, the lighter hits!

Below on the deck, the fuel ignites in a flash of intense orange-red. Instantly, the air around it is sucked towards the ravenous flame that swiftly travels across the accelerant towards the spilling containers and the others that are full. The blaze crawls across the fuel in rushing waves, growing and consuming everything in its path. Then like a pouncing tiger, the flame leaps from the liquid to the air's massed gases by the tanks. It explodes! A concussive blast of exploding metal structures and bursting iterative fireballs engulf everything.

#

Rapidly moving inside amidst the crumbling barn's destruction, McNeil hugs one of the few standing walls, as he runs from the dwelling. Knowing he can't go out the front where the tanks awaits, he charges from the blasted double barn doors and turns heading towards the precipice. He sees Lisette's barely visible footprints from the falling snow heading off into the tree-line. As he emerges from the remains of the barn, machine-gun fire from the tank chews at his heels, spraying up the snow behind him. Hearing the hangar's explosion, he turns back to see the *beast* hurdle from the catwalk up through the hydraulic door's opening, landing in the barn. As the rest of the fuel containers explode, the flames erupt from the hydraulic doors catching the creature in its wake. The flames swell leaping up thirty feet in the air from the hole. Simultaneously they spread out across the barn floor surrounding the screaming brute. Engulfed in a blaze, it bolts from the barn diving in the snow and continuously rolls over to snuff out the flames. Searing and smoking, it rises. Steam engulfs its burnt body. Behind it, a thick black cloud of roiling smoke chokes out the air and blocks the tank's vision. Blasts continue to churn below. In excruciating pain, it tears after McNeil.

McNeil bolts towards the precipice, pumping his legs through the deep snow. The severely burned creature gains on him and it won't be stopped this time. Suddenly, blaring devastation bellows from deep beneath, followed by multiple sporadic explosions. The earth moans. The ground beneath their feet tremors. And as McNeil chugs forward, the destroyed barn and farmhouse's ground begin to drop away. The area implodes. Radiating outwards from the barn, the land caves in and the collapsing earth spreads like a wave. The barn, the farmhouse, the *T-44* and everything surrounding falls into an ever-expanding gaping hole.

Tearing across the open expanse from where the team first came, McNeil charges the edge of the precipice straining to breathe. The thing closes in behind him. The sergeant can hear its huffing breath and footfalls. He knows it's close. Only about twenty feet separates him from a violent certain death. Weaving in and out between sparse vegetation, McNeil abruptly reaches the precipice... There's nothing in front of him. The edge rushes up. It ends. There's only the cliff-face and sky in front. His eyes lock on what's below. Out of room, out of time and with no opportunity to climb down because of the monster right behind, he jumps! Hurtling himself through the open air, he sails off the cliff's edge. Arcing downwards, he falls into the boughs of giant eighty-foot conifers, smashing into the limbs. Tumbling he falls, hitting limb after limb trying to grab hold.

As the creature reaches the last twelve feet of the precipice's edge, it doesn't notice what is rapidly approaching right behind. Dashing, it readies to replicate McNeil's jump, but the ground suddenly falls away. With a deafening wail, the precipice collapses. Its feet are pulled out from under it. It fights to hold onto the disappearing ground, scampering with its legs and hands. Everything falls away. Rock, snow, ice and debris plummets down like an avalanche. The *beast* disappears into a plume of dirt and crystalize backdraft. Dust and disturbed snow rise up from the destruction.

CHAPTER 31 — COLD AND ALONE

Clouds darken the midday sky. A stormfront pounds the area unabated; it has been unrelenting and brutal. Heavily falling dense wet snow obscures normal visibility and an assaulting wind wildly bellows throughout the exposed landscape, making every sound practically inaudible.

From out of a cropping of evergreen trees, a shadow emerges. Cold and alone, McNeil limps from the tree line, leaning into the gale and whipping white. Along his quest, he has trudged for miles trying to find any sign of civilization, but to no avail there's been nothing. He has scaled stone tor formations, nearly swallowed by cracking ice fissures, and had his path hindered by massive snowdrifts. He is wounded, exhausted from exposure and hungry. And due to running from the *beast* and his lifesaving jump, his sutures have torn open on his leg and a thin trail of claret red steadily trickles down behind him.

As he breaks into a clearing, he attempts to see what direction he should proceed, but it's futile. Hanging his head, the want to give up is great, but yet he keeps moving forward. Incredibly weak, he struggles forward. With every labored step his body aches to quit. Suddenly catching his foot on a root frozen under the snow, McNeil stumbles and drops face first into a pile of white. There is no movement. He is at last still.

From over the horizon, the sound of propeller engines swell, shattering the tranquility. He lifts his head. A barely visible billowing fog of snow grows in the distance. Moving swiftly closer, white blurred images start to focus into clarity. Two Soviet *NKL-26 Aerosan* vehicles race towards McNeil's position. An *Aerosan* is basically a wooden box on four skis, with a 10mm steel plate in the front, an aircraft prop affixed on the back and a *DP-27* machine-gun mounted on top. They are a first generation military sled.

With every ounce of strength, McNeil pushes himself up into a kneeling position, and begins to frantically wave. They haven't seen him in the blinding snow. But then… suddenly one of the *Aerosans*' driver frantically points to the other and then in McNeil's direction. The vehicles slightly arc and turn to intercept. At this point, McNeil doesn't care. He just doesn't want to be out here any longer. Stopping just feet from him, the commander and two armed soldiers exit their vehicles, only one gunner remains manning the machine-gun. They approach McNeil kneeling in the snow.

With a smile on his face, the Soviet commander jokingly gives McNeil a sarcastic greeting. He yells over the howling wind, "*Dobryy den' amerikanets*." His comrades laugh at the sarcastic comment, "Good afternoon American." Chuckling, he follows up in English with a thick Russian dialect, "You don't speak Russian do you my friend?"

McNeil stares into him and strains to answer, "No…"

"No matter, you'll learn. Come my friend… you're our guest now." He points to his two underlings, then to McNeil ordering them to take him, "*Voz'mi yego*." The two shoulder their *Mosin-Nagant M1938 Carbine* bolt-action rifles and each grab McNeil by an arm.

As they start to drag him away, McNeil's fading vision catches a flash of movement in the snow. Hardly able to muster a sound, he tries to speak, "Over there…"

From out of seemingly nowhere, with its stealthy approach hidden by the storm, one of the alien creatures attacks! Freed from its concrete cell by the blast, it wants revenge for all the torture and pain… and to deliver it on any human. It doesn't care.

Charging, the beast runs headfirst slamming into the *Aerosan's* flank. Smashing, the wood bulkhead fractures and collapses under the beast's massive weight. The machine-gunner is violently tossed around inside like a ragdoll. Simultaneously, he involuntarily clutches his weapon's trigger, firing hot lead outward and upward into an askew arc. Searing gunfire and tracer rounds rip into one the Soviet soldiers standing in front of McNeil. His back is riddled with holes, and he's thrown forward from the impact. As he drops, other errant rounds slice away at limbs in the trees beyond. Without hesitation, the *beast* clamps its jaws down on the machine-gunners head and rips it from his neck, bathing the sled in arterial spray. The thing then dives from the sled and pounces on the commander who's trying to frantically draw his sidearm. Pinning him, it bites down ferociously. The commander screeches a high pitched bloodcurdling scream that pierces the storm. Now on all fours, the enormous creature picks him up in his maw and shakes him back and forth like a dog toy. Gores spatters the snow around them.

"*Komandir!*", the last Russian solider exclaims, while bolting in a cartridge. Shaking, he jerks the rifle up to his face, tries his best to aim and fires at the hulking animal. The hot lead strikes the *beast* in the neck. It grabs at the wound and roars in pain. Spinning to face its attacker, it hunches and launches itself at the Soviet. As the soldier attempts to bolt in another round, the creature swings wildly as it lands in front of him. It shreds flesh and coat fabric from the Russian's arm, knocking him over. Simultaneously its claws rake across the rifle, throwing it multiple feet through the air into the snow. Scrambling in a flurry of deep red and white, the wounded soldier gazes back in terror trying to escape. It tears into him. The Soviet repeatedly stabs his fighting knife into the creatures torso, but there's no stopping its merciless attack. The soldier's futile screams for help are drowned out by the echoes of snapping jaws and his total evisceration.

During all the commotion McNeil has made his way to the other still functioning *Aerosan.* With everything he has left, he focuses on surviving. He quietly enters the vehicle. Swiftly, he pulls open what he thinks is the choke and then flips up all of the five switches on the dashboard, hoping that one will work. He whispers to himself, "Come on you son-of-a-bitch… start." Surprisingly, there's a pop and chug of a piston. The engine cranks and catches. It starts. As the propeller spins, he yanks the throttle and pulls the joystick left. The sled starts to move.

The creature hears. Slowly it turns from the remains of what used to be a human body. Dropping entrails from its mouth, it moves.

McNeil sees death rushing at him. Although it won't do anything to change physics, he instinctively jolts his body forward rapidly, almost hoping his physicality will cause the vehicle to speed up. Even though the prop's rotation is at top end, the *Aerosan* steadily creeps up towards its max speed against the deep snow.

The *beast* closes. Running at full-bore, it threateningly snarls a guttural hint of McNeil's brutal fate to come. It's wounded and in pain and it wants him dead.

Glancing back quickly, the sergeant sees its gnashing jaws in his peripheral vision. He yells in frustration at the machine, "Move you piece of shit!" Charging at the speeding sled, the thing slams its massive skull into the side of the vehicle. The wood cracks, the vehicle violently jolts from the impact and the creature drops a few feet behind but is still in pursuit. Running alongside on all fours, its determined to catch McNeil. As it dashes over rocks and through the snow, it fights to keep pace. It sees its prey. It won't relent. It closes again and lowers its head ready to deliver the final crushing blow. As it's ready to pounce, the *Aerosan's* automatic gear shift kicks in and the sled lurches forward. Hitting max speed, McNeil and the machine pull away from certain death. The *Aerosan* disappears over the horizon.

The *beast* stops running. It stands against the blustering winds and watches as its vengeance becomes unattainable. Snorting its displeasure, it turns and walks back for the Soviet weapons. Now it needs to escape and hide, until it can find a way off this planet.

CHAPTER 32 — A CHOICE

McNeil is in a prison cell. Battered and fatigued, he lays on the cot unbathed and unshaven. It's been hours since he's been rescued, interrogated and since turned into a captive. Still in the tattered uniform he wore on the mission, he notices how badly he smells. It's not so much the sweat, it's the carnage. He opens his eyes, breaths in deeply and smells the brutal day that transpired earlier still lingering in his clothes. The stench of ground in dirt, gunpowder residue, sweat and coagulated blood all remain. He thinks about all those who were lost and will never go home again… good men… his friends… his "brothers".

Adjusting in pain, he favors his bandaged leg with a pillow underneath. A metal mess-hall tray of half-eaten prison food lays beside him on the floor. This cell isn't in the typical prison, there aren't bars on the door nor are there any making up the walls. It's made of steel plates, rivets, and concrete. This hold is purposely cold and claustrophobic. Only a five by five inch window gives view to the outside world.

The approaching sound of boot-heels striking the concrete floor resonate throughout the hallway outside his cell door. The repeated resolute synchronicity of the steps' gait speaks to the fact that they are military. Drawing closer, McNeil sits up, lowers his leg, and faces his fate. The jingling of keys, the snap of the lock and the squeal of metal hinges proceeds the cell door opening. Harsh light bathes the room as the heavy steel access swings open. “Leave us.”, Colonel Tate commands to his two escort guards, as he enters. His bony frame minimally obstructs the cascading light that silhouettes him. He taps a Chesterfield from the pack, lights up and advances further into the room. Now exposed in full view by the cell light, McNeil looks at up him questioningly. Tate reaches out with his lanky fingers offering McNeil a smoke. The sergeant takes the cigarette and a light but continues to watch Tate suspiciously. The colonel takes another drag and then contemptuously inquiries, “Isn’t it protocol to stand for officers Sergeant? Or did you forget that during your recent travels?”

Exhausted and annoyed, but knowing that he’s right, McNeil puts weight on his leg. His face grimaces, as he holds on to his cot to stand. Lowering his head momentarily, he mouths the words under his breath, “Son-of-a-bitch…”. The sergeant braces to get up in one painful motion.

With the cigarette lightly clutched, Tate holds out his hand to stop. A manufactured grin instantly rolls up his gaunt cheeks, “Don’t get up Sergeant. I was only teasing. I know you’re wounded. And I know what you’ve been through.” McNeil eases back down from being poised on the edge of the cot. “Do you know who I am Sergeant?”

Slightly shaking his head, McNeil replies, “No… Sir.”

“I am Colonel Orenthal Tate from the Office of Special Operations and the commanding officer of this facility. I’m the one who ordered your detention.”

With the cigarette clenched in his teeth, McNeil angrily asks, “Why am I being held here?”

Peering down at him through his wire-rimmed glasses, Tate takes a swift drag and replies with smoke exhaling with each word, “Dereliction of duty. Failure to follow a lawful order. Amongst other infractions. Would you like me to go on?”

“That some bullshit… Sir.”, irked McNeil responds flatly, but emphatically.

“Really…? I’ve read the transcript from our investigators. In your debrief earlier, didn’t you state in your own words that you had conspired with Lieutenant Neuhaus to wrest command from a superior officer, which eventually lead to the death of your whole team?”

“It wasn’t like that.”

Mockingly, Tate continues, “I see. And isn’t it true that you deliberately blew up an alien spacecraft that Major Kowalczyk specifically told you was in our national security interest and was to be recovered at all costs?” The sergeant stares back at him indignantly and in utter disbelief. “And most disturbing of all… didn’t you report that there’s another extraterrestrial creature still running around out there, and you did absolutely nothing to stop it? You… just… ran.”

Incredulous, McNeil shakes his head at the railroading he’s receiving and gibes, “Well, I guess you told me, huh Colonel. So what now?”

“So what now…?” The colonel takes a long deliberate drag and pretends to think, even though he’s known every move on the metaphorical chessboard before making one, “I’m going to offer you your life back Sergeant.” McNeil looks up at him questioningly. Tate continues, “You’ve seen these creatures. You know how they think, you know their weaknesses and most importantly you know the location where you last saw it and direction it was headed. So, the solution is quite simple… You join us in the *OSO*, help us track it down and capture it… then I'll make you a free man."

Now able to see that this was a ruse all along, the sergeant snickers at the set up, "Incredible…" McNeil takes a drag, exhales, and stares Tate directly in the eyes, "I don't think so Colonel. I spent four years over here fighting… I survived that. I faced one of those things and I barely survived that… and now you want me to go back and face another? Only a stupid man tempts fate." McNeil follows up, "And I'm not stupid. In two days I'm a civilian and I want no part of what you're sellin'. I'll take my chances with a court-martial and see what happens. Besides, no *real* Army officer would ever convict me knowing the full circumstances."

"How droll, you think there will be a court-martial. Let me assure you, there won't be. We are in a covert garrison, in an undisclosed location half away around the world and no one even knows you're here. How did you really think this would go Sergeant? You have committed mutiny… a crime punishable by death. Be thankful I've only given you a life sentence. You will sit here indefinitely living out the rest of your days, until you're a lifeless corpse stinking up these drafty halls." Pleased with his move that's one step closer to checkmate, Tate offers, "Unless…"

"Unless I play along?"

"You're a wise man Sergeant McNeil."

"Don't waste your time Colonel. I don't believe you; I don't trust you, and I certainly don't make deals with men who have no honor."

Tate glowers in disappointment, "I expected more from you Sergeant. Neuhaus always said you were a pragmatist. That was one of the things he admired most about you. Are you really going to sit here rotting away over something so provincially quaint as principles?"

"Are you through?"

Tate taunts, "Do you really think clinging to your honor makes you a good man…? Maybe a hero?" Contempt oozes from each word, "Think of your family McNeil. Because they will certainly be thinking a lot about you… when they're all alone and grieving you." The words viciously roil in the sergeant's mind and then he contemplates, *why did he use the word grieving*? He mentally shakes it off, turns his head away and stares up at the moonlight through the paltry cell window. The Colonel continues to toy with him, "Let me assure you McNeil, they won't be thinking that you're sitting in the brig somewhere rotting away. We'll be sending them a folded flag along with the War Department's deepest condolences. For all intents and purposes… in their eyes you'll be dead. Sad as it may be, your family will mourn you and cry over you, but then life will go on. There will be no cards, no letters, nothing. Your children will grow up, your wife will remarry, and she will spend her days in your bed with another man. Be hubristic… be stubborn… be '*honorable*'. But it won't matter McNeil. Time has a way of erasing those with such rigid principles.

Heroes only last in stories and no one will be writing yours." Tate can see the words strike McNeil to his core. Checkmate!

The hatred swells inside McNeil. There's almost nothing worse than losing the love of one's family, except for being forever erased from their minds by another. He wants to pummel this man. He wants to tear him apart. He wants to punish him, but he doesn't even have the strength to stand. The sergeant's mind screams his thoughts, but his lips hold them from escaping for the sake of his family. *You're gonna pay you son-of-a-bitch! Maybe not today, but there will come a day that you will pay! I swear it.* He knows what he must do.

Filled with self-aggrandizement over being so easily able to push McNeil's buttons, Tate pompously reads the sergeant's eyes, the muscles in his face and his body language knowing exactly what he will eventually respond.

McNeil knows he's lost, but he won't just roll over. Curtailing the anger in his voice, the sergeant speaks, "Okay, I'll do it. But here are my conditions…" Tate smiles, impressed by this man's guts to make demands. Unwavering the sergeant states ardently, "I won't wear the uniform for you… that's not gonna happen. I'll be a civilian contractor for the *OSO*, but I want the Honorable Discharge I deserve. And I want to go see my family first."

Amused, Tate tests him, "What makes you think you're in any position to make demands Sergeant? Or that I'd be willing to grant them?"

"You obviously think you need me, or you wouldn't have even cooked up this little scheme. Those are my conditions, Colonel."

With a slight sense of admiration for this man, Tate acquiesces, "Agreed."

Excited at the prospect of seeing his family, McNeil shifts forward on the cot, "When do I get to leave to go home?"

"*TIDCIS* has to strategize, arrange the logistics and to assemble the strike team anyway, so I'll give you two days with your family. But two days only, McNeil. Any longer and your family will be truly missing you. Understood?"

"Understood..."

"Good. I will send someone in here to redress that wound and to clean you up for your travels." As Tate turns to leave, he stops and adds one more point, "One other thing Sergeant… I'm sure I don't have to articulate this, but not a word to anyone about this or anything we do here. You are *OSO* now hence forth. Undertake that distinction appropriately."

McNeil nods a subtle acknowledgement. "Tell me one thing Colonel… was Buchwald in on this or was this all you?"

Tate smiles. With a gleam in his eye, he takes pleasure in answering the question, "Don't worry McNeil, Buchwald didn't betray your friend or your team… that fat old fool was as clueless and in the dark as Neuhaus, his favorite pet. Dinosaurs like him still think that future wars will be won with guns. He doesn't comprehend the true power of technology and intelligence. He is nothing but an unfortunate incumbrance that must be navigated… at least for now."

"What the hell does that mean?"

Mockingly, Tate jests, "You're ruining the surprise Sergeant." His Cheshire-cat grin once again rolls up his face and his eyes glimmer with bliss, "However, seeing that you asked..." He wants to tell McNeil. He's enjoying this. "It simply means that by this time next year we will be released from the aggravating yoke of military command. The *OSO* will become the wholly civilian controlled *CIA*... the *Central Intelligence Agency*... has a nice ring to the name doesn't it?" Taking a satisfying drag of his Chesterfield, he continues, "We will be a truly clandestine entity and the most powerful intelligence agency ever known to man. We will change the face of the world and it'll be glorious. Welcome aboard... Agent McNeil." Not waiting for a comment from the silently astonished McNeil, Tate exits the cell, and slams the door behind. His footfalls echo throughout the hallway as he walks away.

Still stunned, McNeil's mind races. The sergeant may be an agency man now, but he's still imprisoned in his situation. Grimacing, he stands. Turning to face the window, he gazes out at the night sky. The storm has cleared and a shimmering starfield hangs over the clear horizon. The stars twinkle for him in a way that they never have before. He's filled with happiness. He grasps on to the hope that he will soon be home with his family and embraced by the ones he loves. It's been years since he's seen them or touched their faces. His thoughts drift to a better place and time, where they can be all together forever. Everything is peaceful...

Just then, tearing through the heavens, a shooting star burns brightly across the blackness of space. As the falling meteor's white-hot tail spreads, it lingers across the celestial horizon. McNeil's suddenly snapped back into reality and his peaceful thoughts shattered. Fear grips him. His mind suddenly locks on the daunting mission to come… and the ferocious otherworldly *beast* that he will soon face.

THE END

Made in United States
North Haven, CT
17 October 2023

42875088R10173